Sign up for our newsletter to hear
about new and upcoming releases.

www.ylva-publishing.com

Other Books by Tiana Warner

From Fan to Forever

The Road Trip Agreement

Tiana Warner

Acknowledgements

Thank you, Toshi, for helping me bring Ruby's character to life. Thank you for all our conversations, brainstorming sessions, your knowledge, feedback, and for the memories we made on that Oregon coast road trip, which inspired this story. I couldn't have written it without you.

Special thanks also to Laurel Greer for the feedback, the team and editors at Ylva Publishing, and my amazing family and friends, for your endless love and support.

Chapter 1
Coral

"THERE WOULD BE A SIGN if people have died doing this, right?" Coral asked.

On the ground beside her, her camera's red LED blinked.

She hadn't planned to free-fall into a river today, but as she teetered on a muddy bank with her career on the line, it was the only thing to do.

Career was a loose description of what this was, of course. Being a YouTube creator paid, but her parents were keen to tell her it wasn't a real job, and it definitely didn't earn her enough income to live on.

Yet.

After a year of posting daily videos, she had enough data to know the adventurous ones got the most views. This wasn't just a rope swing—it was an opportunity.

"Don't do what I'm doing," she said by way of a disclaimer. "The thing with water is that no matter how beautiful and calm it looks, there can be a lot going on beneath the surface—rocks, logs, currents…"

The waterfall roared, close enough to coat her skin in mist, filling the swimming hole with glacier runoff. To be safe, she grabbed a branch and dropped it over the cliff. It fell for an uncomfortably long time before plunging in. After a second, it bobbed back to the surface and floated gently onward.

"There doesn't seem to be an undertow, and I checked for rocks before climbing up." Her voice was steady, and she flashed the camera her best smile—but inside, her pulse raced. "Ready to jump with me?"

Coral grabbed her GoPro for the extra point-of-view footage. With it safely in a waterproof case and the selfie stick awkwardly between her fingers, she wrapped her hands around the rope. It was grimy, rough, and smelled like the sweat of a thousand show-offs.

After one more deep breath, she backed up as far as the rope permitted. Palms sweating, she gripped tightly, double-checking that both cameras were recording.

She pushed off and swung over the water. As she soared through the air, weightless, the sense of freedom lifted her into the clouds.

She let out an exhilarated whoop.

This was why she'd chosen this life. It was the middle of a Wednesday, and most people were working at their office jobs while she soared through the air in a Pacific Northwest oasis.

Then the water stabbed her every pore, cold enough to be painful.

When she surfaced with a gasp, a dad and daughter picnicking at the river's edge applauded her.

Coral laughed. "Thanks."

She was grateful they were here. If she'd been alone, she wouldn't have jumped. She was all about adventure, not recklessness—for the most part.

Shivering, she sat on the bank beneath the rope and wrapped a towel around her shoulders.

"Okay, that was awesome." She smiled, adding pep for the camera. "The water's an ice bath, if you're into that. I'll share my GPS track on Patreon."

She untied her braid and shook out her blond hair to let the early summer heat dry it. Then she spun the camera to capture the scenery. "Look at this place. How lucky are we to call this home today?"

Everything was lush and bright, from the evergreens towering overhead to the moss on the boulders around the waterfall. The cold mist purified the air, and she breathed deeper to savor it. Hopefully, the microphone picked up the birdsong beneath the rushing water.

Why couldn't her parents understand how important this lifestyle was to her? This was more than a job. She was free to do whatever she wanted and to try new things every day. Recording and sharing her life was fun, and the fact that people paid her for it was a bonus.

She had zero interest in being part of a capitalist, forty-hour-a-week, work-till-you're-dead society.

Except life was getting more expensive, and Vancouver was one of the most expensive cities in the world. She had no desire to move away from her sister and friends, but the longer she tried to live this life, the harder it became to afford food and gas. Her parents might have had a point, but she wasn't ready to give up. Aunt Nina managed to live the life of her dreams—she was in Costa Rica now, probably zip-lining with a sloth or something epic—and if she could do it, then Coral could too.

She smiled. "Time to pack up and head back to the van. I've got a deep-dish pizza waiting for me in the slow cooker."

She turned off the camera, ready to hike back.

After pulling her running pants and compression tank over her damp bikini, she looked up to find the picnicking girl staring at her while her dad rummaged in a cooler. She must have been in her mid-teens.

Coral heaved on her backpack. "Gonna try the rope swing?"

"Are you on YouTube?" the girl asked.

"I am."

The girl crossed her arms and gave her dad a pointed look. "See, Dad?"

He opened his mouth as if to scold her and shot Coral a disapproving glance. "Yes, Avery, but she's probably doing this for fun while she goes to school."

Avery had a desperate look in her eyes that was all too familiar.

"I'm not going to school," Coral said. "And my parents didn't want me to do this either. We made a deal. What niche do you want to get into, Avery?"

The dad shifted, glancing between the two of them. The point of Coral's channel was to prove to herself and others that you didn't have to live according to anyone else's agenda. If Avery wanted to be a creator, then she should go for it.

"Um, fashion." Avery blushed. "I make my own clothes."

"You do?" Coral studied Avery's outfit, an adorable periwinkle tank top with a big bow in the back. "You made that?"

Avery nodded with a nervous glance at her dad.

"It's really good." Then, so as not to come across as a total ass trying to undermine someone's parenting, she said to the dad, "It takes work to build an audience, but you might be surprised at the income that's possible online. Being an artist can be a good career."

The dad's brow pinched. "What deal did you make with your parents?"

Coral fidgeted with the strap of her camera. "I live in a converted van full-time, and they bought it for me to get me started. I wrote a business plan, and we agreed that by the time I turn twenty-four, I need to be earning thirty grand a year. If not, I'll sell the van and work for them."

"Thirty grand?" the dad asked. "You're making thirty thousand dollars a year doing this?"

Coral's insides twisted with something between panic and shame. "Not yet."

His lips tightened into an infuriatingly smug smile. "Your parents set high expectations."

"They own an auto repair franchise, and my older sister's in business school."

"And you didn't want to take up the family business?"

Coral shook her head. She'd seen enough of it growing up, the way her parents worked to exhaustion with endless overtime. Farrah was headed down the same path by going to business school. She'd set her sights on a marketing firm and had already completed an internship that involved staying late every Friday. Why would Coral want that?

"How much longer do you have before you turn twenty-four?" Avery asked.

Coral's insides hollowed out. "A month."

"Do you think you can do it?"

She appreciated Avery's hopeful tone, but it was unlikely. She was going to give it everything she had, starting with today's epic hiking video, but the fact was that she was only pulling in four hundred a month. No matter how she graphed it, she was so far off thirty thousand that she would need a miracle in order to win the bargain in time.

4

"Did your dad fix up the van for you through his business?" the dad asked.

Coral bristled. "My parents got a cheap one for me through *their* business, and I put in a new transmission and did the whole build myself."

"Oh." The dad glanced at his daughter, his face reddening. "Good for you. That's really good."

"Thank you."

There was a beat of silence. Coral stepped toward the trail.

"What's your YouTube channel?" Avery asked.

Coral smiled. "Coral Lavoie Adventures. I'll keep an eye open for Fashion by Avery?"

Avery smiled.

A ghost of a smile crossed the dad's face. "We'll see what kind of deal we can come up with."

Two hours later, when Coral arrived back in the parking lot, she waved to a couple of women who'd set up camp across from her in a teardrop trailer. They had a tripod set up and were obviously in the middle of taking pictures.

"Good hike?" one asked.

Coral wiped the sweat beading down her temples. "Beautiful! There's a rope swing at the end."

"Ooh!" They turned to each other in excitement, launching into a plan to head up later.

Trembling from hunger, Coral cleared a spot on the cluttered counter for her camera and recorded herself taking the pizza out of the slow cooker. Pesto, goat cheese, peppers, kale, artichokes, sun-dried tomatoes, and assorted mushrooms. *Yum.*

"Mm, this looks and smells amazing." She took a bite, struggling not to make moaning sounds and devour it like a Neanderthal. "Wow. That's incredible. I'll share the link to the recipe. Let me know if you try making it."

She wolfed down a few more bites, intending to cut these few seconds out of the video. The hike was longer than anticipated, and she'd never been good at packing her bag properly.

"Anyway, that's it for me today. Tomorrow I've got to pick up a new heating and cooling unit I ordered online. It'll be nice to get some AC in here. Thank you for watching, and thank you to my Patreon supporters. If you like this video, please give it a big thumbs-up and hit that subscribe button. See you tomorrow for another adventure!"

She turned off the camera and shoved an indecently huge bite of pizza in her mouth. Cheese and pesto oozed everywhere, deliciously satisfying. Then she got to work on editing the day's footage.

This video had better do numbers. As much as she hated to do it, she should probably feature a screenshot from the few minutes when she was in a bikini. Time was running out, and she needed to pull out all the stops if she wanted more subscribers.

Was there really only one month left before she had to present a financial report to her parents? Ugh. Thirty more videos didn't seem like enough. How was she supposed to translate her twenty-thousand-strong following into more income in that time? Losing her deal with her parents and losing this van was not an option.

She kicked off her hiking shoes and leaned back on the bench seat, shoving piles of clothes and blankets out of the way. This van was her comfort, her home, her life. Listing it for sale would be like ending a friendship.

There must be some way she could get more followers, more views, and more paying subscribers. Should she find more interesting locations? Do something dangerous? Create drama?

The answer was hiding somewhere. One way or another, she would find a way to keep living the life of her dreams.

Chapter 2
Ruby

"Welcome to Intentional Living with Ruby Hayashi," Ruby said in her most mellow, soothing camera voice. "Tonight, we're making vegan chickpea stew with coconut rice, and we'll serve that with fresh garlic naan I got from Pike Place Market."

Standing at the kitchenette of her camper van, Ruby prepared the ingredients carefully, making sure each shot was perfect before moving on. The mic was positioned to catch every tiny sound, the camera so close that she had to use the knife with her elbow pinched against her side. Three ring lights illuminated the scene from every angle.

With the onion, garlic, ginger, turmeric, red pepper flakes, and chickpeas sizzling in her rose gold stockpot, Ruby held the camera and microphone as close as she dared to capture the sight and sound of the wooden spoon mashing the chickpeas.

"Add the coconut milk—" The words came out too fast, so she drew a breath, took a sip of water, and tried again in a warmer, smoother tone. "Add the coconut milk and vegetable broth to the pot, then simmer until it thickens. It should take about thirty minutes."

While the curry simmered, she captured close-up footage of her home. She misted her herb garden while it swayed in a breeze that rolled through the window. She recorded Calvin curled on the bed, repositioning the dog's ears for maximum cuteness. Calvin didn't move, accustomed to her fussing. It was his price to pay for being ridiculously photogenic, with his light cream coloring and big, expressive eyes. His boxy head and chunky build indicated some kind of pit bull-Labrador mix, though Ruby couldn't be sure without ordering one of those dog DNA tests.

She aimed the camera out the door, adjusted the exposure, and got a gorgeous shot of the Seattle skyline across the water. Trees rustled, and there was the distant sound of campers laughing and enjoying themselves. The evening was perfect.

Perfect, but not good enough, she thought, the words as intrusive as a mosquito buzzing in her ear.

Her stomach churned as she returned to the stove. Her audience had been complaining that she was filming from the same spot all week, but she wasn't about to explain to them why she hadn't moved the van. They came to her channel for a stress-free experience.

Anyway, she should have enough money to fix the transmission within a month or two. She just had to keep her subscribers happy and engaged until then.

She prepared Calvin's dinner and filmed him eating it. His meals were fit for a prince, full of raw, ethically sourced animal proteins, fresh fruits and vegetables, and vitamin powder. He ate slowly, always savoring his meals—kind of like Ruby did. When he was done, she followed him with the camera while he sniffed around the campsite. Her audience demanded at least a few minutes of Calvin footage in each video, and she tended to face a riot in her comment section if she didn't show enough of him.

Their love for her best friend warmed her like hot tea. He deserved his personal fan club. She'd adopted him from a shelter after starting her life in the van at twenty-two—already three years ago—and his loyalty was like nothing she'd ever experienced. He was cuddly, playful, smart, and a great bodyguard for this solo life she'd chosen. His past was a mystery, but the way he flinched at sudden movements and avoided strangers made it clear that people hadn't been nice to him. Ruby had been determined from day one to make up for that tenfold. So what if he was suspicious of strangers and tended to growl at men? Ruby had no men in her life and probably never would, and she preferred not to have random strangers come up to her anyway. As far as she was concerned, she and Calvin were soulmates.

She returned her attention to the simmering chickpea stew, which smelled mouthwatering. She added a couple of handfuls of spinach and let it wilt before serving it over steaming rice and naan.

Before digging in, she spent several minutes getting the perfect lighting for the featured photo.

It was delectable and still hot by the time she started eating it, which wasn't always a guarantee for her meals.

"I'd call this recipe a success," she said to the camera. "Thank you for watching, and please visit my Patreon page for this recipe and other extra content. If you like this video, please like and subscribe. As always, leave a comment if you find a great recipe I should try. Keep living with intention, and I'll see you next time."

She smiled, turned off the camera, and looked at Calvin. "Thanks for being such a quiet boy while I was filming. Want dessert?"

She grabbed Calvin's cookie jar while he gazed at her with big, glossy eyes that reflected the string lights on the ceiling. Whenever he looked at her with such awe, she imagined him wishing he had opposable thumbs so that he, too, could open cookie jars.

After she ate and filmed the cleanup, she gathered her journal, tripod, and Calvin, and headed down to the beach to capture footage of the lapping waves.

Annie and Parm were there, YouTuber friends who'd come to this campground on her recommendation. They were a couple in their late twenties who lived in a converted ambulance, and they'd glommed onto Ruby last year after she helped them dig their vehicle out of deep snow.

She didn't mind meeting up with them once in a while. Though she preferred camping solo, it was nice to know people in the vanlife community.

"What up, Rubes?" Parm asked.

"Probably doing the same thing you are." She held up her tripod. "Calvin, go play."

Calvin trotted into the waves to stand chest-deep and look for fish.

Annie made a zipper motion over her lips and gestured for Ruby to go ahead with the video.

"It's okay. I've got time." Ruby sighed, plunking next to them on the driftwood.

Sometimes, recording every minute of the day was tiring. It was why she'd started recording only in the evenings, giving herself the rest of the day to turn off the camera and live. She still caught herself thinking about interesting shots during the day.

"Did you film today?" she asked.

Annie nodded. "We didn't set up our new fridge properly, so we had a lot of spoiled food to deal with."

"And a mouse got in through a hole in the floor, so we had to patch that up," Parm added.

"Dang," Ruby said. "Sorry."

"It's fine," Annie said brightly. "It made for a dramatic video."

The thing with Annie and Parm was that they always seemed to be in a disaster. Usually, it was an avoidable disaster. Ruby had to stop watching their channel last winter for the sake of her stress levels, when they'd posted a video of them getting stuck in a snowstorm without snow tires, chains, a shovel, or even proper insulation in their vehicle.

But the conflict earned them a lot of views, and she had to admire their willingness to share all of it on a public platform.

Ruby smiled. "Sometimes, I wonder if I should make my video style more like yours."

"What, a constant shitshow?" Parm asked.

"Just…open. Truthful."

Ruby's style was obviously successful—she had one of the most popular vanlife pages on YouTube and had gotten awards for it—but sometimes, it felt like she was lying to her audience. Like, she couldn't talk about her broken van and money stresses because that would ruin the perfect image she'd created. She'd worked hard to create all of her videos in the Japanese style she used to watch with Dad—simple, minimalist, aesthetically pleasing, with long silences to give people time to appreciate the views. Her channel was a place people could come to escape everyday life, to get cozy in a camper van, cuddle up with a sweet rescue dog, and eat delicious, ethical comfort food. Chaos and mechanical failures had no place here. Not in the van, not on her channel, not in her brain.

"You know, Rubes, I don't think anyone's online presence is fully honest," Parm said. "Like, you don't get into the challenges of living off-grid, but we make a big deal out of minor things all the time for the sake of views. Nobody on social media is truthful all the time. It's just the way it works."

"I guess."

Still, Annie and Parm's subscriber count wasn't dropping. They didn't get comments calling their videos monotonous.

Was Ruby's method of telling half the truth failing her? Should she change her approach?

Annie squinted suspiciously. "Are you having a platform identity crisis?"

"Maybe a little." Ruby rubbed her hands over her face. "Are my videos getting boring?"

Annie and Parm gaped at her.

"Girl, you're approaching a million subscribers," Annie said. "Nobody thinks you're boring."

"But I've been posting the same type of video every day for three years. Should I do something new?"

"Not if it's working," Parm said.

"Hm." That was exactly the problem. It wasn't working anymore. Something about her channel was failing to attract new viewers, which was detrimental because this was her only source of income.

And with the van's transmission sounding like a wrench got stuck in a blender, she needed more income *badly*.

But how could she get more subscribers and views? Should she start dumping her problems onto her audience and calling it conflict?

No. She wasn't ready to get personal on camera. The invisible wall between herself and her audience was nice.

Maybe she just had to embrace something different. There must be a new angle she could take in her videos, right?

"Anyway, we haven't made dinner yet, so we'll let you make a video before it gets too dark," Annie said, patting her boyfriend's knee.

"Yeah, and I've got to fix the frying pan first," Parm said. "The handle broke off this morning."

"Oh. I forgot about that."

They stood.

"Have fun," Ruby said.

"By the way, we're going kayaking tomorrow, if you want to come," Annie said. "There's supposed to be a pod of orcas in the area, and we want to see if we can find them."

"At a respectful distance," Parm added.

Ruby smiled. "Thanks. I'll see how I feel tomorrow."

She probably wouldn't—and they probably knew that. She wasn't a good swimmer and had never been the type to hop in a kayak and track down killer whales. Plus, did she trust their kayaks not to have holes in the bottom?

While they retreated to their campsite, Calvin stared at her from the waves with his head down and his tail wagging slowly.

"Oh, I know that look." Ruby stood, leaving the camera on the ground. "You want a piece of me?"

Calvin bowed into a play stance, and for a moment, they stared at each other, frozen.

She crouched abruptly, and he exploded, zipping over the shoreline in a burst of energy.

A laugh bubbled up inside Ruby as her pup zoomed in a wide circle, barking. He became a blur of paws, a lolling tongue, and flapping ears.

This life was everything she wanted, and she couldn't let it go. She had Calvin, friends, nature, and she could park her house wherever she pleased.

Now, if only she could figure out how to keep her channel alive so she could keep living this way.

Chapter 3
Coral

CORAL PARKED IN KITSILANO AT noon, where the beach was packed and volleyball games were underway. She slid open the side door, bringing her audience through every step.

"I'm meeting up with my sister, Farrah, for some beach time today. She goes to UBC, so Kits Beach is our usual spot." She turned the camera to give her audience a view of the busy grass area, footpath, and the sandy beach beyond it.

"Coral!"

Across the street, Farrah strode out of Starbucks.

Coral waved. "There she is!"

Farrah held up two iced coffees and did a happy dance through the crosswalk. She wore jean shorts and a white tee with a neon-green bikini top visible through the thin material. Her blond hair was mostly roots as it swung in a high ponytail—she hadn't had much time for things like haircuts and self-care during this final year of university.

"I would've bought them!" Coral said as she accepted her drink.

"It's fine. I won a gift card at a department fundraiser last weekend."

"Nice. Thanks."

"So you want my advice, huh? Come here for some of my genius business school wisdom—"

"Okay, let's not get carried away," Coral said teasingly. She shut off the camera, intending to leave out the real reason why she was meeting her sister today. As far as her viewers needed to know, they were just hanging out.

They found a spot on the grass and flopped down on the blanket. Coral lay on her stomach in her bikini top, intending to multitask and work on her tan. Farrah did the same, lamenting how pale she was because she had no time for the outdoors. Around them, the smells of everyone's barbecues mingled, and so did their music. A few guys were playing catch dangerously close to people's heads.

Coming into the city was nice, but sometimes, it was a little crowded. It reaffirmed Coral's decision to live on wheels.

"So." Coral opened her laptop. "Help. I need money by the end of the month or else I owe Mom and Dad a van."

"You're liking nomad life, then?" Farrah lifted her sunglasses to the top of her head, revealing the bags under her eyes. She looked more worn down every time Coral saw her—but thankfully, the stresses of school hadn't quashed her bright personality.

"Definitely."

"Not surprised. Remember when you spent a weekend living in the treehouse?"

Coral laughed. "Remember when you turned your bedroom into a store and made us all buy snacks and books from you?"

"Living our destinies."

Coral let her head fall forward so her nose pressed into the blanket. "Now, if only my destiny involved earning an income."

Farrah tugged the laptop closer. "I can help you look at your finances and do some marketing, but I honestly don't know how much help I'll be. There's no *hashtag-vanlife* class in my program."

Coral lifted her head. "That's fine. I just need someone to brainstorm with."

"What are your streams of income?"

"YouTube, Patreon, affiliate links, merch, ad revenue…"

"Can you show me what other vanlifers are doing? Who are the best ones?"

There were a few options for the most popular channels, but one came to mind first. She'd been catching Coral's attention for a while, both as an idol and a nemesis, depending on whether Coral was feeling inspired or jealous that day.

"Ruby Hayashi's channel does really well." Coral navigated to her YouTube page. "Hers is a lot different from mine, but she focuses on the minimalist angle. I don't think I've ever seen her go on a hike."

She clicked the featured video, and Ruby's gorgeous face filled the frame. Coral's stomach did a weird twisty thing as a familiar mix of admiration and envy filled her. On top of being stunningly beautiful, Ruby was a genius when it came to building her platform. She was also fun and interesting to watch, and apparently, she was a great cook. What *didn't* she have?

Farrah reached forward to brighten the laptop screen. "Hot damn, look at that van."

"I know," Coral said begrudgingly.

Ruby's van was the same type as hers—a bed at the back, kitchen on one side, bench and dinette on the other, lots of cupboards and drawers for maximum storage space. Having watched Ruby's van tour, Coral also knew there was a toilet tucked away under the bed—a luxury worth having—and no shower, which meant she also relied on campgrounds and gyms for hygiene. Their vans' similarities ended there. Their layout was mirrored, so entering from the side door, Coral faced the bench, while Ruby faced the kitchen. Their choice of interior design was also different. Coral's was geared toward practicality, with a roof rack on top for a paddle board and a lot of hiking gear everywhere. Ruby's was about the aesthetic, all cream colors with wood accents, cute succulents on the wall, a fruit net, woven baskets to hold everything, rose gold knobs, fairy lights, and a chic black geometric pattern on the white bed linens.

"Do I make my van more like hers?" Coral asked, frustrated by the idea of redoing her interior.

Farrah tilted her head. "You know your market better than I do, but the way you've positioned yourself, I'm sure your audience values practicality over aesthetics."

"Yeah. That's true. But if it's not about aesthetics, what does Ruby Hayashi have that I don't?"

Farrah clicked on Ruby's About page and pointed to the date. "She's been doing this longer than you, for starters."

"But she didn't start posting daily videos until recently. I've got more content out of the gate."

Farrah clicked on her latest video. "On first impression, she's also got a lot more finesse than you."

Coral opened her mouth to argue, but she couldn't deny it. Ruby's videos were flawless. Her production was meticulous—the lighting, the dishes she used, her choice of music, the video transitions, and a million other things.

"What software do you think she uses?" Coral asked.

"That might not be relevant. She's got a blueprint for success. Look at the way she moves, even. It's pleasing to the eye."

It certainly was. Ruby was born to be in front of a camera, with her shapely lips, distinct cheekbones, dark eyes, and long, silky black hair. She was slim and graceful, moving around the kitchenette with the poise of a ballerina. Her voice was like warm butter, and she'd probably taken professional voiceover lessons.

"Also, she has a cute dog," Farrah said. "Look at that smooshy face!"

"Calvin." Coral gave a wistful sigh. The dog definitely drew people to her channel. His giant eyes, flappy little ears, and big smile made Coral miss Oliver, the Labrador they grew up with.

"I guess I could try to copy what Ruby does," Coral said, unconvinced. "It'll be the combination of everything that makes her so successful, right? Bright lights, rose gold, plants, soothing voice, cute dog, artistic close-ups—"

"But that isn't you. I think you need to stay true to yourself."

"Then what should I do? How do I get that many followers"—she pointed to the screen— "while living in *my* van and going on hikes instead of cooking perfect meals?"

They lay in silence while everyone played catch and had obnoxious barbecues around them. It was hard to think with so many people encroaching on her space.

She opened a new tab. "Let me show you a few other channels, and we can figure out a pattern."

They watched more videos, coming to no conclusions, before Farrah stopped her. "Here's an idea. Remember when Mom and Dad partnered with a marketing firm to get their business name out? Maybe you could consider reinvesting some of your income into marketing the same way they did. Ads and publicity."

Coral hummed. "I don't know if ads would work."

"How do others promote their channels? Could you get on someone's podcast?"

Coral sat up and crossed her legs, Farrah's words sparking an idea. "Hey, what if I partnered up with someone who has a bigger audience? Other creators team up sometimes. They show up in each other's videos, take road trips together, promote each other's channels... I can find someone who's willing to do cross-promotion."

Farrah's eyebrows shot up. "Ooh, that's good."

"The question is, who? I should find someone who has a similar audience to mine, right?"

"Or the opposite."

Coral squinted at her. "Really? Why?"

"You have your niche cornered, so see if you can corner a different one. You need a new audience."

"Okay. See, this is why I need you." Coral flipped through the dozens of open browser tabs. One creator stood out above all the others, and she always had. She was more talented, charismatic, beautiful, and, yes, more popular. Partnering up with her would be any creator's dream.

Coral's heart fluttered at the prospect of emailing her. It would be a long shot.

"I'll message Ruby." Heat rose in her face at the boldness of her words.

"Ruby? This Ruby?" Farrah pointed at the screen.

Her surprise didn't help Coral's confidence.

Yeah, I know she's way out of my league. But why not try?

"I mean, she'll say no," Coral said modestly, "but I have to start with someone, right?"

"Well, she would definitely give you a boost in exposure..." Farrah made a face that might have been a doubtful grimace.

Footsteps stopped beside them. They froze.

"Can I interest you two in a barbecue?" He was a tall, broad-shouldered Asian guy with more abs than seemed possible and not a single hair on his chest. He motioned behind him, where about a dozen guys and two women in their mid-twenties were hanging around a folding table covered in food.

"H-hi," Farrah said breathlessly and then seemed to catch herself. She dipped her chin toward her shoulder and flashed a cheeky smile. "Throw in some drinks and I'm sold."

He smiled and stood taller. "Cool."

Coral gave a little cough, and Farrah cast her a guilty glance.

"I mean—we're busy with something, but maybe in a few?"

The guy nodded. "For sure. We'll be here."

Farrah watched him go wistfully.

"You're drooling," Coral murmured, clicking on Ruby's About page.

Farrah swatted her.

Coral nudged her back. "Almost done here, and then we can go say hi."

"It's fine if you don't want to. I don't want to torture you."

"Maybe one of them has a gay sister."

"That'll be our opening line when we go over."

Coral laughed. She made it to Ruby's page and paused, her heart jumping.

"Here's a question," Farrah said. "I get why it would help your channel to partner up with Ruby Hayashi. But what does she get out of it? What's your pitch to her?"

Coral plucked at a loose thread on the blanket. "It would be... fun?"

Farrah rolled over to tan her front and pulled her sunglasses down. "You're good at a lot of things, and I think making business proposals is one of them. It's why you're here right now instead of at university like Mom and Dad intended."

"You think I should send her a business proposal?"

"She's obviously smart and good at what she does. I think the best way to catch her attention is to make sure she sees your value."

Coral nodded. "Okay. That's a good idea."

Her gaze locked onto an email address on Ruby's page.

For business inquiries.

This qualified.

Farrah angled her face toward Coral and opened her eyes. "Sis, I have full faith in you, and I think you'll figure out how to keep living in a van if that's what you want. But say you decide…" She trailed off, apparently searching for the right words.

"You're wondering what I'll do if I can't manage to make enough money from this."

"Yeah." Farrah pursed her lips, looking a little guilty. "Do you have a backup plan?"

"I'll start thinking about one if things don't pick up." Coral searched her sister's face. Seeing Farrah go through university gave her zero motivation to do that herself.

"You don't have to jump into a forever career immediately. You can do whatever feels right for now until a new job speaks to you."

Coral nodded. "For now, I like what I'm doing. I might be a little broke, but I'm happy. I have freedom. I go on a different adventure every day. That's worth more to me right now."

"And what about a side hustle? Freelancing? Selling crafts on Etsy?"

Coral shook her head. She'd considered other sources of income, but everything took up valuable time that could be spent building her vanlife platform. "I want to put all of my time and effort into my channel. This is my calling."

Farrah hesitated. "Okay."

Coral squinted at her, not sure how to interpret the hesitation. Did Farrah really believe in her, or was she just saying she did?

"University is worth it in the end," Farrah said. "It's a few years of hard work, but you end up with a good job with a good salary."

"In an office."

"Office jobs have good perks and benefits."

"I don't want—" Coral huffed, trying to get the edge out of her voice. "I'll think about it."

Farrah let out a breath too. They were both getting defensive—and maybe Coral had taken a few shots at her sister's life path.

"You could get into a trade," Farrah said.

"Just drop it, okay? I'm focusing on this right now. I'll make a backup plan later."

Farrah fell silent, closing her eyes and continuing to work on her tan.

Coral copied Ruby's email address.

"You can go over and say hi to those guys now," Coral said. "I'll be over in a minute."

Farrah sat up and fixed her hair. "Sounds good. Do I look okay?"

Coral pretended to be repulsed. "Ew. Did you have an allergic reaction to something?"

Farrah elbowed her and stood up.

While she strode over to the guys, Coral opened a new email. With a nervous flutter in her chest, she pasted in Ruby's address and began typing.

Chapter 4
Ruby

As Ruby sagged under the weight of her grocery-filled backpack, dripping in sweat, she had to admit that her broken van was a many-layered problem. With this transmission failure, her home, her ride, and her income had all been compromised.

Right now, the most pressing crisis was her ride. Her van hadn't broken down in the most convenient spot. Yes, she was at a campground, but it took an hour to walk to the nearest grocery store, and right now, her back was suffering for it.

She got back to her campsite, and Calvin began barking from inside the van as her footsteps crunched on the gravel.

"Hey, buddy! It's me."

She hated leaving him while she went for errands, but tying him up outside the grocery store would be worse. At least the van was air-conditioned and comfortable.

She opened the door, and he jumped on her, whining like she'd been gone for a week.

"Hi, hi, hi! I missed you too." She dropped the grocery bags and rubbed his thick neck with both hands while the force of his tail made his whole body wiggle. "I got you more peanut butter."

She put away the groceries, then flopped onto the bed. Calvin hopped up beside her, delighted by the spontaneous cuddle time.

"Mph." She hugged him close and buried her face in his neck. "Calvin, I think we have to move the van."

It was technically drivable, but the automatic transmission was stuck in first gear, which meant she would have to roll down the side of the road with her hazard lights on. Would she get a ticket?

It was a risk she would have to take. She couldn't afford a tow truck.

Plus, the campsite charged her for every day she stayed here, and she could probably find somewhere free to park instead. The options for free overnight parking near civilization were limited, but she could usually find a department store parking lot in a pinch.

"Yeah, because that view would keep my audience happy," she mumbled.

Her phone lit up with a new email with the subject line, *Road Trip Proposal.*

She was about to swipe it aside for later when the sender caught her eye. Coral Lavoie. Why was that name familiar?

She opened the email.

Hi Ruby,

My name is Coral, and I make vanlife videos in Vancouver, BC. My channel is Coral Lavoie Adventures.

Ruby tapped the attached link and came to her YouTube page. There was the familiarity. She was the pretty vanlifer who was always doing outgoing things. Wasn't she the one who went viral when her van got stuck on the highway between mudslides for two days last year?

Ruby went back to the email and read on.

I started gaining a following a couple of years ago when I documented a backpacking trip through South America. When I got back, I decided to get into vanlife, so I did my own build and have gained 20k subscribers over the last year. I'm looking for the next opportunity to make more exciting content and have a proposal for you. Would you like to go on a road trip down the Oregon coast together?

Ruby's insides twisted. Together? Like, caravan? Or live in the same van?

A firm "no" rose inside her. Either way, that sounded like a nightmare. She'd chosen solo vanlife for a reason, and she had no desire to let someone invade her personal space and wreak havoc on her peaceful life of solitude.

I've attached my stats, analytics, and demographics. I'm guessing there is some overlap with yours, as well as room to expand. I think we would complement each other's channels, and there's potential for both of us to expand our audiences.

Let me know your thoughts!

Coral

Well, she was definitely business-minded.

Ruby flipped through the attachments. They shared a lot of the same demographics, but Coral was focused on a more outdoorsy set of keywords. Her audience was more into hikes and campsites in the Pacific Northwest.

If Ruby wanted to promote her channel to a new audience, this would be a good way to do it. Could she expand into a more adventurous niche? She had everything she needed—the van, the dog, the camera equipment.

She returned to Coral's YouTube channel and clicked yesterday's video.

"Welcome to another episode of Coral Lavoie Adventures! Check out my morning view." Coral turned the camera to the open back of her van, which looked over a sparkling river. "For breakfast, I'm having overnight oats with cinnamon and apples." She raised a mason jar with a tiny spoon sticking out. "Then I'm headed to Kitsilano Beach."

The glimpse of the van didn't entice Ruby to accept her offer. The place was cute but not the aesthetic Ruby's followers had come to expect. The bed was unmade, she had hats hanging everywhere, and there was no unified theme or color scheme. Were those hiking poles leaning against the wall?

She clicked off her phone. Why was she even considering this? A shift like that would be jarring to her followers, who'd come to expect a certain style.

She sat up and rubbed her face. "Okay. Let's get off our butts. Time to move into town."

Calvin gazed at her. He rolled over with his legs up, a plea for a belly rub.

Ruby obliged.

Moving into Seattle wouldn't solve the problem of being stuck filming from the same location, but right now, she had to think about survival. Groceries and other essentials would be easier to walk to if she parked in the city. She could pretend this was all intentional—a special urban miniseries.

So she secured loose containers, clothes, and her fold-out table, unplugged the electrical hookup outside the van, put Calvin's bed between the seats and called him into it, and slid into the driver's seat.

The van spluttered and groaned to life, and when Ruby hit the gas, it predictably stayed in first gear. She accelerated as much as she dared without putting too much strain on it, but the van was definitely a goner.

She couldn't even curse this problem for coming out of nowhere. It'd been six months since the van started running a little rough, and the mechanic told her it would need a several-thousand-dollar transmission repair. It'd been a month since it started rattling every time it switched gears. It was the sort of problem that made even the most inexperienced car owner cringe. She'd thought she would have enough money to fix it by now—but in waiting, she'd let the problem get worse.

Unfortunately, Ruby hadn't budgeted for a broken van when she started helping Mom pay her bills. Whenever she considered that she might have to choose between continuing to support Mom and fixing the van, she broke out in a cold sweat. She needed a working van in order to help Mom—but she couldn't fix the van if she kept sending all her savings to Mom. What was she supposed to do?

The cold sweat started up again as she took the ferry back into the city. There, she rolled along in the slow lane with her blinkers on and heat rising in her face.

God, please, nobody recognize me.

The van ran obnoxiously rough, stubbornly in first gear, and Calvin kept looking up at her as if to say, *Are you sure the engine is supposed to be making that sound?*

When she stopped at a red light, the van shuddered, and with a final lurch, it died completely.

"Fuck," she whispered.

Cars honked and swerved, apparently angry at her for her van's death.

Calvin picked up on her mood and went to sit at the back of the van, looking at her with concern.

"I think we need a tow truck, boy." She let out a breath, forcing herself to stay composed.

Since adopting him, she'd learned to process her emotions better because he was so sensitive. She'd begun questioning whether problems were worth getting worked up over, and nine times out of ten, it was better to take a deep breath and stay calm.

But her home and livelihood stalling at a busy intersection? This was pushing her to the brink.

She inhaled deeply. And then again. Her throat and chest became painfully tight. It was getting hard to breathe.

"Do I tow it to a mechanic?" she asked no one.

Bringing it to a mechanic would solve nothing when she didn't have enough in her bank account to pay for the repair yet. She needed somewhere free until she could get it fixed.

She turned in her seat and met Calvin's big eyes.

"We'll get it towed to Mom's. Should we go see Grandma?"

Calvin perked his ears and tilted his head, which made Ruby smile. He might not like very many people, but he sure loved Grandma.

Ruby wouldn't be able to make vanlife videos from a parking garage, but she could continue some cooking videos from Mom's kitchen.

Her "Seattle in June" miniseries was going to be pretty different from her usual content. Hopefully, her audience didn't revolt.

So, resigned to defeat, she called a tow truck, bidding farewell to the sad remnants of her savings account.

Mom greeted Ruby with a cry of delight. They wrapped their arms around each other in one of their usual long hugs in which they swayed back and forth until one of them lost their balance and broke away, laughing. Then Mom turned to Calvin and spent just as long petting him and giving him kisses. He wiggled and whined in excitement.

"This is such a nice surprise."

"Just thought we'd come stay with you for a bit. I need a break from living in a box."

It was all the explanation Ruby was willing to offer. Telling Mom the van was broken would put pressure on her, and she was already stressed from moving. Knowing that her daughter was facing a financial hiccup would be unhelpful.

"I wish you'd warned me you were coming." Mom was flushed, a glint in her eyes that might have been panic. She fluffed her dark, shoulder-length hair and tugged her forest green cardigan closed over her old pajama shirt. "It's a bit of a mess in here."

That was a light way of putting it. The place looked like it had been visited by a tornado, followed by a larger, angrier tornado.

The one-bedroom condo, which had been bright, open, and minimalist when they'd viewed it a few months ago, was crammed full of boxes. The TV was on the coffee table, clothes spilled out of bins, and wood shavings and drywall covered the linoleum floor. Trinkets and doilies cluttered every surface. And the kitchen—oh, the kitchen. Cupboards were open with nothing inside, dirty dishes filled the sink, and takeout containers overflowed in the trash.

It was normal for a move to be messy, of course—but this was so completely unlike Mom. For Ruby's entire life, Mom had kept her home spotless. No mess, no dust, and definitely no overflowing trash. Ruby had taken this meticulousness with her into the van, making sure everything she owned had a purpose, sweeping and cleaning several times a day.

"You told me you had the unpacking covered." Ruby tried not to make the words come out wrong, but it was hard with this enormous amount of guilt roiling inside her. She should've insisted on helping, or at least called to check in more. "I thought Yui was coming to help," she added and then felt even worse for trying to push blame onto their family friend.

"Her kids are sick, so she had to postpone. I'm fine. I'm chipping away until she can come next week."

Ruby scanned the drywall dust on the floor. *Chipping away at what, the walls?*

Calvin flopped down on a pile of coats, settling in.

Mom was lying when she said she was fine. She fidgeted with her cardigan, her gaze darting around the condo as if she was trying to decide how to tackle the endless mess.

Ruby opened a bin. "Well, I'll help you in the meantime."

"No, no—"

"Come on, it'll be fun!"

Mom knew better than to protest. She smiled and pulled Ruby into another hug.

Over Mom's shoulder, Ruby's gaze drew to the fridge. It seemed that the first items Mom had unpacked were photos of Ruby and Dad. There was one of the two of them hugging in the backyard of the house she grew up in and one of all three of them on Orcas Island when she'd been twelve. It'd been four years since they lost him to cancer, and the ache in Ruby's heart when she looked at these pictures would probably never go away. Mom insisted she was all right, but Ruby could see how much it hurt to lose her soulmate. Her parents met at fourteen when Dad's family immigrated from Osaka to Seattle. Mom's parents were Japanese and Italian immigrants, and at that time, she rarely met other kids who shared her Asian heritage. So when a new boy from Japan showed up in class, it didn't take long for them to forge a friendship. They started dating when they were twenty and got married at twenty-two. They liked to joke that it was love at first sight, but they were both too shy to say anything for six years.

Seeing the family photos made Ruby soften. Who cared about a little mess, anyway? They would have fun unpacking together over the next few days.

"How's business?" Ruby asked as they broke their hug.

Mom put a box labeled *kitchen* on the counter. "Better. I've got quite a few customers coming in these days. Probably the summer crowd."

"That's great!"

The tea lounge had been struggling, but with Ruby's help to pay the bills, Mom's business had been able to stay afloat. But she still worked seven days a week instead of hiring more staff, which would hopefully change one day.

"I've been giving your tea a shout-out in my videos," Ruby said. "Lots of comments from people saying they're excited to check it out."

"Aw, thanks. I have noticed a lot of online orders."

Ruby started filling a drawer with utensils.

"How long are you planning to stay for?" Mom asked. "The pull-out couch is being delivered tomorrow, and you're welcome to stay on it as long as you want."

Ah. So we'll be sharing Mom's queen bed tonight.

"I'm not sure. I haven't decided where I want to go next. Maybe I'll stay with you for long enough to get you organized, and then—"

"Ruby, stop. I've told you I don't want you to slow down your life on account of me, and I mean it. Go live your adventure." Mom nudged boxes around until she found the bear-shaped jar she kept for Calvin's biscuits. She fed him a few while he wagged his tail and pawed her for more.

Ruby kept organizing the utensils. A compromise would have to do. "Okay. But at least let me help you for a couple of days."

Mom hesitated, then nodded. "Thanks, love."

That bashful look was familiar. Mom hated asking for help but was always grateful for it. It'd taken months to convince her that Ruby was earning enough to help out with her expenses and the mountain of medical debt. But Ruby's platform was doing well, and she wouldn't have been able to live with herself if she hadn't used some income to help Mom stay on her feet after Dad died.

If only she had some savings to spare.

It's fine. I'll have enough money to fix the van after the next couple of payouts.

She just had to keep her channel alive until then. Somehow.

Could Mom handle all of the expenses for a couple of months if Ruby paused her end of things?

Ugh, she couldn't bring herself to ask.

While they unpacked, Ruby couldn't help worrying about what she would do next. She couldn't record videos here. Her minimalist channel would die under the weight of all of Mom's stuff, even if they managed to unpack and get organized at lightning speed.

Could she get the van towed somewhere else?

No, what a waste of money. The only place she should be towing the van to was a shop.

She needed somewhere else to film. Somewhere that would make her audience happy—and hopefully earn her more paying subscribers so she could hurry up and get the van fixed.

That email from Coral Lavoie drifted forward in her mind's eye.

Maybe she couldn't afford a new transmission, but she could afford one road trip.

The idea of partnering with someone wasn't bad. She could move her stuff into someone else's van and pitch it to her audience as a change of scenery. In terms of Coral being the person to partner with… well, why not? She could get over a messy van, right? She'd been doing the same thing for three years, and this could be the perfect chance to try something new. Hadn't freedom and unpredictability pulled her into vanlife in the first place?

"You're not lonely, are you?" Mom asked, arranging her collection of porcelain dolls inside a glass cabinet.

Ruby stared at her. "No. Why?"

"It's okay if you are. I know you have Calvin but…you've chosen such a solitary life."

Oh. She probably thinks I came to stay with her because I got lonely in the van.

"You know I'm an introvert," Ruby said brightly.

Mom smiled. "Do you ever think about dating?"

"Mom, oh my God." Ruby's insides might as well have caught fire. She went to get another box to hide her burning face in.

Sure, she thought about it, but she only had to spend two days on a dating app to know it wasn't for her. She could think of a lot of things she would rather do than have a shallow texting conversation with a random woman an algorithm matched her with.

Besides, she didn't have room for a relationship in her life. She was a nomad, and when she was home, it was to see Mom and help her out—like she was doing today.

Mom kept stuffing trinkets into the glass cabinet until they all bumped against each other—the decorative plates she and Dad brought back from Japan, the round, red Daruma doll with *perseverance* inscribed on the belly in kanji, a framed wedding photo, teacups. "I just want you to be happy. Even introverts get lonely."

"I have friends!" Ruby drew a breath to get rid of the defensive note in her voice. "Also, I might not be living in solitude for much longer. I just got an email from another YouTuber who wants to go on a road trip together."

Mom raised an eyebrow. "Yeah? That sounds fun."

Ruby's insides twisted. Why had she brought that up? She wasn't even sure yet whether she wanted to go.

She began putting away mugs. "Maybe."

"You don't think so?"

"I don't know. I'm not sure if it'll be jarring for my followers to watch me take a road trip when they're used to watching me cook and water my herb garden." It was a feeble excuse. She could cook and water an herb garden from anywhere. A road trip didn't have to interfere with her aesthetics.

Mom twisted her mouth as if to suppress a smile. "I'm sure they'll love it. Your followers like you for you."

"Hm." It was a nice thing to say, but the internet was an unforgiving place, and it might not be true. She couldn't predict how her audience would react to change.

Mom faced her, pausing her efforts to fit an entire tea set into the overflowing cabinet. It was an old, cracked set that had been mended with gold. "Ruby, isn't your channel about living intentionally and making decisions based on what brings you fulfillment?"

"Yes…"

"Well, are you still happy and fulfilled making videos in this style, or do you want to try something else?"

Ruby gaped. Okay, Mom had a valid point. Here she was touting about living with intention, and yet she was failing to consider what she truly wanted right now.

Aside from needing to break the monotony in her videos, she was ready for something new and exciting. The prospect of taking a road trip with another creator put a spark in her chest that hadn't been there in a long time. After living in a comfortable routine, leaping into the unknown had appeal.

Maybe sometimes, living intentionally meant making a change. If Ruby paused to listen, her heart was telling her to mix up her routine. She could listen to that urge while staying true to her life philosophy. She *should*.

Mom seemed to consider her silence as an answer. "You can leave your van in my parking garage while you go. Be free."

"But what about you?" Ruby asked, the words coming out in a rush. "I'll be driving too far away to come home quickly if you need—"

"Ruby, I, too, have friends. I'll be okay if you're doing a little trip a few hours away."

It was hard to believe she would be okay because Ruby always seemed to find out by accident when Mom was in a pinch—like today, popping in, only to find out she desperately needed help unpacking. Even finding out Mom was in financial trouble took months longer than it should have.

"But you never call your friends when you need them," Ruby said. "You never even call *me* when you need me."

Mom opened her mouth, closed it, then said, "I guess I should stop wondering where you get your independence from." She sighed. "How about this? I promise to admit when I need help if you promise to go on that road trip."

Another compromise.

They exchanged a smile. Watching from the pile of coats, Calvin wagged his tail.

That night, after Ruby edited the day's video on the kitchen island, she opened YouTube and went to Coral's channel. Scrolling through her latest videos, her brain stalled at a thumbnail of Coral in a bikini.

Well, the image had certainly caught her attention, and it seemed to be raking in a decent number of views.

The video was from a few days ago, and it promised a hike to a waterfall with a swimming hole.

Ruby skimmed through the video and stopped when Coral set her camera on the ground and gave a big thumbs-up, casting a cute smile. She walked to the edge of the cliff and looked down.

God, this girl was going to jump into that freezing river.

"There would be a sign if people have died doing this, right?" Coral asked, and Ruby couldn't help smirking.

As much as Ruby hated to admit it, she needed someone bold to help her break out of this shell she'd been hiding under. She'd gotten comfortable living quietly, losing touch with the more outgoing aspect of vanlife.

Coral grabbed the rope swing, backed up, and leaped off the cliff, letting out an exhilarated scream that Ruby felt in her chest.

Ruby smiled at her laptop.

Yes, Coral Lavoie might be exactly what she needed to give her online platform new life.

Chapter 5
Coral

CORAL'S CONVERSATION WITH FARRAH NESTLED into her brain, running on a loop. *"Do you have a backup plan? What about a side hustle?"* As much as she wanted to scoff and ignore these questions, they were realistic, and she was running out of time to come up with answers.

Was she being too stubborn? Should she listen to what her parents were trying to tell her?

After a fitful sleep, she awoke at dawn and grabbed her phone, typing out an email before she lost her nerve.

Hi Aunt Nina,

How's Costa Rica? I have a vision of you sitting in a mossy forest surrounded by sloths. Say hi to them for me.

I wanted to get your opinion on something... You know that agreement I made with my parents for my camper van? My time's almost up, and I don't know if I'm going to earn enough income to uphold my end. But I really don't want to give up and sell the van. I want to live like you do, going on adventures, doing what makes you happy. The thing is, living that way is harder than I thought it would be. There are so many reasons to quit. Do you think I'm making a mistake? Should I stop clinging to the fantasy of being a nomad?

Sorry to dump this on you. No rush getting back to me.

xo

Coral

She sent it and grabbed her camera, ready to start her day with a video.

As she was in the middle of telling the camera about her morning hiking plans, her phone lit up. The name caught her eye, and she lunged for it with a gasp, ruining the shot.

It was Ruby.

Sitting cross-legged on the bed, her heart thumping, she read the email twice.

Hi Coral,

Your timing is good. I was just thinking that I wanted a change of pace for my channel. So, I like your proposal. I'm in if: (1) we use your van, (2) you're okay with my dog coming with us and understand that there's a chance he won't like you, (3) since money and IP are involved, we write up a real agreement that says what we're both expecting to get out of this, who owns the rights to the footage, etc.

Thanks,

Ruby

"Holy crap!" Coral exclaimed.

She said yes! Ruby Hayashi was up for a road trip!

These conditions were all doable—and very meticulous, which fit what Coral knew about her.

It was as if the universe had replied to her email to Aunt Nina: *no, Coral, you aren't wrong for wanting this life, and your patience will be rewarded.*

Coral typed a reply, her fingers clumsy in her excitement.

Hi Ruby,

(1) Yes, we can use my van, though frankly I'm not sure why you'd want to. (2) Dogs love me, and of course Calvin is welcome. (3) Sure, we can sign an agreement.

-Coral

A tap dance was happening in her belly. Was she seriously about to go on a road trip and share a van with *Ruby Hayashi*? She'd totally expected a rejection. She'd even spent last night making a list of other people to email.

With energy buzzing through her, she returned her attention to the camera. Her smile came more easily than a minute ago. She positioned her ponytail in front of her shoulder again and hit record.

"I'm waking up at Alouette Lake today, and I'm planning to head out to try one of the tougher hikes—"

Her phone lit up, and she lunged for it again.

Hi Coral,

Per your second point, those are the famous last words of every person who's been bitten by a dog. Anyway, I made a slide deck last night with my thoughts on what the road trip could look like. Let me know what you think.

Thanks,

Ruby

Coral grinned. A slide deck? How adorable. And she'd made it last night, which meant she'd gone to bed excited about the idea. This boded well.

Ruby,

Okay, I won't touch Calvin without his express permission. Also, I can't believe you made a PowerPoint presentation to plan a road trip.

Coral

The reply came in seconds.

I plan all my trips that way. It helps me figure out where I'm going, and at this time of year, we'll need to book our campsites in advance. How do you figure out your trips?

-Ruby

I tend to wing it.

-Coral

Why am I not surprised to learn this about you?

-Ruby

Coral laughed and opened the slide deck. Maybe traveling with an uptight person would make for a fun dynamic in their videos.

She couldn't help noticing that Ruby never explained why she didn't want to use her own van, but Coral wouldn't pry. Ruby must have had her reasons—maybe she didn't want to put that much mileage on it.

Each slide had the destination, a picture, a map with the driving time, and possible landmarks to see. Ruby had made slides for several spots down the Oregon coast and Northern California and then different spots while they headed back up the coast. She'd picked campgrounds in state parks, which, in Coral's limited experience of camping in the US, were incredible places to stay. It would be more expensive than stealth camping for free in random parking lots and side streets, but Ruby must have had a good reason for this decision.

This plan had better work or else this road trip is going to drain my bank account for nothing.

As Coral browsed the destinations and imagined exploring all of these places, a flutter of excitement went through her. This plan would give them ample opportunity for good content. They'd have to talk about whether Ruby was okay with them veering off schedule here and there. Coral tended to decide where to stop on the fly, depending on when she got tired of driving and which parks or landmarks caught her eye.

If they knew each other better, she would tease Ruby for being a nerd and making such a detailed itinerary. Instead, she replied kindly.

Ruby,

This itinerary looks great. I'm excited. Should we have a video call to draft up our official Road Trip Agreement?

-Coral

She called Farrah, ready to burst.

"Ruby Hayashi said yes!" Her voice filled the van. "We're going on a road trip down the Oregon coast and into California."

Farrah screamed. "That's amazing! Wow, we haven't been to Cali since Disneyland."

"Right? We won't drive that far south, but wait until you see the places we're going." Hope filled her like an inflating balloon. There were so many hikes to do, views to seek out, and landmarks to explore.

"You think you'll get enough subscribers to hold up your end of the bargain with Mom and Dad?" Farrah asked more seriously.

Coral's stomach squirmed. "I think so. I'm guaranteed to nab at least a few of her followers, right?"

Farrah paused. "I have no idea. But if she's got a million, then even a tiny percentage would be huge. There's no way this can go wrong."

Coral flopped back onto her pillows, letting out a breath of relief. The promise of reaching Ruby's huge audience was more than she'd hoped for.

"And anyway," Farrah added, "let this be about the trip itself, not the number of subscribers you'll nab. Don't be like Mom and Dad."

Coral huffed out a laugh. "I will not be like them! I'm living the dream."

"So are they, if you ask them. But work's work and play's play. If you spend all your energy thinking about business on this trip, you're going to forget to experience it for what it is. You're going to get home and realize you missed out on something good."

Coral sighed. "Farrah, it'll be impossible not to have fun."

This was the road trip of all road trips. The entire Oregon coast and into California? How awesome would that be?

"So a professional approach worked?" Farrah asked.

"Oh, yeah. She wants to make an official agreement. It's smart, right?"

"Definitely. You should have everything in writing in case things go south between you—or in case you end up fighting over video rights or whatever."

There was a pause. Coral's heart stumbled. If things went south between them, would her entire online career be over? What if they ended up hating each other and Ruby's entire audience turned on Coral?

"Speaking of contracts, does Ruby know about your agreement with Mom and Dad?" Farrah asked.

Coral wrinkled her nose. "No, and I won't tell her. She doesn't need to know how desperate I am for more subscribers. And I don't want to give her the impression that I'm using her."

"Aren't you both using each other?"

Coral chewed her lip. "I guess so."

"And that's fine. It's a win-win."

Was it, though? Why *did* Ruby agree to this? What could she hope to gain from Coral's comparatively tiny audience?

I'll have to ask her.

A deep voice in the background asked Farrah if she wanted pancakes.

Coral froze. "Oh—my—God. Is that Beach Guy?"

Farrah giggled. "Maybe."

"Dude."

Her sister had hit it off with the guy who'd said hi to them on the beach, and Coral had to admit he was a catch. He'd been cool and funny.

None of the guys that day had a gay sister or knew any single queer women at all, but Coral hadn't really expected it. Anyway, living the nomad life made it hard to have a relationship.

"What's his deal, again?" Coral asked.

"His name is Paul, and he's a personal trainer."

"That would explain the physique."

In the background, Paul asked if she wanted coffee.

"Anyway, I'll leave you to your romantic pancake breakfast," Coral said.

"Okay. Later, turd."

"Bye, loser."

When they hung up, Coral had a new email.

> *Yep. I'm around now if you want. Or tonight. Or whenever.*
> *I have no life.*
>
> *-Ruby*

Coral laughed. This Ruby seemed different from the one who calmly talked about how to prune a tiny tomato plant.

With a nervous flutter in her belly, Coral replied to say she was free now. She fixed her ponytail and adjusted her shirt, suddenly conscious of how frumpy she looked—which was absurd because she'd just been on camera moments ago and hadn't cared then.

The link to the video chat arrived in her inbox, and her heart thrummed.

Adventure awaited. This was how she would win the bargain with her parents and keep control of her own life. She had no other option.

Chapter 6
Ruby

"THAT WAS QUITE THE SLIDESHOW," Coral said in greeting. She was seated on her bed, propped on one arm with her legs folded beside her. "I like how many of the pictures featured dogs."

Ruby grinned, pleased she'd noticed. "That's what I typed in to find each photo. The landmark name plus *dog*."

Something about talking to Coral one-to-one instead of watching a video made Ruby's belly do a strange twist. It was hard to pinpoint why. Maybe it was the unique sensation of talking to a low-key internet celebrity.

"Is that so you can make sure the spots are all pet-friendly?" Coral asked.

"Yes, actually. I've been disappointed in the past when places I wanted to visit didn't allow dogs."

Coral shrank back, her lips parted in an expression of disgust. "Like where?"

"A lot of beaches, some parks, hikes, pedestrian trails. You'd be surprised."

Coral shook her head. "The horror."

She looked incredibly cute in a slouchy, pink off-shoulder shirt. Her blue eyes glimmered behind full lashes, and her hair was in a high, messy ponytail. The bed was rumpled behind her, like she'd been curled up in it a moment ago.

A crease appeared between her eyebrows. "Where are you?"

Though Ruby had turned on the blurry background to hide Mom's messy living room, it was probably obvious she wasn't in the van. Her laptop was on the coffee table, and she was cross-legged on the floor with Calvin snoozing next to her.

"My mom's place in Seattle. She moved in recently and needs help unpacking." It was true, even if that wasn't her original reason for coming here.

Mom had left at six to open the tea lounge, and Ruby had already unpacked several boxes. She resolved to do as much as possible before Mom returned home at five.

With grueling business hours like that, no wonder Mom hadn't had time to unpack. Ruby ached for a day when she could help Mom reduce her working hours—even retire when she was ready for it—but that sort of wish was impossible for everyone except millionaires. The best she could do was keep helping Mom pay her bills until the tea lounge bounced back.

"That's nice of you," Coral said.

"I guess." Ruby didn't consider it to be *nice*, more of a given that she should help her mother with this sort of thing. "How about you? Where are you parked today?"

"Golden Ears Provincial Park. It's like an hour east of Vancouver."

The place sparked a memory. "Oh, I've been there!"

"Right! That Canadian road trip last summer. I watched—I mean, um, I subscribe to your channel, so I saw…" Coral flushed and shifted so she was cross-legged.

"I'm flattered you watch my videos," Ruby said. "And thanks for emailing me about this. It'll be fun. I've never been down the coast."

"Yeah, for sure. Same." Coral fidgeted with something off camera. "Hey, can I ask, like… What are you hoping to gain from this road trip?"

Ruby rubbed at an imperfection on the coffee table. Was she willing to confess to a stranger how much of a lie her channel was? Was it safe to share that she needed to boost her viewership or else risk financial trouble?

Easy answer.

She shrugged. "I want a change of pace. It's been three years of making the same videos, and I think it'd be nice to introduce something new. The road trip idea sounds fun."

There. It was the truth, or at least most of it.

Coral nodded. There was a pause.

"What about you?" Ruby asked, maybe a little late.

"Same. Change of pace. Expand my audience. Maybe I'll learn a thing or two from a pro."

"Well, I hope I can be the change of pace you need."

Coral smiled, her face brightening. "I'm feeling pretty confident."

Now, if Ruby could say the same. She'd probably feel better once they had the agreement nailed down and she could get a better understanding of what she was getting into.

"Do you think I could see your van?" Ruby asked. "I couldn't tell from your videos how everything was situated." She needed to know what an average day in Coral's van looked like.

"Oh." Coral looked past the laptop, her gaze darting rapidly— hopefully not from mess to mess. "Yeah. Sure. I haven't cleaned up yet today, so it's in a bit of disarray…"

God, help me.

"It's the same kind of van as yours, just with a mirrored layout, I think." Coral pointed, her hand coming into the wobbly frame. "Dinette—"

The dinette had a dirty bowl and spoon on the table and clothes all over the bench.

"—some storage below it—"

A pair of hiking boots was in the middle of the floor, positioned as if Coral had kicked out of them one at a time on her way to the bed.

"—kitchenette—"

Nearly every cupboard and drawer was ajar.

"—swivel seat up front—"

The passenger's seat had a dripping-wet jacket hanging over it, water pooling on the floor.

"—and that's all there is to show, I guess."

Ruby's heart beat faster. There was no unified color scheme, and nothing seemed to be in its place. It was, however, the type of van Ruby was used to, and despite the mess and the total lack of aesthetics…she could picture herself living in it. Traveling with Coral. Seeing new sights and trying new things. It was a change she needed, even if it made her vision blurry to look at it.

Coral spun the laptop back around to face her. "Anything in particular you want to see?"

"No." Ruby's voice came out a little high. "Thanks. We'll be able to fit both of us and Calvin, no problem."

"Totally. We can leave behind anything we don't need, anyway." Coral looked down. She spread her fingers over the bed beside her, flattening the wrinkled sheet. "Um, one more thing. Are you fine sharing a bed?"

Heat traveled into Ruby's face so fast, it was like she'd stepped inside a fireplace. She was going to have to be okay with cuddling up next to a stranger and fast. "Sure. We're going to have to, right?"

The way Coral's mouth opened let Ruby know this response had sounded a little cold. She tried to amend it. "I mean, yeah, I'm fine sharing a bed with you. Are...are you fine with it?"

"Yeah, totally," Coral said quickly.

A pause.

"As long as you're okay with snoring," Coral said. "Gentle ones. Little bunny snores."

Ruby laughed. At least one of them wasn't painfully awkward.

"Oh, and cold feet," Coral added. "And I might elbow you in my sleep by accident."

"Wow, you're really selling this."

"And you should probably also add to our agreement that we each get 50 percent of the covers because I will *totally* hog them."

They laughed.

They were definitely both blushing. Coral fidgeted with the sheets beside her.

"On the topic of the agreement..." Ruby moved the video call to the left side of her screen and opened the document alongside it. "I found a template online that we can work from."

"Awesome. Thanks for doing that."

"No problem. We just need to settle a few things. Outside of the 50 percent blanket shares, I'll put that we're going for ten days in your van... We each hold the copyright to our own videos... We agree

43

to be in each other's videos and pictures... Nobody owes each other royalties... There are a bunch of other legal clauses that we shouldn't have to enact unless one of us decides to be an ass."

Coral opened her mouth, and it was a moment before the words came out. "You were on the honor roll in high school, weren't you?"

"What?"

"Nothing. What else is in the document?"

Ruby almost smiled. "Are you calling me a nerd?"

Coral laughed. Her whole face changed when she did, making her even cuter. "You're very organized. It's good. Nothing wrong with that."

"Good." Ruby patted Calvin, tearing her gaze from the screen for a few seconds.

"How much recording do you do in a day?" Coral asked. "Like, are you fine with me busting out the camera during everything important, even if it's a crisis?"

Though Ruby's instinct was to restrict how much they recorded, the point of this trip was to change up her usual content. She would have to learn to grab the camera during a time of stress instead of tucking it away. "Sure. We should add that to the agreement. Everything gets recorded—but each of us has the right to decide if we don't want a particular personal crisis documented."

Coral's gaze darted as if trying to find a flaw in this plan. She nodded. "Fair enough."

As Ruby typed a note, her stomach twisted at how vulnerable she was about to become for the cameras. *Everything gets recorded.* God, she'd better not regret this.

"Does the rest of the agreement sound fine, then?"

"Yep," Coral said confidently. "I can have my parents' lawyer look it over and get it back to you in a couple days."

Her parents had a lawyer? Wow, her family must have been well-off. Did she just live in a van for kicks?

"Sure. Thanks." The thought of money reminded Ruby of another important thing to agree on. "Also, we'll add something about expenses. We'll split the cost of gas and oil changes or whatever. But what if the van needs some kind of repair? How will that work?" Ruby had no problem pitching in, but if there was a preexisting problem with Coral's van, then it probably wouldn't be fair for her to pay for it.

"Don't worry about that."

Ruby waited for her to go on. When she didn't, she said, "Are... you sure?"

"Yep, I can do those things. All good."

"Do them how? Like, pay for repairs with a ginormous savings account, or—?"

Coral smiled. "I do my own maintenance."

"Oh." A jolt of guilt went through Ruby for making assumptions. She pictured Coral in overalls, her hands grimy, doing her own oil changes and stuff. The image was...hot. She cleared her throat. "Okay, I'll put in the agreement that you'll handle all repairs, then."

"Yep. Hey, one more thing—you put down state parks for all of our destinations. I'm wondering if we should do more stealth camping."

"Why?" Ruby had stealth camped more often than not, but this trip wasn't necessarily the time and place for it.

"Well, we both run vanlife channels, so we should do things that are purely vanlife, don't you think? We should show the unpredictability and cost-effectiveness of staying in unconventional places."

"Being cost-effective sounds good," Ruby said, a casual understatement, "but I think we shouldn't waste time trying to find a free place to sleep when we could be getting great footage of the parks that people are more likely to stay at. Like, we need to share an experience that anyone can have, and the average person will stay in state parks. We'll be able to use the park names as keywords."

Coral tilted her head. "Okay. You're the pro."

Ruby's insides twisted with sudden uncertainty. What if Coral's idea to stealth camp was the better one? Should Ruby trust her instincts, or were her instincts leading her down the wrong path?

God, nothing about having a platform was easy. What was the best way to get more followers?

"Well..." Her heart jumped. "We could stealth camp a little bit. I guess. We want to reach a broad audience, right?"

"What if we prebook our campsites for the first half and wing it for the second half?" Coral suggested.

Ruby considered. That wasn't bad. It would give them a chance to explore both ways of traveling. She nodded. "Sure. I like it."

"Cool. Anything else we should put in the agreement?" Coral leaned sideways so her shoulder peeked out of her sweater.

Ugh, she's cute.

Ruby hummed, averting her gaze from the video as her brain seemed to sputter and stall. Maybe she'd overstated how satisfied she was being single. If talking to a pretty girl was wreaking this much havoc on her, it was probably time to get out there. She could try downloading a dating app again once this road trip was done.

They decided on a few more details, like when and where to meet, and after ending the call, Ruby drew a breath and reached down to pet Calvin. "This is a good decision, right?"

He gazed up at her, the whites of his eyes showing.

She stretched. "I guess we'll find out."

What if she and Coral were so different that they ended up hating each other? Could she handle a whole road trip with this girl?

She had the sensation of hovering at the edge of a whirlpool, ready to get sucked into a place where she would lose everything.

Then again, she also had a lot to gain.

They were leaving in four days, which meant she had that amount of time to finish setting up Mom's new place. She could do it. She could balance everything.

But first—a nervous swoop went through her gut—she had to record a video to tell her audience a change was coming.

Chapter 1
Coral

Hi Coral!

I said hi to the sloths for you, and they told me to tell you "Hhhiii Cccooorrrraalll." I think they wanted to say more, but I ran out of time to transcribe it. I hope you'll come with me next time I visit—I think you'll really like it here. We can go canyoning down some waterfalls together.

Now, buckle up for my unparalleled wisdom.

People with unconventional dreams have to fight ferociously for them. You should've heard your grandparents fight me when I told them I was going to spend my twenties backpacking.

You want an unconventional lifestyle, and given the way your mom is, I can see why she wants you to stop. Growing up, she prioritized school over everything—friends, sports, even sleep. I'm not surprised she has a hard time understanding someone who doesn't put her career first.

People are always going to try and stop you. They're going to be jealous, or they won't understand why you want to live the way you do, and their defense against that is to try and force you to fit into society's mold. Don't let others stop you from living a life that makes you happy. People have tried to pressure me into buying a place, getting married, having kids, etc., etc., but what I do with my life is none of their business. Since I decided to ignore other peoples' visions for me, I've never been happier. This is my calling, the same way vanlife is yours.

Keep doing it. The means to do so will make itself known in time.

Love,

Auntie N

WITH FIERCE DETERMINATION IN HER heart, Coral set off for Seattle on the morning of the road trip. Aunt Nina's email was exactly what she needed. This idea would work, and by the time she returned home, her means to keep the van and keep this lifestyle would make itself known.

She spent the drive jittering with nervous excitement, and by the time the navigation app told her she was three minutes from her destination, her heart was in her throat.

Ruby had booked their campsites for the first half, and, admittedly, it was nice to know in advance where they would sleep. Coral normally lived day-to-day, so Ruby's plan would be a fun change, freeing her to get excited about each park they would be staying at.

When they'd ended the video call the other night, it was with mixed feelings. Though Ruby was as uptight as Coral had guessed, there'd been something intriguing about her. She was thoughtful and smart, and Coral was interested in learning more about who she was off camera.

Coral parked in front of the brick condominium marked with a pin on the map. She set her camera on the dash and hit record. Time for the big reveal.

"Those of you who've watched my videos know that I'm all about seizing the day and living adventurously. Right now, a road trip is calling to me." She didn't need to force any enthusiasm into her tone, letting her anticipation shine through. "I'm excited to tell you that I am about to meet up with *the* Ruby Hayashi—and, of course, her dog,

Calvin—for a road trip in my van. Get ready to explore the natural wonders of the Pacific Northwest coastline with us!"

When she turned to the building, her stomach flipped. Ruby stood out front with a big smile, her camera up. She waved. She must have seen Coral park and had come down to greet her.

Coral waved back, her face tingling. This was the first time she'd set eyes on Ruby in real life, and she was somehow even prettier than her videos let on.

She grabbed her camera, got out of the van, and kept recording. "There she is! Wow, this is so exciting to meet her in real life. Hi, Ruby!"

There was something about Ruby that cameras couldn't capture. She carried herself with easy confidence. Her dark hair was in a thick braid, managing to catch the light on an overcast day, and she wore tiny exercise shorts and a neon yellow tee. It was a practical outfit for all of the moving around and packing they were about to do and also *very* flattering.

Coral had worn jean shorts and a gray flannel shirt, which suddenly felt drab next to Ruby's sunshine-bright appearance.

"No problems at the border?" Ruby asked with a dazzling smile.

"Oh, I've always got problems at the border. They see the van and assume I'm trying to illegally live here." Coral stepped in for a hug, then regretted it as Ruby tensed. But Ruby hugged her back, probably because the cameras were rolling and their first meeting had to look friendly and energetic.

"I was thinking we could pull your van up beside mine in the parking garage," Ruby said, getting right to business. "We can store anything we don't need in my van while we're gone—"

"Sure." Coral rummaged in her backpack, desperate for an energy boost. She'd already driven for three hours, and the day hadn't even begun. "Want a snack?"

"Um, no. Thanks." Ruby looked at Coral's granola bar offering as though the idea of having food right now were inappropriate. "Anyway, we won't need anything wintery, and we'll have a lot of duplicate items, so we can leave those behind. I have some labeled moving boxes we can use."

"Mm." Well, she certainly was organized. Though it wouldn't kill them to have a less-than-perfectly organized van.

Coral took a huge bite of the granola bar, studying Ruby's camera setup. It was an expensive-looking one with a Rode mic on top, which Coral should have expected, given the quality of her videos. Maybe Coral's reluctance to spend too much money on a camera was her first problem.

"So...I'll let you into the parking garage?" Ruby asked.

Coral hopped back into the van, her mouth too full to answer.

Ruby motioned for her to drive around the corner. There, Ruby clicked a fob to open the metal gate. She guided Coral to park in an empty spot beside her van.

Coral hopped out into the cool, dimly lit parkade. "Where's Calvin?"

"Still in my mom's place. He doesn't like to be more than six feet from me, so he'll just get in the way while we're moving stuff."

"Cute. Well, I'm excited to meet him." Coral addressed her camera. "Now for the hard part: moving *two vans* full of belongings into one. Think we can do it?"

Ruby faced her own camera. "Time for my favorite minimalism exercise: sorting through everything I own. I love doing this once in a while to evaluate which items no longer serve me."

They turned off the cameras and faced each other.

"Hi for real," Coral said.

Ruby's lips twisted, and she dropped her gaze like she was suddenly shy. "Glad you found the place okay."

Her lips had such a nice shape. Coral had noticed it before in her videos, but it was more pronounced in real life.

Both of their energies shifted a little, which was interesting. This wasn't their first interaction, but it suddenly felt like they were meeting for the first time.

It would be fun to get to know each other's off-camera personalities. Coral tried to be herself in her videos as much as possible, but a person's energy in front of a camera was always different.

Coral studied the dim, dank parkade. "Think we should do all of our moving outside for better lighting?"

"No," Ruby said. "This is fine. I've got ring lights."

The firm refusal caught Coral by surprise, but she shrugged. "Okay."

So Ruby was going to be a little inflexible about things. Good to know.

Ruby wasn't kidding about the ring lights. She had not one, not two, but *three*, which was another bit of insight into why her videos were of such good quality. They lit up the vans from every angle.

Coral also set up her GoPro to capture a timelapse video while they worked, and once the lights and cameras were ready, they stood between the vans with crossed arms. This shouldn't take long—an hour or two to shuffle things from Ruby's van to Coral's—but the work that needed to be done hung heavily between them.

"Let's start with the kitchen," Ruby said. "I post recipes, so I need a certain set of things."

Coral motioned for her to go ahead.

Did Ruby seem tense? She was definitely tense.

Maybe she was stressed about this big change to her channel. Coral watched her video yesterday announcing a surprise was coming, and she could tell Ruby had been uncomfortable speaking in a more lively, less polished tone than usual. The comments beneath the video had been interesting—her most loyal fans vowed to watch everything she created, while others were concerned they were losing the channel they'd signed up for. It twisted Coral's stomach to read those. One person wrote an essay about how they'd come here to watch soothing videos and learn vegan recipes, and if Ruby was about to change that, then she'd just lost a follower.

How could people act so entitled about free content? It was infuriating.

It was also a harsh reminder that Coral had the better end of this deal. Once she posted today's video, her viewers would be unanimously excited to see she was embarking on a road trip with one of the internet's biggest vanlifers.

Ruby furrowed her brow as she rummaged through Coral's cupboards and drawers. "You don't have cutlery?"

"I have a spork. It's multipurpose."

Ruby picked up the red utensil. "This looks like a toy. Or the kind of spoon used to feed babies."

"It's practical. And a baby could not be trusted with the fork tines. What do you have? A full set of rose gold silverware?"

Ruby flushed.

"You have rose gold cutlery?" Coral exclaimed.

"It goes with my aesthetic!"

Coral grinned. "Okay, feel free to take over my kitchen with all of your stuff. I think you'll be disappointed with my thrift store skillet and one wooden spoon."

Ruby beamed. "Cool. Thanks."

While Ruby migrated her kitchen over to Coral's van, Coral packed up everything she wouldn't need. Ruby seemed to tense up whenever Coral brushed past her too closely, which was a little annoying.

Yeah, I'm not used to sharing a van either, but you'd better start getting used to being in close proximity.

With the kitchen done, they turned to the clothes.

Ruby opened the compartment over the bed. "Where do you keep the rest of your wardrobe?"

"That's it."

"What? Where are your socks and like…bras?"

Coral shrugged. "My socks are at the back, and I don't wear bras."

"You don't—what?" Ruby's gaze fell to Coral's chest, and then she seemed to realize what she was doing and blushed.

"I mean, I wear sports bras and bralettes." Coral tugged aside her shirt collar to reveal a strap of the Calvin Klein beneath it. "But these B-cups don't really need much support. Also, underwire is torture. I'd rather free the nip when I'm not exercising."

Ruby's gaze traveled to several places in the van, like she was looking at everything in it except Coral. "I guess I can reduce my bras to one or two."

Coral moved her winter clothes, shoes, and equipment to Ruby's van, keeping only what she would need for this trip. Even that needed careful paring down until both of them were disgruntled by the pitiful amount of clothes they would be able to bring.

They each checked the time, a tense silence stretching between them. It was past lunch.

"Okay…" Ruby scanned the tiny space, her brow pinched. "Do you really need this many hats? What is that at the foot of the bed, a cowboy hat?"

"It's for my road trips into Alberta and stuff."

"Well, we aren't going to Alberta, so we can take this out."

"But—" Coral started, then closed her mouth when Ruby cast her an exasperated look. Fine, it was clutter. There was probably no point in arguing that it looked cute in photos.

"Do you need this many tools?" Ruby asked, peeking under the sink.

"Yes," Coral said firmly. On this issue, she would not waver.

"An entire toolbox, though?"

"You never know what breaks."

"But—"

"I'm not taking out any tools. We might—we *will*—need them. You should know how often things break in a van."

Ruby nodded and shut the cupboard, apparently reading Coral's tone correctly.

They had an unsatisfying lunch made up of snacks, determined to finish and get on the road before it got too late. Rolling into a campsite after dark was never fun. Why was this taking so much longer than anticipated? Weren't they both supposed to be minimalists?

After lunch came the rest of the van—toiletries, technology, and other belongings that took up way too much space. Ruby's politely phrased opinions about where things should go were getting terse. Admittedly, Coral was getting grumpy too. They were two hours behind schedule, all because they were both apparently failed minimalists and had very different ideas on what was essential.

"All done, then?" Ruby said finally, crossing her arms.

Coral rubbed her face. "I think so."

It was three o'clock, and Cannon Beach was four hours away. They would have time for one rest stop at best.

Coral stretched, trying to regain some of the earlier light-heartedness with a big smile. "With your decor in here, I admit the van looks a lot better than it did."

Ruby offered a small smile in return. "I'm impressed we fit everything."

"So your van will hang out here until we're back?"

"Yep." Ruby shifted on her feet. "I'll get Calvin and we'll go?"

Coral nodded, drained and already eager to get to the campsite.

"By the way…" Ruby hesitated, seeming to contemplate her next words. She went to the cameras and turned them all off. "This is one of those things I don't want to film."

Chapter 8
Ruby

CORAL TILTED HER HEAD, LOOKING bemused. "Why?"

"I need to focus on Calvin and not the cameras. The thing is, he's scared of strangers. I need to make sure your first meeting goes well." Nerves writhed in Ruby's gut. If Calvin didn't trust Coral, then what? Maybe she should have introduced them before they'd packed the van. Then if it was a disaster, she could call off the whole trip.

Except what a sad reason to cancel a trip.

No, she had to make this work. Ruby would always have new people in her life—hopefully a girlfriend one day—and Calvin needed to learn how to trust them. A road trip with Coral would be good for his growth.

And if Ruby was honest, this trip would be good for her own growth. She was already agitated over the thought of sharing a van with someone for ten days. But discomfort was a good thing, right?

It'd better be. Otherwise, I don't know why I'm making myself suffer like this.

"Is he protective of you?" Coral asked, more curious than alarmed.

"More like mistreated in his previous life." Ruby let out a breath. "I think he'll be okay with you because you're like..." She motioned up and down Coral's body. "Tiny and feminine and nonthreatening. But we'll take it slow."

Coral's lips quirked.

Ruby fidgeted with her keys, heat rising in her cheeks. Well, it was true. Coral had a gentle, breezy air about her that Calvin would probably like, and she was tinier in real life than the cameras let on.

Her oversize flannel shirt kept slipping off one shoulder and came low enough to hide her jean shorts, giving the appearance that she was wearing no pants at all. Just smooth, bare thighs with a golden tan.

"If you think I'm nonthreatening, you've obviously never seen me fight for the last scoop of chocolate chip cookie dough ice cream," Coral said, thankfully seeming oblivious to Ruby's gaze.

Ruby returned a tentative smile.

"Anyway, I brought Calvin a bribe." Coral rummaged in her backpack and withdrew a sandwich bag of bone-shaped cookies.

"You bought dog treats?"

Coral nodded. "Is that okay?"

"Yes. Of course." Well, that was sweet of her. Mom always teased that the way to Ruby's heart was through her dog's stomach, and she had a point.

This gesture made her warm up to Coral by several degrees, which was much needed after that stressful experience of packing the van. Coral had a lot of energy and a habit of getting too far into Ruby's personal space.

Also, fine, Ruby had failed the test of not getting attached to items. She'd tried to bring the entire contents of her van over to Coral's and make everything fit perfectly into a space that wasn't her own. But how could she leave behind her aesthetics, like her beloved plants and everything in her kitchen?

Ruby went up the elevator and entered the apartment to find Mom reclining on her new couch, reading a book by the light of the lamp she'd had for as long as Ruby had been alive. After four days of unpacking and cleaning, there wasn't a box in sight, and Mom had finished arranging her art and trinkets with renewed energy.

The place would never be her childhood home, but it had potential to feel like home in its own way.

"Please call me if you need me, okay?" Ruby clipped on Calvin's leash. "Or your friends? Remember our deal."

"I will. But with the place looking the way it is, I think I'll be living in paradise. Be safe on your trip."

"I always am." She hugged Mom goodbye, waited five minutes while Mom fussed over Calvin, then headed back down the elevator.

When Calvin saw Coral by the van, he froze, his tail rigid.

"It's okay," Ruby said. "She's a friend."

Calvin gave a low growl, a barely audible rumble in his throat.

"Don't," Ruby whispered. "Please?"

Calvin looked up at her, and she walked forward with him, trying to relax.

"So, Calvin's got trust issues, huh?" Coral's voice was a lot softer than it'd been all day. She sat calmly on the step of the open van. "What else do you hide off camera, Ruby Hayashi?"

"Side effect of being a rescue dog," Ruby said, dodging the question. "People weren't nice to him, so here we are, bribing him with cookies before he agrees to be around strangers."

"It's okay. I wouldn't want strangers patting me on the head without permission either." She reached into the bag of dog treats. "Want me to toss these on the ground?"

"Yes, please. Just a couple of strides away."

Coral did so, and Calvin ate them with enthusiasm. After a moment, he looked at Coral with less suspicion.

"When I was seven," Coral said, "a metal gate in a playground hit me on the back of the legs and made me fall. For a year after that, I refused to walk through gates without my sister behind me for protection. So take it from a girl who spent a year afraid of gates because one hurt me: I get why you'd be afraid of strangers, Calvin."

Ruby couldn't help smiling a little. "You can gradually bring him closer now. Just let him come to you, and don't pet him."

Coral tossed the treats closer, and Calvin gained confidence as he realized this was a fun game.

Ruby came to sit beside her on the van step. "I was afraid of sunflowers at that age. My mom had some on the kitchen table once, and I cried so hysterically that she had to get rid of them."

Coral giggled. "Where'd that fear come from?"

"No idea. My parents were flabbergasted."

"I mean, I guess they are a bit creepy."

"They totally are!"

"Is the fear still there?" Coral nudged her teasingly. "Just a little bit?"

"I prefer tulips."

Coral laughed, revealing a subtle pair of dimples Ruby hadn't noticed before.

She kept hand-feeding Calvin while he inched closer.

Ruby's heart seemed to expand as Coral moved so gently in Calvin's presence. So she *could* be calm. Maybe the excess energy was something she adopted for cameras. Or maybe this calmness was a great effort for her. Either way, it was nice to pause and talk to her a little after the stress of packing the van.

When Calvin sat in front of Coral in his signature "feed me" pose, relief washed over Ruby.

She relaxed her shoulders. "Well, you've been deemed not a threat if he's willing to beg from you."

"Yay," Coral whispered, tossing another treat right by her toes.

They sat for another minute while Calvin hovered within touching distance.

Coral fed him one more treat. "We'll be friends, Calvin. You'll see."

Ruby grinned, her heart swelling. "Thanks for cooperating. Some people don't listen and try to pet him before he's ready, so I stopped trying to introduce him to strangers. You're the first new person he's met since..." She trailed off with a shrug. The last person was a girl she'd dated briefly a year ago, but she didn't feel like getting into her love life right now. "Should we hit the road?"

At these words, Calvin did a full-body wiggle, ready to go.

Coral checked the time. "I don't know if we'll have time to stop for groceries at this rate."

No, they wouldn't. Dammit, packing the van had taken way longer than planned.

"I've got enough food for tonight," Ruby said. "We'll stop tomorrow."

"Works for me."

They met each other's eyes, and a swoop of anticipation went through Ruby's middle.

Here we go.

The van was packed, their campsites were booked, and there was no turning back.

First stop: Cannon Beach.

Chapter 9
Coral

THE OVERCAST DAY TURNED WINDY, tugging the van back and forth as Coral drove them down the I-5. Calvin stayed alert on the floor between them, unsure of his new surroundings.

"So, Ruby, what's your story?" Coral asked, gripping the wheel with two hands while they swayed like a train car.

Ruby looked at her suspiciously, resting a reassuring hand on Calvin's back. "What story?"

"You know, your life. Who are you? What shapes you?"

"Why?"

Okay, so Ruby was uptight *and* guarded. Or maybe just shy? But they had to start somewhere if they wanted to enjoy this trip. They were about to get to know each other's bathroom habits, after all.

Coral turned down the music. The gusty wind replaced the guitar twangs of "Send Me On My Way" by Rusted Root—part of her specially made road trip playlist. "What do you mean, *why*? We're about to spend ten days together. Let's get to know each other."

"I thought you said you've seen my YouTube videos."

"Yeah. That's why I contacted you."

"Then you already know about me."

Coral snorted.

"What?" Ruby asked, a defensive note in her voice.

"Your entire life is portrayed in vegan recipes and a rescue dog?"

Ruby scowled. "What's your story, then?"

"I'm still in chapter one."

"What's that supposed to mean?"

Coral lifted a shoulder. "My parents wanted me to go to university, but instead I'm living in a van so I can do whatever I want and follow my whims. And in doing so, I'll create my story."

"I see." Ruby reached into the backpack at her feet and pulled out a bag of trail mix. "Don't you think it's a little grim to assume you haven't done anything meaningful yet and you're still waiting for something to happen that qualifies as a life story?"

"I'm not even twenty-four yet."

"And? I'm twenty-five, and I consider my life well-lived so far." Ruby shook her head. "See, this is the whole reason I made my channel—" She stuffed a handful of trail mix in her mouth and held out the bag.

Coral took a handful. A mix of salty sweetness met her tongue— almonds, cranberries, pumpkin seeds, chocolate, and something cinnamony and crunchy. Toasted quinoa? Definitely a homemade mix. Dang, this girl was a good cook.

"People let life pass by," Ruby continued, "waiting for the big stuff like expensive vacations and professional achievements, when, really, the day-to-day stuff is where the meaning is. Your routine of waking up and eating breakfast while the sun rises. Taking your dog for a walk. Telling your friend how your day was. Looking at the first dusting of snow on the mountains. Simple things make up everyday life, and that's what we have to be intentional about appreciating."

Coral grinned as Ruby finished her impassioned monologue. She was talking a little higher and faster than before, maybe getting more comfortable. Her tone was somehow even more pleasing to the ear than when she put on her camera voice.

"What? Why are you smiling?" Ruby asked.

"I've never seen you fired up."

Ruby settled deeper into her seat. "Mellow is my brand."

"I know." A gust of wind tried to pull the van onto the shoulder, and Coral tightened her grip on the wheel. "I get what you're saying, but the big stuff is where the memories are. Think of your best memories. They're big events, no?"

Ruby tilted her head. "Maybe to some extent."

"Traveling to new places," Coral said emphatically. "Holidays. A time you tried something crazy like bungee jumping."

"So you think people who don't take big vacations have a meaningless life without memories?"

"Of course not. But everyone has big moments in their life, and those are their best memories."

"But big moments aren't your *everyday life*. Those are pivotal points in your story, sure, but they aren't your story in itself."

They fell silent. Clearly, they were both set in their beliefs. Ruby's happened to be wrong, but whatever.

Calvin's big eyes were on Coral. She took her left hand off the wheel to reach for the dog treats she'd left in the door. His ears went up as the bag crinkled, and when she offered it to him underneath her arm, he took it gently.

Another inch closer to friendship.

"Your rant leads me to think you have a good life story, then," Coral said. "A lot of little things that you attach value to."

Ruby put the bag of trail mix in the cup holder and leaned back against the headrest. "Sure. My earliest memory was when I was about five, and it was the first time I saw a spider web—huge, perfect, dew on it, a fat spider in the center. It sparked an admiration for nature that I never let go of." She paused, maybe letting the memory take form. "My other early memories are of my dad playing airplane with me, swinging me around until we were both dizzy. In second grade, my teacher used to hug all of us at the beginning and end of each day. Well, she gave us a choice, and I always chose the hug. I still remember the way it felt. I think that's why hugs are so special to me to this day. My mom and I hug a lot."

Coral waited, something tightening in her chest after hearing Ruby talk about her early memories so openly. She really did seem as thoughtful and introverted as she let on in her videos. But there was something sad beneath her tone, maybe some kind of ache for the past. Coral didn't know enough about her to decipher it.

Ruby stayed quiet, her face angled away. They passed a couple of massive elks grazing by the roadside, which they both looked at in silence. Coral had time to admire the way their thick manes rippled before they whipped past.

Ruby didn't seem to want to go on, so Coral said, "My dad used to swing me around like that too. He stopped when it started to hurt his back. He said being able to work was more important than my desire to fly through the air." It still hurt to think of the moment he told her they couldn't do that anymore, but it had been nice while it lasted. "And my first memory is of a rotting tree stump."

Ruby looked at her. "What was special about it?"

"I wanted to see what was inside. My parents didn't know where I went for an hour and freaked out trying to find me. Meanwhile, I was twenty feet away inside a stump."

Ruby cracked a smile. "Adventurous from a young age."

They turned off the I-5 and headed west toward Astoria. The tall trees on either side of the highway cut the wind, letting them cruise along peacefully. Calvin put his head down and fell asleep, his breaths deepening.

"I do like your philosophy, for the record," Coral said. "Living with intention. Focusing on the simple things."

"Thank you."

Coral tried to live with intention too, of course, but Ruby took it to the next level. Who talked about their life in terms of tiny details like that? All of Coral's best stories centered around noteworthy events, like places she'd traveled. But maybe Ruby had a point. It was easy to forget to appreciate everyday routines. Hanging out with Farrah and playing video games wasn't noteworthy, but it was fun and an important part of her life.

"I guess my life story involves a lot of afternoons outside," Coral said. "Hide-and-seek with my sister as a kid—I'm sure she cheated and never really counted to a hundred—plus backyard camping, helping my Aunt Nina with her garden, and weekend walks along the river with her."

Ruby smiled. "Sounds like a good one."

"Can't complain," she said because the alternative was to get into how hard it was growing up with parents who weren't home enough, weren't emotionally available enough, and were more focused on their business than their kids.

They stopped at a gas station for fuel, coffee, and a bathroom break, then got back on the road. The landscape oscillated between picture-perfect oceanside marshes and wooded corridors. Ruby filmed it, promising to share the footage with Coral so she could add it to her own videos. Finally, they came to the long bridge leading to Astoria. The wind gusts pushed them harder than ever as they drove across. Seagulls fought against it, hovering beside the van.

"Not the best day for driving," Ruby murmured as she filmed. With the other hand, she patted Calvin, who looked around whenever they got hit with a gust.

Coral wasn't concerned. Better weather would come.

At the end of the bridge, colorful homes and buildings came into view, speckling the green hillside. They spiraled down into the town, where the ocean's whitecaps stretched for miles.

Coral let out an excited squeak. "Astoria! My inner *Goonies* fangirl is bursting with joy."

Ruby smiled. "I was so into the romance between the jock guy and the cheerleader as a kid."

"Me too!" Coral still remembered the flutter in her belly when she watched that movie—one of her first experiences of having a crush on a girl. She rolled down the window and leaned her head out. "Hey you guyyys!"

"Shh!" Ruby sank lower in the passenger's seat, laughing. "I'm sure the locals just love hearing tourists scream that line every day."

The sound of Ruby's laughter warmed Coral's chest, making her grin.

"You have a Canadian accent, by the way," Ruby said.

"What? I do not."

"You do. It comes out in the way you say some words. I think it's the O sounds, like *Astoria*, and *holiday*, and *outside*, and…"

"Yes, I pronounce my O's." Coral lifted her chin. "And?"

Ruby laughed. "It's fine. I like it."

Coral opened her mouth to defend herself, and the words sank in. She grinned.

As they wound closer to Cannon Beach and the sun dipped lower over the beautiful Oregon coast, she felt a little more confident in her decision to ask Ruby to be her partner on this road trip. So far, so good. She was trying not to approach this dramatically, but this really had to go well for her channel. Her lifestyle, her van, and her entire future depended on it.

Chapter 10
Ruby

THEY MADE IT TO CANNON Beach after six, which was exactly the sort of time crunch Ruby wanted to avoid, but there was no use moaning about it. They would just have to skip exploring the town tonight.

"Will there be time to see the town on the way back up the coast?" Coral asked, apparently worrying about the same thing as they parked as close as they could to Haystack Rock.

"Yeah. We can just see the beach tonight."

Coral let out a slow breath. "This is why I like to keep a flexible itinerary. You never know what kind of delays will come up."

"Well, my itinerary is the reason we have a campsite reservation tonight," Ruby said defensively.

"True..."

Sure, maybe Ruby had to work on the skill of *winging it*, but planning had always served her well. If it were up to Coral, they would be struggling to find a place where they would be allowed to park overnight right now.

She fed Calvin dinner, letting him eat while they changed into warmer clothes and gathered their cameras and bags. She was starving, but she and Coral would have to eat later.

When they stepped out of the van, they were immediately buffeted by the wind.

"Holy crap!" Coral shouted, zipping up her sweater. "This is going to be interesting."

"Yup." Ruby buried her nose in her windbreaker so she could breathe.

Sure enough, as they crested the coastline, the wind hit Ruby like a full-body punch.

Her breath caught as she took in the scene ahead of them.

Stretching out to infinity in either direction, ferocious waves rolled into the shore, frothy, powerful, and spectacular. The continuous roar pounded in Ruby's ears, a sound like nothing she'd experienced. The beach was more immense than she'd imagined—an endless expanse of hard, wet sand.

"Wow," she whispered, the word getting swept away.

In the distance, Haystack Rock jutted out from the mist, everything she'd dreamed of and more. She filmed the view for a long moment, taking it in.

Then a gust of sand hit her, and she turned sideways, shielding her eyes. "Argh!"

Coral let out an exhilarated laugh. "This is wild!"

Calvin stood regally on the dune, squinting, his little ears flapping. Ruby bent to take a video.

"Do you think this counts as gale-force?" she shouted as she stood back up. The wind whipped her hair in all directions, and she struggled to tame it into a bun.

"Definitely. Come on!" Coral took off at a run.

Calvin looked at Ruby, his tail wagging, and let out an excited bark.

"Okay." Ruby unclipped his leash. She braced herself against the wind, then took off after Coral.

Calvin bounded beside her, barking like this was the best day of his life. He'd never had so much space to play before, and seeing his pure joy made Ruby's heart soar.

Seagulls speckled the top of Haystack Rock, tiny white dots that put in perspective just how big it was. A smattering of people stood at the base, taking photos, staying cautiously back from the surf.

Coral whooped, raising a hand in the air. Then she stumbled as the wind tried to push them back the way they came. She laughed.

Ruby stopped beside her, adrenaline pumping through her veins, while Calvin zoomed in circles around them like a greyhound on a racetrack.

"I can't believe I'm looking at this in real life," Ruby said. "The rocks are exactly like the pictures. Even the mist."

Coral grabbed her wrist and pointed. "Look at the way the water crashes into them."

She let go, and Ruby's arm tingled where her hand had been.

They stood admiring the view while the wind and waves roared. Their cameras stayed up, recording every second. The good parts could be edited and trimmed later.

"Ow, sand in the eyes!" Coral turned into Ruby, covering her face, nearly ending up in Ruby's arms.

Ruby's heart thrummed. She put a hand on Coral's shoulder, turning her away from the wind. "Stand here and I'll take a video of you. Let your hair down."

Coral took out her ponytail, letting her blond locks whip around her head. She looked beautiful as she put her arms out and laughed, leaning into the wind.

They took several photos and videos of each other—Coral also wanted a picture with Calvin—and then a selfie of all three of them, which wasn't good enough quality to post but would stay in their phones as a memory.

When they'd gotten all the footage they could, they put their cameras away and kept gazing out at the water.

"Did you ever see *The Last Unicorn*?" Coral asked over the wind.

"Nope."

"There's a part where unicorns gallop out of the sea, and they materialize from white frothy waves, just like this." She motioned to the shoreline. "This view makes me think of unicorns."

God, this girl was all rainbows and sunshine. It was sweet, but nobody could be that happy all the time. What was hiding underneath?

"It makes me think about how many ships must have sunk against rocks like these," Ruby said.

Coral chuckled.

A strong gust hit them, and Coral let out a shriek, grabbing Ruby's arm for balance. Ruby laughed as they stumbled in the wet sand. Her heart skipped in exhilaration.

"You gotta admit, the wind makes for a cool view," Coral said.

"When your eyes aren't stinging and full of sand, sure."

Coral laughed.

They walked on, their heads bowed, Calvin still galloping around them.

"I always feel so lucky that I get to do this sort of thing every day," Coral said.

Time to dig beneath this bubbly outer layer. Also, Ruby had a genuine question. "Do you ever worry that doing this is setting you up for career failure?"

"Like, not giving me transferable life skills?"

"Yeah."

Coral walked in silence for a moment, her arms crossed as she hunched against the wind. "I've spent all my energy trying to figure out how to make this my career, so I haven't thought about much beyond that. I guess I assumed I'd figure it out in time. Why? Are you worried?"

Shivering, Ruby pulled up her hood and tightened the strings, not caring how dorky it looked. "I've been living in a van and documenting my journey since a little after high school. I worked in a cafe for a bit and quit when my channel started paying well enough. But sometimes I worry that I don't have any skills or education to fall back on."

"You're sounding like my parents."

"Really?"

Coral hesitated. "They aren't exactly on board with my plan."

"Oh." Okay, here was something real about Coral, and not at all what Ruby had expected. Maybe Coral's situation was a little different from the idea Ruby had formed of her living in a nice van with the full support of her wealthy parents. "What if your parents are onto something? They have years of wisdom on us."

"Don't even. Besides, if you're making a lot of money from your platform, you could invest it and earn interest or something, right?"

Ruby let out a humorless laugh. "If I had anything left over to invest, sure."

Coral gave her a double-take. "I thought you were, um, well-off."

"I thought the same about you," Ruby admitted.

"Me? Oh, hell no. I have yet to figure out how to earn a living doing this."

"There's the million-dollar question."

Damn, she'd definitely judged Coral earlier. Coral wasn't just some spoiled girl whose parents had given her a van. She was working to build a career out of her interests, and wasn't that everybody's dream?

"You've got a ridiculous number of followers, though." Coral's brow pinched in confusion—and maybe that was a little flash of alarm in her eyes. "Doesn't that equate to income?"

Frowning, Ruby pushed her hands deeper into the pockets of her hoodie. She might as well admit the truth. It wouldn't do her any good to keep it from Coral, and it might feel good to tell someone. "My mom needs help paying the bills, and by the time I'm done helping her, there's nothing left to invest."

Well, part of the truth.

Coral's gaze darted between Ruby and the sand. "Sorry."

"It's fine."

They walked on in silence, getting further from Haystack Rock.

"My mom runs a tea lounge in Seattle," Ruby said, worried she hadn't portrayed Mom in the best light. "She's doing great, and it's a good business, but—" *How to explain this without talking about Dad dying?* "Um, she still needs my help."

It was hard to share the most personal details of her life with someone she didn't know well. Talking about feelings didn't come naturally.

Coral was quiet for a minute. "Well, we have a lot of motivation to go viral, then, don't we?"

Ruby smiled, grateful Coral wasn't prying. "We sure do."

It was too dark to see what Nehalem Bay State Park looked like as Coral backed into their campsite. They'd been quiet during the half-hour drive from Cannon Beach, both of them in desperate need of dinner and a break.

"Should we hook up?" Ruby asked.

"What?" Coral looked at her sharply.

"Hook up the van? You said you have an electrical hookup, right?"

"Oh. Yeah." Coral's cheeks reddened for some reason. "I'll do it. It'll take two minutes."

"Okay. I'll start dinner. Can I cook for you?"

"Really?" Coral paused with a foot out of the driver's side door. "You don't have to—"

"I like cooking, and I want you to try this recipe. It's really good. I've got enough ingredients for two."

"Okay. Cool." Coral's shoulders relaxed. Maybe she'd been stressing about what she would eat when they hadn't stopped for groceries. "Thanks."

Ruby let Calvin out to sniff around and pee while she texted Mom to tell her they'd arrived safely. Mom replied immediately with a hugging emoji and several hearts.

"Coral, I'll have the camera rolling while I cook," Ruby called as she set up the camera and lighting, "so don't say anything incriminating for the next half hour."

"Noted," Coral said from outside. "I'll wait until you're done before broaching the subject of where we'll hide the body."

Ruby smirked.

She finished setting up and hadn't even started recording yet when Coral came inside.

I guess I'm recording with an audience.

This would be weird—especially when she had to do retakes. Would Coral judge her for being a perfectionist? How many takes did other people tend to do?

Trying to push aside her doubts, Ruby checked her hair and hit record.

"We've arrived at our campsite, and I'm going to make Mediterranean pasta for dinner," she said to the camera, hoping her nerves didn't compromise the video quality.

Coral said nothing, minding her business on the bed with her laptop.

As Ruby boiled the noodles and began sautéing the garlic and onion, it was hard to stop her gaze from darting to Coral. Coral didn't seem to care about Ruby's filming, so why was she self-conscious about it?

She filmed a close-up as she stirred in the tomatoes and kalamata olives, aware of Coral's lingering gaze.

"It smells amazing in here," Coral said with a moan.

"I've never cooked with a pretty girl watching," Ruby said with a nervous laugh. "I feel like I'm forgetting everything and losing charisma."

Her cheeks warmed as the compliment came out. What possessed her to throw in the word *pretty*? She could've just said "with an audience."

Coral's lips curved into a little smile. "Your charisma seems fine to me. Would it help if I put on headphones so I can't hear you?"

"It's okay. I'll have to get used to this." Ruby turned back to the camera. "Next, I'll add white wine, tomato sauce, and balsamic vinegar."

She'd never noticed before today how much her tone shifted when she was talking on camera. Was that weird and embarrassing?

When the noodles and sauce were ready, she mixed them together, plated the food, and topped the dishes with fresh basil.

"Dinner is served!"

Coral jumped off the bed, clapping her hands excitedly. "Yum! Thanks so much for cooking, Ruby."

"Of course. Do you mind if I keep rolling while we take our first bites?"

"Go ahead. God, this looks amazing."

Ruby glanced at Coral's reaction as they dug in. She loved this recipe, but not everyone had a palate for vegan food.

Coral's eyes lit up. "This is really good," she said through a mouthful.

Ruby exhaled into a grin.

It was nice to share a meal with someone other than Mom for once. Maybe Mom had been a little bit right about her solitary life. There was a chance Ruby had been lonely without realizing it.

"Will you be offended if I grate cheese on top of mine?" Coral asked.

"Go for it. I mean, the pasta's perfect as is, but if you want to ruin it with—oh, God, cheddar? I thought you'd at least make it Parmesan."

Coral shamelessly grated a block of cheddar cheese over her bowl, smiling impishly. "What would you do if I added ketchup?"

Ruby clutched her stomach and groaned. "You're the worst."

"Don't panic. I won't."

Calvin watched her grate the cheese, tilting his head, and Coral picked up a shred that fell on the table. She held it up, asking Ruby a silent question. Ruby nodded.

Coral offered it to Calvin. He hesitated, then slunk forward to take it gently.

Ruby couldn't help smiling as Coral offered him another one and then another, until his tail gave a little wag and he stopped backing up between bites.

"See? Trust isn't so hard," Coral whispered.

After dinner, they did their video editing and social media—Ruby in the swiveled passenger's seat, and Coral on the bed at the opposite end. Calvin lay on the floor between them. The only time they broke the silence was to warn each other if they were going to start adding narration and then to record the narration.

"The beach was so flat that I'd *love* to bring a bike here and ride for miles..." Coral said in her typically excited, animated tone.

"It's hard to convey how vast the beach is..." Ruby said, mellow and calming, leaning closer to the mic for a warmer tone.

Close to midnight, Coral flopped back on the bed. "Done. Where are you at?"

"I could be done." Ruby rubbed her eyes. She'd been checking and replying to comments, but that was an endless task, so it was better to call it a night.

They took turns using the campsite restroom to shower away the sand and salt. Coral went first, returning fresh-faced.

As Ruby went next, her heart beat faster, and it took her a moment to understand why: they were nearing the moment when they would have to share a bed. They were about to spend the night lying next to each other in a bed barely big enough for two.

"Who cares, right?" she whispered to her reflection, taking out her toothbrush.

This might be easier if Coral wasn't so charming. But sharing a bed with a childhood friend at a sleepover and sharing a bed with a woman who she happened to be a little bit attracted to were two different things.

Ruby tamped down the flutter inside her, furious at it for being there. This trip was a *business agreement*.

When she returned, Coral climbed into bed first, not meeting Ruby's eye. She wore an oversize T-shirt with a *Lavoie Auto Repair* logo and teeny-tiny shorts that all but disappeared beneath it.

Ruby let out a breath and climbed in after her. Ordinarily, she didn't wear pants to bed, but she'd put on checkered flannel pants tonight with her tank top.

They left three-quarters of the bed between them, lying faceup on the furthest edges.

Okay. This is fine. I can fall asleep like this. I just won't move.

Coral let out a soft giggle.

"What?" Ruby asked.

"This giant gap between us."

"You'd rather spoon?"

"I'm fine with it…" Coral swept a hand over the empty space. "My grandma called it leaving room for Jesus."

Ruby burst out laughing. "Your poor grandpa."

Coral laughed too, and the sound was so contagious that it took them a long minute to calm down.

Ruby grinned at the ceiling, a little more relaxed. It felt good to be like this with Coral. They needed it after such a long day of traveling. It felt like a week ago that they'd met in the parking garage to consolidate their stuff.

"Good night, Ruby," Coral said, her voice carrying across the empty expanse they'd left for Jesus.

Ruby grinned into the darkness, her heart full of something like adventure. "Good night, Coral."

Chapter 11
Coral

AFTER STOPPING FOR GROCERIES AND gas, Coral and Ruby continued down Highway 101, winding along the scenic Oregon coast, passing towns so small that they came and went in a breath. They took turns driving, giving both of them a chance to take footage out the window to try and capture that elusive viral content.

"Okay, would you rather adopt ten dogs or zero dogs?" Coral asked from the passenger's seat, continuing a long game of Would You Rather. She was having way more fun with this than she'd expected when she'd suggested it. Based on how animated Ruby had become, it seemed that she was too.

Ruby hummed, tapping her fingers on the steering wheel. "Ten. I'd rather have too many dogs than zero. Though I would have to sell my van and drive a converted school bus."

Coral nodded. "True. One dog is—Oh, wow, look at that view!"

It was the fifteenth time one of them had said it during the drive down the coast, but it was hard not to be in awe at the dramatic rocky shoreline and the huge waves rolling in. Plus, all of the rivers and bodies of water speckling the land were too gorgeous not to point out.

They gazed at the waves crashing into the shore until they rounded a bend and it fell out of sight.

"Would you rather..." Ruby chewed her lip. "Okay, would you rather get rid of all of your socks or all of your underwear?"

Coral gave the question serious consideration. "Underwear. I could live if I had to go commando, but if I didn't have socks, I'd get so many blisters that I would probably never be able to hike again."

"Makes sense. I'm not as much of a hiker as you, so I'd choose the opposite. I could survive in sandals."

"Fair. Hm… Would you rather eat for free at a Michelin-starred restaurant, or have a night of amazing sex with your celebrity crush?" Coral asked.

Ruby paused for a fraction of a second. "Free Michelin meal."

Coral put down the camera and turned in the passenger's seat to face her. "Really? You'd choose food over sex?"

"Hundreds of dollars' worth of a world-class meal? Yes."

Coral looked her up and down, then faced forward again, unable to stop herself from making a smug expression. "I see."

"What?"

"Nothing."

"What?" Ruby exclaimed.

"Well, there are two possible explanations here. Either you don't have a celebrity crush…or you haven't had good sex."

Ruby opened her mouth, incredulous. "Excuse me?"

"Yes, I think it's the latter," Coral deadpanned.

"I've had good sex!"

"Not good enough that you'd choose it over food."

"World-class food."

"It's still just food."

"It's about the whole dining experience," Ruby said emphatically. "Meals come with multiple courses, drinks, dessert, candles…the whole VIP experience."

"Sex comes with foreplay. And if you're with someone good, it's pretty much a VIP experience." Coral waggled her eyebrows.

"Oh, stop it." Ruby let out an awkward giggle. "Also, the celebrity sex would be meaningless. I need it to mean something if I'm going to enjoy it."

"Fair."

Ruby looked ahead, her lips curved upward. She had a freckle by her temple, right at the top of her cheekbone. Loose strands from her ponytail fluttered across it as the wind whipped through the cracked windows. "Maybe *you* haven't had good food. Ever think about it that way?"

"I've had good food."

Ruby shook her head. "Now I have to pull out all my best meals for you."

"I look forward to it."

Something fluttered in Coral's midsection in a way that only a conversation about sex could do. And something about sex plus Ruby. She picked up her camera again to distract herself with the view before her brain could go down that totally inappropriate road any further.

"Who have you had all these VIP experiences with?" Ruby asked. "Are you in a relationship?"

Coral smirked. So Ruby was still thinking about it too. "Single. I've had two partners. Three, technically, but the first doesn't count because he was a dude, and it was *not* great sex. The other two were girls, and that, my friend, is where you get the VIP experience."

Ruby gave her a double-take. No, not a double-take—more like a seven-take. Her lips were parted, a question forming behind her eyes.

"What?" Coral asked.

"You're—I didn't know—Are you a lesbian?"

Coral raised an eyebrow. "Um, yeah. You didn't know?"

"No. Why would I know that?"

"I've talked about it on my channel—" Coral's insides twisted as she realized she'd made an assumption. "Sorry, I guess you wouldn't know if you haven't seen my channel."

Ruby was quiet again. Coral would've given her lunch to know what she was thinking.

"I never talk about relationship stuff in my videos," Ruby said finally, "but I'm a lesbian."

Coral's brain stalled. "Shut up. Are you serious?"

"Why wouldn't I—"

"I had no idea!" The little sparks inside her roared to life. Not only was Ruby beautiful and established but she was also into women? Was this goddess real?

Stop it. Her sexuality shouldn't change anything.

Their partnership was a business agreement. Hitting on her would be like hitting on a coworker. Out of bounds. Inappropriate.

"Why does it matter?" Ruby narrowed her eyes suspiciously.

Coral smiled. "I'm just excited that we're both queer. For our channels. Maybe we should use this marketing angle—"

"No," Ruby said firmly.

"Why not?" Coral exclaimed. It was a valid suggestion.

"There's no point. I'm perma-single anyway, and my sexuality shouldn't matter to my viewers."

"It does and it doesn't. It's part of your identity. My viewers love it when I share personal details."

Ruby pulled over at a rest stop called Boiler Bay, which had to be the most gorgeous view yet—a high cliff overlooking a turquoise bay.

"We're two girls on a road trip, and that's our angle," Ruby said.

"Two lesbians," Coral murmured.

They got out and walked over to lean against the wooden fence. Even Calvin seemed enraptured by the view, poking his head between the railings to look down at the water. Below, the waves crashed against the jagged, rocky shore and sent up sprays so high they drew gasps from everyone standing with their cameras. The frigid mist bathed Coral's cheeks and coated her tongue in salt.

"Just keep our angle as two vanlifers partnering up, okay?" Ruby said. "It's not that I'm closeted, but I don't want to pigeonhole myself. My niche is *female intentional living vanlifer*, and adding *lesbian* in there will narrow my audience too much."

"Okay. I disagree, but okay." Maybe this was another one of those things that Coral was more open about than Ruby. That was fine. So she wouldn't talk about it in her next video. There were lots of other topics to cover, right?

Ruby faced her, crossing and uncrossing her arms. "Are you really that naïve?"

"Tell me."

"We're posting content on the *internet*. There are so many trolls and creeps who would fetishize us. I already have to block weirdos on a daily basis. This would be like…" She shuddered and faced the water again, frowning.

Heat rose in Coral's face. She hadn't considered that part—and wouldn't have experienced it to the same extent as Ruby, with her platform being smaller. "I'm sorry."

Ruby didn't meet her eye. The wind whipped locks of hair around her face as she scowled at the view. "It's fine. Part of being a creator, right?"

They watched the scenery for a moment, silence stretching between them.

"What about all of the people who would feel inspired and uplifted?" Coral asked gently. "A few years ago, how would you have felt to see someone on YouTube who shares your identity?"

Ruby finally looked at her. "I would've screamed, probably."

Coral smiled. "Those are the people I'm doing this for. I want to *be* the representation I've always wanted. Know what I mean?"

Ruby studied her, her brow pinched. She gave the subtlest of nods.

"I'll let you decide," Coral said. "I understand either way."

Ruby twisted her lips into a small smile. "Thanks."

They stayed to watch the powerful waves froth and crash for a while. The calm beaches back home had nothing on this, and Coral broke out her camera for some epic footage. The pleasant sound purred in her ears, soothing and energizing all at once.

Ruby walked back and forth with Calvin, letting him stretch, pausing here and there to take photos and videos. She moved with the grace of a dancer, just like Coral had seen in her videos. When she stopped to fix her ponytail to tame the windblown locks, Coral had to force her gaze away from her arms and neck.

Business agreement aside, Ruby was way out of her league. She was older, more established, more interesting, more confident, more *everything*. Coral was embarrassing herself by even thinking about this.

"Shall we?" Ruby asked, startling Coral back to reality.

"Yep!" Coral said with a bit too much enthusiasm.

They hopped back in the van and continued on, Ruby taking the wheel.

Was Ruby right that they should stay in a *female vanlifer* lane and avoid inviting more creepy comments? Or could they stand to gain something from openly talking about their sexualities?

The latter put an excited skip in Coral's chest. Going on the road with a successful creator was great, but there was potential for more exciting videos something more than an ordinary road trip series.

How much better would their videos do if their viewers knew they were both single, both into women, and sharing a bed every night? And what sort of traction could they gain within the queer community?

Coral would let the subject drop and give Ruby the space to consider it, but they'd gone past a point of no return with this discovery—and the tiniest seed of an idea was sprouting in the back of her mind.

Chapter 12
Ruby

"I'M SORRY THERE'S A LAYER of dog hair on everything." Ruby tried to wipe it all off the bench seat, but it was hopeless. Coral's van had been infiltrated.

"It's okay." Coral laughed. "I don't mind. Honestly."

They'd arrived in the Oregon Dunes, marked by the obvious presence of deep, tan-colored sand everywhere. Their campsite was in a beautiful wooded oasis called Umpqua Lighthouse State Park, where tall trees cast them into a patchwork of sun and shade. The air smelled crisp and clean, and the surf roared in the distance.

Coral went to fill the water jugs, which had grown dangerously empty on the long drive, while Ruby plugged in the van's electrical and swept out the ecosystem of dirt that had collected on the van floor. She put away the clothes strewn across the bed and threw out the receipts and wrappers Coral tended to toss everywhere, leaving the van in a more acceptable state. Letting out a breath, she turned off her camera.

Something like frustration twisted in her gut. Would filming this ordinary camping setup be interesting enough? Why should their viewers care? Yesterday's video had gotten an average number of likes and comments, and her follower count hadn't grown by anything significant. With such mediocre results so far, Coral's idea to be open about their sexualities on camera grew roots in Ruby's mind.

She'd refused for a good reason. There were few things as creepy as having a random guy DM her, asking if she was alone or saying he saw her earlier or trying to find out where she would go next. Days like that made her grateful for Calvin and bear spray.

But those things were sadly unavoidable on the internet, and whether she opened up about her sexuality on camera or not wouldn't change the fact that those creeps would always be there.

Coral had a point about becoming the representation she'd always wanted to see. When she considered how her younger self would have reacted at seeing a sapphic Asian American YouTuber, the decision became easy. She could make a difference for people who shared her identity. Plus, getting personal on camera earned views; scrolling through vanlife channels on YouTube offered all the proof she needed.

She'd never considered talking about her personal life on her channel until recently. Her content had always had a different purpose. What would she say? She really was perma-single and had no intention of changing that. Life was too complicated without bringing dating into it.

"Should we explore the campsite?" Coral asked.

Ruby checked the time. It was a little early to start dinner. "I'll get Calvin's leash."

At the mention of his leash, Calvin jumped up and down, excited to explore.

They went for a walk, spying on everyone's campsites and admiring the different motorhomes and trailers, and then followed a path down to Lake Marie. It was a glassy, quiet pool that looked totally untouched despite the well-used trail around it. They raised their cameras to capture it.

"This would be such a good lake for paddleboarding," Coral said longingly. "Look how smooth it is."

"I've never tried paddleboarding. Am I missing out?"

"You'd love it. It's like meditating."

Ruby imagined herself trying to stand up on a floating board while Calvin sat at her feet. "Until you fall in."

Coral tossed a pebble into the water, watching the ripples spread. "On a lake like this, you wouldn't fall in."

"I'd find a way."

Coral laughed. "You don't strike me as clumsy."

"Not clumsy, just no experience with anything physical."

"Your parents didn't put you in sports?"

Ruby shook her head, ignoring the pang that still came when people said *parents*, assuming she had both.

Maybe it would be fine to tell Coral about Dad. After spending these last couple of days with her, she felt more ready to trust her with the personal details of her life.

They kept walking around the lake, and Calvin searched for a break in the bush so he could jump in.

"Well, I would argue that paddleboarding is one of the least physical activities you could do...except I've had my struggles," Coral said.

Ruby smiled. "What happened?"

"Once, and only once, I went out on a lake when it was windy. I was overconfident about these bad boys." She flexed and patted a bicep.

Ruby laughed.

"No matter how hard I paddled, I couldn't beat the wind," Coral said. "I was too exhausted to paddle back, and I got blown so far from where I started that it was hopeless. So I got out of the water on someone's private property, slogged through blackberry bushes with my board, got all cut up and bloody, and came out on a side street. I had to hitchhike back to my campsite. A nice family in a Jeep stopped and saved me."

Ruby gawked at her. "Okay, I would've cried."

Coral laughed. "I almost did."

"I'm not sure if the near-drowning or hitchhiking is the scarier part."

Coral shrugged. "I've had to hitchhike a couple of times while traveling abroad. There's always a bit of trepidation—horror stories creeping into the back of your mind—but it's always worked out."

Her phone beeped, and she took it out to reply to a text. Her cheeks lifted as she read whatever message she'd received, her lips making a heart shape.

She had to be one of the most interesting people Ruby had ever met. Ruby had never even tried paddleboarding, never mind having an adventure where she nearly got stranded. As for hitchhiking? She'd rather walk than trust a stranger with her life.

Hearing little details of Coral's travels and adventures forced to mind the possibility that Ruby was, in fact, boring. She didn't have mishaps to share. She couldn't think of an interesting story about herself if she tried.

Calvin found a gap in the trail and plunged into the water with a splash. He swam in a circle with pure happiness in his eyes, making Ruby and Coral both laugh as they filmed him.

Coral's phone beeped again. She stopped walking to reply, that little heart-shaped smile reappearing on her lips.

She noticed Ruby watching her and said, "My sister. She's got a new boyfriend."

Ruby looked away, heat rising in her cheeks over being caught staring. "Oh?"

"Well, sort of. She barely has time for him with school." Coral rolled her eyes. "She doesn't have time for anything she enjoys."

"I think being busy is just life, isn't it?"

Coral tilted her head. "I don't know. Seems worse for some people. I feel like I've got time with this minimalist lifestyle, don't you?"

"Meh. I live minimally, but I still don't have time for a social life."

"Not even dating?"

Ruby shook her head. "Especially not dating. I've got better things to do."

Things meaning helping Mom, and, realistically, that was probably the whole list. But it was important.

Coral nodded. A crease appeared between her eyebrows as she studied Ruby.

What was she thinking about?

Ruby checked the time. "Anyway, let's get back, and I'll start dinner. How do you feel about sushi bowls?"

Coral's expression softened, and she grinned. "Yum! But are you sure you don't want me to cook tonight?"

Ruby nodded. "I need the content for my channel."

Back at the van, Coral stayed outside with Calvin while Ruby set up her ring lights and camera. Narrating every step, she put on rice, then prepared a tray of cubed tofu and yams in a blend of spices.

"Make sure you don't skip the ginger," she told the camera, holding up the little glass jar.

Next, she sauteed shredded cabbage, carrots, and edamame with a bit of soy sauce.

This recipe looked fantastic and was sure to get hits. But would it be enough?

Guessing what videos would go viral was an impossible science—but maybe Coral was right, and it was time to try something drastically different. Something adventurous. At the very least, Ruby shouldn't be so reluctant to open up about her personal life on camera.

She couldn't deny that her aversion to getting personal on camera ran deep. It was the threat of opening up about painful things to strangers—like losing Dad. Internet strangers weren't her therapists, and she didn't owe them any personal confessions.

But bringing up one aspect of her personal life didn't mean she had to talk about all of it. She could choose what she wanted to share. She didn't have to talk about things that hurt.

Would that be welcomed by her viewers? Or would they roll their eyes and migrate to a different channel to give them the content they wanted?

The latest comments she'd gotten contradicted each other, with some people excited about the road trip and others keen to tell her how much they didn't want change.

> *Please don't stop making your usual content! I live for quiet time with Ruby & Calvin!*

> *Ooh this is amazing. My bf and I are thinking of doing the same road trip. Can't wait to see your videos!*

Frustration simmered inside her. How was she supposed to keep as many subscribers as possible happy? Why wasn't there a formula she could follow to gain new people while keeping the old ones?

She mixed rice vinegar into the cooked rice, then spooned it into two bowls. She topped it with the tofu, yams, and vegetable mix, then sliced and fanned out half an avocado on each bowl.

"Now each bowl gets a sprinkling of seaweed," she said to the camera. "For that, we'll use nori."

She toasted two sheets of nori, then crumbled it on top, followed by a dash of toasted sesame seeds. Finally, she dolloped vegan sriracha-mayo on each like a cherry on top.

It was beautiful. A rainbow in a bowl.

She scowled.

Now let's see if viewers care.

Chapter 13
Coral

WHILE RUBY MADE DINNER, CORAL set up their campsite. She put down a bamboo mat so they could be outside without shoes, and she'd just draped a tablecloth over the wooden picnic table when her phone beeped with another text from Farrah.

Anyway, how's it going with Ruby Hayashi? Is she awesome?

Coral hovered her thumbs over the screen, not sure how to reply. Yes, Ruby was awesome. She was as polished and perfect as her videos, and once in a while, she let Coral see the real person underneath—the person who helped out her mom, who worried about the future of her career, who braided her hair before bed and slept in a camisole and flannel shorts.

Coral kept her reply simple.

It's been fun! Ruby's cool, and Calvin is the cutest. He makes me want to adopt a dog.

She went to get the fairy lights. As she strung them up outside the van, Farrah's reply came.

Do it!! Get a bernedoodle.

Coral smirked, shaking her head.

Ok, chill, bernedoodles are thousands of dollars. I was thinking a rescue. Calvin is a wounded soul.

Aww. Does he like you?

Coral looked down at him, where he lay sprawled in the dirt, still damp from the lake. He lifted his head to meet her gaze with his giant seal eyes, then sprawled flat again. She smiled.

Getting there. We bonded over cheese.

And Ruby?

It took Coral a second to understand what Farrah was asking. *Did* Ruby like her?

In the van, Ruby moved around the kitchen and narrated her recipe for the camera.

Despite a bit of friction yesterday as they'd packed the van and arrived late to Cannon Beach, things seemed to be going well. They'd shared smiles and laughs and had conversations about real life. Ruby had even opened up about her mom. She was just reserved, and that made her hard to read.

It also made her intriguing.

Yes, Ruby likes me too.

Coral shifted on her feet, this conversation making her face hot.

Ruby stepped outside with two bowls in hand, grinning. "Nice setup!"

"Thanks." Coral told Farrah she had to go and put her phone away.

Ruby tilted her head and flashed a cute smile. "Dinner is served."

They set up a camera on the picnic table and settled in.

Coral took a bite, and, *wow*, it tasted unbelievably good. "Okay, this competes with sex," she said begrudgingly.

"Ha!" Ruby fist-pumped.

"*Competes.* I didn't say it won out."

"I'll take it."

They ate to the sound of chirping birds and rustling trees, and Ruby paused once in a while to fiddle with her camera.

It was interesting how she hadn't changed anything about the mellow cooking videos she posted. And actually, Coral hadn't done anything different with her own videos either. Both of them were posting the same style, stuck in the same ruts, just with a different backdrop. Wasn't the point of this trip to change things up and produce exciting content?

"How was the reception on the video you posted yesterday?" Coral asked.

Ruby shrugged. "Meh. You?"

"Same." Coral hesitated. She wanted to do something adventurous with Ruby tomorrow, but she was afraid of the answer. Trying to keep her tone light, she said, "Maybe tomorrow you should post a video of us in a dune buggy instead of another recipe."

Her light tone didn't work.

"My followers want the same sort of content as usual," Ruby said, a little snippy. "I've had a lot of comments asking me to keep doing the same thing. I can't afford to lose my existing audience."

"Okay, sorry. I just thought you wanted something different."

"I don't see you doing anything different. Maybe you should try savoring the small stuff instead of trying to make everything into a big adventure."

"I enjoy the small things!" Coral said, the words stinging. "But adventures make for the most memorable parts of any vacation, and you know it. When was the last time you did something adventurous?"

Calvin looked between them from his spot in the dirt, his ears perked, like he was trying to figure out why their voices had gotten louder.

"Living in a van is adventurous in itself," Ruby said.

Not the way you do it, Coral wanted to say. Instead, she said calmly, "I'm going to rent a dune buggy tomorrow. Will you come with me?"

Ruby glared. The way her face pinched when she was angry was cute, which made it hard to be irritated with her.

Her gaze darted over Coral's face. "I get your point about adventures making good memories. But I don't know how much I would like riding in a dune buggy."

"At least try it. You can post the dune buggy video *and* a recipe."

There was a pause while Ruby seemed to search for an argument. "I'll think about it."

That was something.

After dinner, they began editing the day's videos in silence. Coral wanted to ask Ruby for advice—there were a lot of features she didn't use, and she wasn't even sure whether she was using the best software—but Ruby looked too deep in thought to be interrupted, so Coral kept her questions to herself.

Then Ruby asked, "Do you think I should stop using a soft filter on my videos? Would that make it look a little less polished and more…different?"

Wait, did Ruby Hayashi, video editing expert, just ask Coral for advice?

Coral hesitated. "Um—maybe? Are you talking about adding color corrections?"

"Yeah."

Coral shifted on the hard bench, crossing her legs. "I think your editing style should stay the same because that's your brand. If you want to be different, it's about the content itself. Trying new things, you know?"

Ruby chewed her lip. "Yeah."

"Your editing is perfect, Ruby. Actually, I was hoping you could give *me* some advice on that part. I barely add filters and don't know what visual style I'm going for."

Ruby stood. "Sure, I could show you."

Coral shuffled over as Ruby came around the picnic table to sit beside her.

As she sat next to Coral so that their arms brushed, Coral's heart did a little skip. She leaned away for some reason, as if in silent apology for touching Ruby.

Dammit, why does she have to be so pretty? I'm acting weird.

"What programs do you use?" Ruby asked.

Coral showed her, and they descended into a crash-course on video and sound editing. She took notes, astounded by how much Ruby knew, and wasn't surprised to learn that Ruby had taken a few online courses on the topic.

Should I be taking courses too?

Maybe that would be a good way to convince her parents she was making a viable business decision.

"You're a godsend," Coral said after an hour. She'd thanked Ruby profusely and still fell short of expressing how grateful she was. The footage she'd taken today looked astronomically better, like she'd sent it to a production team. They'd created a bright, pink-tinted filter that she could start using on all of her videos for a consistent tone.

Ruby met her gaze. "No worries."

"Now, any hot tips for marketing?" Coral asked with a hopeful smile.

Ruby tilted her head. "Just send it out into the world and hope for the best."

Chapter 14
Ruby

"Come on, you got tons of good comments!" Coral exclaimed from the bed, using her laptop to scroll through the comments on the video Ruby had posted last night. "Look at this one. *Another amazing video, Ruby. You make me want to go to Cannon Beach. Keep shining that inner and outer beauty!* Aww, that's nice, right?"

Ruby rubbed her hands over her face, slumping against Calvin on the bench. It was sweet of Coral to point out the positive comments, but she didn't get it. "That was from Mrs. Peppermint, and she comments nice things on everything I do. I'm talking about the overall reception." Yesterday's video hadn't performed any better than the first. Sure, there were nice comments, but her stats hadn't gone up. In fact, they were continuing on the downward trend they'd been on for two months.

Was this whole road trip a waste of effort?

Crap, crap, crap. I'm so screwed.

"How was your reception?" Ruby asked, trying not to spiral.

Coral wrinkled her nose and slapped her laptop shut. "I mean, I've got more followers thanks to you, but my stats aren't as great as I'd hoped. But this is only day three, so maybe we just need time."

"Maybe."

Hopefully. What else were they supposed to do to make better content?

But that, of course, was the ultimate question that loomed over creators everywhere.

With a sigh, Ruby got up to prepare Calvin's breakfast. He watched her eagerly, his ears perked.

Thankfully, Coral didn't bring up the top comment under the video:

You two are so cute together!

Ruby wasn't sure how to interpret that, nor how to feel about it. "Cute" could mean a lot of different things. Was it something about the way they interacted? What did they mean by *together*? And why did so many people reply to voice their agreement?

They ate breakfast and got ready for the day, then drove a few minutes down the road to the dune buggy rental place. Coral would rent one for a couple of hours, and Ruby would…do something else?

Ugh.

Last night's conversation lingered in Ruby's stomach, churning, unsettled.

It was time to do something adventurous. She wanted fresh content, and this was a good opportunity. Her original plan was to walk around the dunes, but she had to admit that a dune buggy would be a better way to see the famous landscape. Coral had an air-conditioning unit, so Calvin could stay safely in the van while they went. She had no excuse.

Coral parked the van and turned to Ruby, a question in her eyes after that silent drive over.

"Okay, I've made up my mind." Ruby braced for an explosive reaction. "I'll rent a dune buggy with you. But don't expect me to be a daredevil—"

"Yes!" Coral leaned closer like she wanted to hug Ruby, but there was too big a gap and a dog between the seats. The little dimples in her cheeks made an appearance. "Oh my God, I'm so excited. This'll be fun."

"And a little expensive."

"Not so bad if we share. Also, we're using it for our channels, so it's a tax write-off." She winked.

"Yeah…" Ruby grimaced. Tax write-off or not, she prayed that dropping a hundred or two hundred or whatever would be worth it.

They went inside the office, and the whole time while they signed forms and handed over their drivers' licenses and credit cards, Ruby's insides became more jittery. The safety video made everything way worse. This was dangerous! What if they hit a well in the sand and tipped over? What if the vehicle landed on her and she broke a bone?

As they went back outside, Coral nudged her gently. "I can see you panicking, and you need to stop. Families with children do this all the time, and we'll go slow."

"Okay," Ruby said, unconvinced.

They followed a truck and trailer to a staging area down the road and through a landscape that felt more like being in the desert than the Pacific Northwest. They left Calvin in the air-conditioned van with water and a peanut butter ball. A guy who must have been around their age—and who was definitely flirting with both of them—showed them which buttons to push. In way less time than Ruby felt comfortable with, he drove away, leaving them with a two-seater dune buggy, helmets, and goggles.

"That's it?" Ruby asked, her voice coming out high. "We just get in and go?"

"Yup." Coral slid into the driver's seat. "Come on. I'll drive first so you can see how easy this is."

Ruby looked around. They were in a parking lot, which was in the middle of the most sand she had ever seen in her life. It was soft and deep, like a tropical beach. Trees obstructed her view, and curiosity urged her to get in the buggy so she could see what lay beyond them.

"Okay," she said weakly.

Coral pushed a button, and the dune buggy roared to life. Ruby couldn't stop herself from murmuring, "Oh my God, oh my God…" as she slid into the passenger seat.

With a lurch and an exhilarated laugh from Coral, they set off, heading into the enormous expanse of the Oregon Dunes.

Coral had her GoPro strapped to her chest, and she'd propped her phone in front of them to capture their faces. Ruby vowed to capture extra phone footage later—for now, she was too busy gripping the seat.

As they emerged from the trees surrounding the parking lot, the view made Ruby's breath catch. Endless hills of sand sprawled out on either side. Ahead, a steep slope led up to a ridge topped with trees. Tire tracks covered every square foot of sand, making Ruby wonder what this place would look like unsullied. Plastic bottles and trash confirmed her suspicion that a lot of people saw the dunes as a dirt bike track instead of a natural wonder.

Coral accelerated, taking them up the first massive dune.

Ruby grabbed her arm. "Slow down!"

Coral laughed. "Ruby, a child just booted past us."

She wasn't wrong. A boy who couldn't have been older than nine zoomed ahead on his ATV, an orange flag flapping on the back, followed a moment later by his even younger sister, and then his parents in a two-seater dune buggy.

"Then follow the kids," Ruby said. "I don't want you to hit those crazy dips they showed us in the safety video."

"Follow the kids? You got it." Coral accelerated hard and steered into their wake.

Ruby screamed and gripped Coral's arm tighter. Coral cackled, which made Ruby's scream turn into an exhilarated laugh.

Maybe she didn't need to hold onto Coral's arm, but she liked it. Touching her was easy and comfortable.

At the top of the dune, they could see the extent of the recreation area, and it was like they'd taken a wrong turn and landed on Mars. They bumped over the landscape, getting faster as they both gained confidence. Ruby had to admit that Coral did a good job of not driving into hazards.

At the end of the recreation area, where a tsunami siren towered over the landscape, they parked on top of a dune to take in the scenery and have a break from the machine's noise and vibrations.

Ruby let go of Coral and relaxed, shaking out the tension in her shoulders.

"This is fun, right?" Coral asked. It was cute how her whole face brightened when she was exhilarated. She clearly thrived on stuff like this.

"Yes. Fine, I'm glad I joined you," Ruby said reluctantly, returning her smile.

They removed their helmets and goggles and sipped their waters.

Coral stopped the GoPro recording, and Ruby reached forward to pause the recording on the phone.

"Hey, I'm sorry I snapped at you when you brought up this idea," Ruby said. "I'm just…a little stressed about my income lately."

Coral waved a hand. "I'd hardly call that snapping. And so am I. Side effect of an unsteady paycheck, right?"

God, she was so easygoing. It was a nice quality.

They watched a group of teenagers blow past, doing wheelies and donuts—a level of bravery Ruby would never have.

"The thing is…" Ruby swallowed hard. The full truth was on her tongue, ready to come out. This could be the first step to opening up more about her personal life. Telling Coral felt safe, harmless.

And when she considered it, she *wanted* to share this part of her life with Coral. She rarely felt comfortable enough to open up to someone she just met, and it would feel good to let Coral into her mind a little more.

Coral waited, giving her full attention. When she wasn't smiling for the camera or talking excitedly about something, the angles of her face were softer, rounder.

Ruby drew a breath. "My dad died four years ago and left my mom with debt. It wasn't his fault—it was mostly medical bills. My mom struggled to support us, especially when the tea shop took a hit in the crappy economy. So, when my channel became popular and I started earning money, I was able to help out. I could pay my own expenses and more. But it's hard sometimes, supporting two people and a dog while living in Seattle. That's where my stress comes from. It's just hard."

She couldn't hold Coral's gaze after spilling all of that, so she angled her face away as if taking in the view of the coast.

"I'm sorry about your dad," Coral said. "Thanks for telling me. I get the financial strain, believe me. Vancouver isn't much different in terms of the cost of living."

Ruby pressed her lips together, trying to smile.

"That's a lot to take on," Coral said.

"It's been all right. I just don't have a savings buffer."

This was putting it lightly, but she'd hit her limit on personal confessions. To admit her van was broken was to open a can of worms she wasn't ready to face—about her family, about money, about her deepest fears and anxieties. She didn't need Coral to know she'd been putting up a front, and she definitely didn't want to start crying in front of her.

Coral nodded. A group of people on dirt bikes zoomed by, their engines so noisy that Ruby winced.

When they'd gone, Coral said, "I'm here if you need to talk about stuff."

"Thanks." Ruby was grateful that Coral didn't make this awkward with a pitying look or empty words about what her dad would have wanted. "Should we keep going?"

"Sure. Do you want a turn driving?"

Ruby hesitated. A video of her driving a dune buggy would make good content. She should do this.

Be brave.

"Yeah, okay."

They swapped seats.

"I bet your mom's super proud of you," Coral said as she put her helmet back on. "Kicking ass with your platform and all. How many parents can say their kids help support them? That's usually reserved for pro athletes and celebrities, you know?"

Ruby did take a lot of pride in being able to support her mom. Her chest swelled at Coral's kind words. But with that pride came a lot of responsibility and stress. Nothing was simple when money was involved.

"She was concerned about me living in a van at first, but she just wants me to be happy and safe. She actually bought me Calvin."

"Really?"

"She said I could pick out whatever dog I wanted, as long as it was big." Ruby laughed at the memory. "She was expecting me to choose something like a well-bred German Shepherd, but I wanted a rescue. So I picked the dog who needed me most. He was at the shelter for over a year before I adopted him."

"Over a year?" Coral exclaimed.

"Not many people want pit bull-type dogs, especially not one who's been abused and doesn't like men. But there are a lot of them. It was heartbreaking to choose just one when so many need homes."

Coral paused in setting up the cameras. "There are a lot of dogs who don't like men?"

Ruby shrugged. "The shelter told me a lot of fearful dogs prefer a feminine presence."

"Hm…" Coral tilted her head thoughtfully.

Ruby glanced over, her finger hovering over the buggy's start button. "What?"

"I've just decided that one day I'm going to open a dog rescue that specifically finds homes for dogs who are afraid of men. *Rescue Dogs for Lesbians.*"

Ruby burst out laughing. She pushed the start button, and the buggy roared to life. Coral turned on the cameras and sat back.

There was that topic again. The elephant in the room.

She couldn't help imagining a scenario where she and Coral had met under different circumstances, like in a coffee shop. Of course, this road trip was for a professional purpose, so the idea of anything sparking between them was off the table. Besides, Ruby had too much to worry about with Mom, and she wasn't lying when she said she had no time for a relationship. Between Mom, Calvin, and her channel, that was one hundred percent of her time and energy.

But in other circumstances…

Stop it. No use thinking about what-ifs.

"You have to give it gas to move," Coral said teasingly.

Ruby gripped the wheel. "I'm psyching myself up."

She accelerated so slowly that Coral dissolved into laughter. She leaned across to grab Ruby's arm, a sensation that sent a pleasant jolt through Ruby's chest.

Ruby smiled reluctantly. "I live at my own pace!"

She drove along the top of the dune at a crawl before taking them down the slope.

"Try going into the trees." Coral pointed to a trail off to the side. "You can go nice and slow in there, and we'll get to see some fun detours."

Ruby steered them into the trees, where they wove along paths between clumps of bushes. Her heart beat faster. "Okay, but we can't turn off the path. If there's a huge drop at the end of this, we're screwed."

"Oh, stop it. There wouldn't be so many tire tracks through here if it ended in danger."

They came to a big, sloping turn around a tree, and Ruby slowed down.

"Keep your momentum," Coral said.

"We're on an angle!"

"And we're about to be on a steeper angle if you—oh, God."

"Shit!"

Agonizingly slowly, the dune buggy lost traction on the right wheels, and Ruby could do nothing to regain their balance. She leaned to the right, and so did Coral, but the buggy kept tipping as if in slow motion.

"What do I do?" Ruby cried.

The buggy fell onto its side, and Coral landed on top of her. Their faces brushed, and their hands scrambled for grip, and for a moment, Ruby swore her fingers closed around Coral's boob.

"Sorry—"

"Oof!"

"I'm stuck—"

"Grab onto this—"

Their noses bumped. In a tangle of limbs, they got free of the cab and rolled onto their hands and knees in the deep sand. The buggy lay shamefully tipped on its side, the engine still running. Coral reached over and turned it off.

Ruby gasped for breath. "You said the trees would be safe!"

"If you drive like a normal person, yeah!"

"Since when is going slowly more dangerous than going fast?"

"You lost momentum!"

They glared at each other, and Coral had so much sand on her face that Ruby couldn't help breaking into laughter.

They both laughed harder, sitting back, until they were wiping gritty tears from their eyes.

"I'm sorry." Ruby rubbed her face in embarrassment. Of course she would do something like this. This was why she avoided doing wild and outgoing things—they always seemed to end in disaster.

Coral got to her feet and extended a hand to help Ruby up. "Don't apologize, babe. These things are inevitable, and based on that safety video, they get tip-overs all the time."

Babe. Ruby's belly flipped as they clasped hands.

"I guess." Ruby sighed and pulled out her phone. "I'll call the rental place."

"You okay?" Coral asked.

"Yeah. I just feel like a kid about to get in trouble."

When the reality of the moment sank in, she couldn't help smirking. She'd wanted a story, an adventurous mishap that would make her interesting like Coral—and here it was, lying in front of her in the form of a rolled-over dune buggy.

"Look at the bright side..." Coral nudged the sideways vehicle with the toe of her hiking boot.

"Good content?" Ruby said with a grimace.

Coral swept a hand beneath the blinking red light on her GoPro. "*Excellent* content."

Chapter 15
Coral

BULLARDS BEACH STATE PARK WAS a gorgeous campground with a picture-perfect hike to the beach. As the sun dipped lower, they ate dinner and edited their videos on the picnic table, leaving the van's back doors open to let the crisp forest air flow through. The routine was easy and comfortable, as if Ruby had always been part of Coral's life in a van.

Before setting off in the morning, Coral oiled the hinges on a squeaky cupboard, then knelt to tighten another one that kept swinging open whenever they hit a bump. She waved off Ruby's offer to help, rummaging for the Phillips screwdriver. "I'll be two seconds."

Her camera rolled to record the repair. Amid the fun and adventure, she liked showing her audience the realities of this lifestyle.

"I can top up the water while you do that," Ruby offered.

"Sure." Coral passed her the jugs from under the sink and paused the recording. "Hey, I meant to tell you, I got a good response on my video editing. Some people actually said they could tell you helped me." She grinned. They'd given each other feedback last night, and Coral had released hers into the world with confidence. The collaboration had paid off.

"Glad I could help. I actually got compliments for showing a different side of me, so…I guess our plan is working."

She got out to fill the jugs, Calvin at her heels. It was cute how he never let Ruby out of his sight.

The words "our plan is working" were subjective. They still hadn't broken that invisible barrier that would bring them more income. But if they continued to be strategic, maybe that wasn't far off. Rolling over in a dune buggy had certainly helped their views go up.

By the time Ruby came back in, Coral was putting away her tools.

"No more swinging!" She made jazz hands by the closed cupboard, and Ruby humored her with a gentle golf clap.

"Bravo."

They put everything away in preparation for the drive, and Ruby pulled Calvin's bed to its traveling spot between the seats.

What Coral had purposely avoided bringing up was the slew of other comments she'd been getting. Ruby was getting them too—Coral had checked her dune buggy video early this morning. Their viewers were *not* subtle.

> *Omg I can't handle the amount of flirting in this video. Kiss already!*

> *Cuuute!! Now admit you have secret crushes on each other!*

> *Anyone else screaming over the fact that the two of them are sharing a bed every night?*

And possibly the most embarrassing of all: a comment from Aunt Nina.

> *Burrito Blake?*

It was an inside joke from several years ago. They'd gone to a bouldering gym and noticed how many attractive people were there, so they came up with a code. One would nudge the other and murmur "Burrito Blake," and the other would know there was an eligible date nearby. Neither of them got anyone's number that day, but it was the birth of a code word that never failed to make the other laugh. Coral couldn't even remember what burritos had to do with it.

Aunt Nina was obviously implying that Ruby was a Burrito Blake—an eligible single that Coral should check out.

She cursed the heat rising in her cheeks and glanced at Ruby. Was she thinking about the comments too, or did they not bother her?

Based on the palpable awkwardness in the van and minimal eye contact, Ruby was definitely thinking about it. *Ugh.*

"Ready?" Coral asked as Ruby hopped into the passenger's seat.

"Hit it."

The casualness was so forced that Coral might have smirked if she wasn't so busy blushing.

Well, she hadn't been wrong when she thought their viewers would have something to say about the two of them sharing a bed. And they hadn't even talked about their sexualities on camera. People just drew their own conclusions—maybe misinterpreting their adrenaline as infatuation in the dune buggy video.

They continued down the 101 to the tune of "Pompeii" by Bastille. After driving for hours each day, they hadn't even crossed two states and the amount of unpopulated land was astounding. A lot of it was deforested, which was sad to see, but a lot had also been preserved. Coral could never get sick of gazing at the forests, ocean, and wetlands. The flat horizon drew her gaze, so different from the views back home in Vancouver.

"Why is it that we have to spend *millions* of dollars for a tiny sliver of an ocean view back home when there are hundreds of miles of empty land with even better views all down the coast?" Coral asked, baffled.

Ruby shook her head. "No idea. But I'm glad this coastline isn't full of cities."

The world felt pure, peaceful, limitless. It felt good having someone to experience it with. Coral loved the freedom and independence of traveling alone, but sometimes it was nice to have somebody to share thoughts with. Even if it was a simple nudge and a "Look at that!"

They pulled off at Port Orford Heads State Park for a rest, where they walked down the nicely groomed trail toward a viewpoint. Calvin took the lead, followed by Ruby and then Coral. A breeze helped cool down what would have been a stiflingly hot day.

"How long do you think you'll keep living in a van?" Ruby asked in a trying-to-sound-casual tone. Maybe she worried about the future?

Coral hummed. She hadn't thought much about it. "Right now I'm just focused on being able to keep living in one, never mind the end point."

"Oh. Do you think if we don't get more followers on this road trip you'll have to give it up?"

"Well…" Should she tell Ruby? Why not? Ruby had opened up to her, and part of her really wanted to open up to Ruby about her own life. "To be honest, I made a deal with my parents that if I earn enough money by the end of one year of van living, they would let me continue. Otherwise, I have to sell the van and work for them."

Ruby gasped. "Sell your van?"

"Yup. They bought it for me in the first place, and this was the deal."

Ruby whistled. "Damn. When's your deadline?"

"My birthday. July second."

"I guess we really have to figure out how to get more followers, then."

"Tell me about it."

Coral tried not to feel hopeless about their prospects, but with nothing going viral enough to make a difference, it was a little worrisome.

They walked on in silence. The trail was gorgeous and well-maintained, leading them under canopies and through meadows.

"So you're not judging me for using you?" Coral asked.

"What? Oh. I didn't think about it that way. I think we're both using each other, don't you?"

Coral's lips twitched. "Glad you think so."

As the trail wove through a meadow, the view of the ocean became so breathtaking that they both stopped to take a few pictures. Calvin sniffed the side of the trail diligently, his nose working overtime—there must have been the scent of other dogs on the bushes.

Coral considered asking Ruby how she planned to respond to all of the comments accusing them of flirting, but she couldn't bring herself to do it. What a perfectly awkward topic to ruin a hike.

"Your parents sound pretty business-driven," Ruby said.

Coral scoffed. "They're ridiculous. Like, yeah, they run a successful company, but it's ruining their lives. They never go on vacation, they have no hobbies… If my sister and I want to do something fun, it's on us. Last year, neither of them even remembered it was my birthday until my sister yelled at them for it."

"Wow. I get why you chose vanlife."

"I *refuse* to be like them."

They took more pictures. The view kept getting better and better.

"It sounds like you and your sister are close," Ruby said.

Coral smiled. "Yeah, Farrah's great. Sometimes I worry she'll go down the same path they did, but…she's aware of their issues, so maybe that will save her."

"And she has you to give her a reality check."

"She does."

"Do they give her a hard time too? I imagine she never had to make a van-related agreement with them."

"No, they approve of her university plans. But they still put a lot of pressure on her." Coral sighed, sick of talking about her parents. "Anyway, what about you? How long will you keep living in a van?"

"I don't know," Ruby said thoughtfully, "but one day I'd like a cabin on a lake. A real cabin."

"Not one of those big, fancy houses that people call cabins?"

"Exactly." Ruby looked back with a grin. Calvin chose that moment to stop and pee on another bush, and Ruby tripped over him. "Dammit, Calvin!"

Coral laughed as Ruby regained her footing.

Ruby shooed Calvin onward. "I had a friend in high school who told me her family had a cabin on a lake, but it was a house. A mansion. I was disappointed not to find a log home or a yurt when we got there."

Coral smiled. "So, what kind of home would you put on your lakeside property?"

"A tiny house. Like a converted storage container, or maybe an A-frame."

"Oh, that sounds nice." Coral sighed wistfully. "I'd want something like that too. I don't imagine living in a van forever, to answer your question, but I'd want a small home somewhere remote. I'd want to build it myself."

"Really? That'd be cool. I saw a YouTube video of a guy who built his own cabin in the middle of nowhere."

"I think I saw that guy!"

"Too bad I have no idea how to build anything."

"We could figure it out together," Coral said and then flushed at her assumption that they would stay friends. Would they part ways at the end of this road trip, or could building cabins together be in their future? She knew what she hoped for. The question was whether Ruby felt the same.

Ahead, Calvin barked.

Ruby raced to catch up. "Oh, we made it!"

Coral picked up her pace to follow.

At the end of the trail, the view was breathtaking. Far below, massive rock formations jutted dramatically from the sea. On the left, waves roared into the bay, white and frothing. On the right, a long beach stretched out. Mist turned the whole view into a dreamy haze.

"Look, seals!" Ruby exclaimed, grabbing Coral's arm and pointing downward.

Calvin poked his head through the fence to look down too, his tail wagging.

"Aww!" Coral leaned over the fence with her camera, zooming in on the dozen seals basking on a rocky plateau while waves crashed around them. "Wow, isn't it gorgeous?"

They filmed and took pictures, then put the cameras away to enjoy the view without them.

Something unidentifiable expanded in Coral's chest as they stood next to each other, gazing at the view. It was nice to get a peek at this side of Ruby and the dreams she had for the future. Was it weird to hope to be part of it? They'd only known each other for a few days, but something about this friendship promised more—like they could easily stay in touch after the road trip was over.

Back at the van, they had lunch and then continued down the winding coast, passing more breathtaking views of beaches with enormous rock formations. A viewpoint called Natural Bridges actually made Coral weak in the knees as they gazed down at the waves ebbing and flowing through massive rock archways. She took so many pictures and videos that she was sure she would hate herself later when she had to sort through them all.

They arrived at Harris Beach State Park, where they had tofu souvlaki for dinner and got to work editing the day's videos. It had been a perfect day full of ridiculously photogenic scenery, leaving Coral giddy.

This content *had* to get a lot of views.

Except what was so special about it in the public's eyes? Other people shared shots of this same scenery. Other people did this same road trip. Why should people watch Coral and Ruby's videos when there were other options?

Coral patted the bed beside her. "Do you want to film a recap of the day with me?"

Ruby looked at her. They hadn't done this yet, so it probably came as a surprise.

"Sure." Ruby came over, fixing her hair along the way.

A little victory jump happened in Coral's middle.

They started recording, and Coral put on a big smile. She clapped her hands together. "Today was an *incredible* fourth day on the road. My favorite part was Port Orford. Between the hike and the view at the end, it was just..." She swooned, falling over onto Ruby.

Ruby laughed, nudging her back to where she came from. "Port Orford was amazing. It's hard to pick, but that might've been my favorite too. The gorgeous walking path added to the experience."

"When you weren't tripping over it," Coral said.

Ruby shoved her. "That was Calvin's fault!"

Coral dissolved into laughter.

When they were done and their videos were out in the world, Coral turned to answering the comments on yesterday's video.

The most popular comment made the heat build in her cheeks.

Ughhh I ship these two so hard.

Was she imagining the awkwardness in the van again?

When she dared to look up, Ruby was definitely blushing. Her comments must have been along the same lines.

"I'm going to get ready for bed," Ruby said abruptly, slapping her laptop closed with extra force.

Coral chewed her lip, the sprouting idea in the back of her mind growing larger. She might have been onto something before.

If they wanted more followers, they had to post videos that were exciting and unique. They had to give their viewers something emotional to cling to. Above all, they had to give their audiences what they wanted.

And based on the comments...it was becoming very obvious what their audiences wanted.

Chapter 16
Ruby

IN THE CAMPSITE NEXT TO them at Harris Beach State Park, a twentysomething couple in a camper van was doing a photoshoot. Through their open back doors, Ruby could see the guy taking a photo of his partner as she lay on the bed in a thong bikini bottom and white crop top.

Ruby looked at Coral to find her staring at them too. She laughed, startling Coral.

Coral smiled guiltily. "What?"

"I think we're both distracted by the view."

The campsite was top-notch—big, grassy, and overlooking a sapphire blue ocean with a gorgeous pattern of rock formations. It offered a perfect photo op as the sun set over the water.

The guy saw Ruby and Coral looking over and nodded in greeting. "Gotta get those clicks."

Coral laughed. "Don't we know it. For social media?"

"Yeah, sorry," the woman said, blushing. "We're almost done here."

"Don't apologize. I've done the same thing. What's your handle?"

Coral walked to the edge of their campsite to talk to them, leaving Ruby to watch in awe as Coral managed to strike up a conversation with total strangers.

How did she just boldly talk to people like that? What was her secret?

While Coral chatted, Ruby opened the back of the van and began setting up their campsite.

"…we're out of here at the crack of dawn," the guy said, "but I recommend heading down to the beach before everyone else gets up. Totally worth it."

"Thanks!" Coral said. "Enjoy the rest of your trip."

When she came back to the van, Ruby shook her head. "It took me weeks of running into the same couple before I finally talked to them. You did it within a few minutes of us getting here."

Coral shrugged. "I just like meeting new people."

Thinking of Annie and Parm made Ruby wonder what they were up to. She looked up their channel. Not surprisingly, their last video was titled *Our Floor Is ROTTING! | VANLIFE NIGHTMARE.*

She closed the app without watching the video, in no mood to spike her stress levels by witnessing everything that could go wrong in a camper van.

In the morning, they took the guy's advice and walked down to enjoy the beach and take footage before everyone else got up.

Coral threw her hands in the air. "First ones here."

Ruby let Calvin off-leash for a zoom. He did a figure-eight around both of them, goading them into playing with him.

She grinned. It was progress that he wanted Coral to play too.

In the peaceful silence, they raced across the beach and climbed on top of the huge rocks, taking a thousand pictures and videos in the hopes of getting that one perfect shot.

Ruby chased Calvin, getting his energy out before the day's drive. He fed off her, barking, rearing up on his hind legs to bat her with his paws.

Coral laughed and raised her camera as she watched them roughhouse. "This is the side of you that you should show more of on your channel!"

"I want my viewers to think I'm interesting, not nuts!" Ruby shouted back, running beside Calvin over the wet sand. It splattered against her legs, but she felt invincible in her waterproof shoes.

Or did Coral have a point? Sharing this might be off-brand for her, but she'd been going off-brand more and more without disastrous consequences. "Okay, I guess I can include a little bit of this."

Calvin barked, challenging her.

She crouched. "Come at me, bro."

Calvin crouched too.

It was a perfect summer day. A warm breeze pulled the waves against the sand, carrying with it the scent of the ocean and the taste of salt.

"You sure get a lot of exercise keeping this dog entertained," Coral said as Calvin trotted over to her. She let her hand fall to her side so he could sniff it.

He sniffed—and then sat down beside her, leaning against her leg. Ruby caught up, wheezing. Holy crap, he was touching Coral! "Good boy, Calvin!"

Coral's eyes lit up. "What does this mean?"

"Crouch down and see what he does."

She did. He looked at her, his tail wagging so it made a *pat-pat* sound against the wet sand.

Ruby nodded. "You can pet him. Just not on top of the head."

"Yay," Coral whispered, rubbing Calvin's chest. "Gross, you're covered in wet sand and slobber. Why couldn't you do this when you were clean?"

Calvin looked over at her with a big smile and a lolling tongue.

Ruby's chest seemed to expand, her heart swelling as she watched him finally trust Coral. He turned his gaze back to Ruby, and she imagined him saying, *See how easy this is? Now, your turn.*

She did trust Coral. It was clearer by the day that she could tell Coral anything. So, yes, she would tell Coral about her broken van and everything that led her to keep that a secret. As soon as she was ready to open those floodgates.

He stayed there for a minute while Coral scratched his chest and neck and then seemed to have enough and walked away.

Coral's eyes went big and watery. "He trusted me, Ruby!"

"About time. Good boy, Calvin!" She invited him closer and patted one of the rocks. "Come on up."

He obediently climbed up and stood tall and regal. Pictures of him tended to get just as many likes as the ones of Ruby, if not more, so she took as many as he would allow.

Coral watched them with a vacant gaze. What was she thinking so hard about this morning?

She blinked and met Ruby's eyes, seeming to come out of a reverie, and pointed to the waves. "Hey, use your fancy waterproof shoes to get a little further into the tide, and I'll take an artsy video of you."

"Sure."

Ruby walked back and forth a few times, gazing at the scenery, and then Coral played the video back to her.

"Looks perfect."

They swapped, and Ruby filmed Coral walking along the beach and climbing onto a rock to look at the ocean. Coral knew how to work her angles for the camera. Ruby watched her through the lens, trying to focus on composing the shot instead of on how attractive the subject was.

Coral waved her over. "Come up here with me!"

Ruby hesitated. The tide was rising around the rock Coral stood on. It would take one big wave to splash over the rock and pull them into the current. Then again, the water was pretty shallow. She was probably overthinking this.

"Okay." Ruby left her expensive camera safely away from the water, then scrambled up to follow Coral to the edge of the rock.

Calvin jumped up behind her, trotting along at her heels.

It was a beautiful place to stand. Perched above the water with waves splashing a couple of feet below, she felt like a mermaid.

The spray dampened Ruby's face. She licked her lips, tasting salt.

Coral hummed a tune from *The Little Mermaid*, and Ruby laughed. "I was just thinking the same."

"Imagine tenting up here," Coral said.

"Yeah, until you wake up and the tide has come in and you're stranded. It's already coming up, look."

Calvin looked down at the waves, and then at Ruby, and then pointedly trotted away. He hopped back into the sand, where he turned to gaze at them with concern in his big eyes.

Ruby was about to tell him to stay there when Coral gasped.

Ruby's heart leaped into her throat. She spun back in time to see Coral duck.

A huge wave hit the rock and sprayed over their heads, drenching them both.

Ruby screamed.

"Cold!" Coral cried.

Clutching each other, they raced off the rock and back to Calvin.

"I knew we would get drenched up there!" Ruby exclaimed, wiping her face with trembling hands.

Coral laughed, combing her fingers through her matted hair. "That was freezing!"

"You're not even wet!" Ruby wrung out her T-shirt. "Look at me."

She flicked her wet hands at Coral, who shrieked and backed away. "Don't you dare."

"Get over here! That rock was your idea." Ruby didn't know what overcame her—maybe it was the adrenaline at work—but she started chasing Coral in a circle. She caught up in a few strides and wrapped her in a hug, forcing some of the icy ocean spray onto Coral's half-dry shirt.

"I hate you," Coral moaned.

Ruby let go, satisfied to see that Coral was *almost* as soaked as she was.

Still laughing, they shook out their hair and aired out their shirts, turning into the wind.

Feeling Coral's gaze, Ruby looked up with a smile. Coral blushed and looked away as if she'd been caught staring. She motioned to Calvin. "No wonder he didn't stay on the rock with us."

"He definitely thinks we're idiots."

Something about this was...nice. Being here with Coral. It was fun and comfortable.

Coral stooped to pick up her GoPro, which Ruby hadn't noticed she'd planted in the sand.

Oh, crap.

She'd caught *all* of that on video.

Why did Ruby have to clutch her like that when the wave hit them? Why did she have to chase her, and then hug her? This would give their audience so much fodder. And they definitely did not need it. She'd gotten more comments than ever saying that she and Coral were flirting. Even her die-hard regulars were calling out the way she acted around Coral. Mrs. Peppermint said, *Coral seems lovely, and you two look happy together*—which for her was basically accusing them of banging.

Why did people have to see romantic subtext where there was none? It happened all the time in TV shows—people shipping two characters because they saw what they wanted to see. Now they were doing it with two vloggers.

She'd been ignoring the comments, but it was getting harder. Now people said her silence confirmed their suspicions. Should she post a video or a comment explaining that she and Coral weren't hooking up?

How embarrassing.

As they gathered their things and walked back along the beach, Coral cleared her throat. "Hey, about those comments…"

Ruby stopped walking. Oh no. Here it was. Awkward conversation, straight ahead, no U-turns.

"How do you feel about them? Does it make you uncomfortable?" Coral turned to her, and her face was beet red. She looked like she was having a hard time swallowing.

"No. It's fine. I thought about it, and…" Ruby's mouth went dry. "You're right that sharing my sexuality would be good. For myself and for any followers I can inspire."

Coral's eyes lit up. "You're sure?"

Ruby nodded.

"Okay." Coral shuffled her feet. "Then I think we should roll with it."

Ruby stared.

Um, what?

She narrowed her eyes. "Roll with it *how*?"

"Like…" Coral huffed and kept walking, like she couldn't stand still while talking about this. Around them, more people were arriving at the beach. "Of all of the things in our videos, the idea that we could be flirting is dominating the comments. It's catching people's attention. So I think we should use that to our advantage. We should pretend we're flirting and—"

"*What?*" Ruby's voice carried far and wide. A nearby family stared at them.

"—kiss on camera," Coral finished, facing her and giving a nonchalant shrug.

Of everything Coral could have said in response to those comments, this was *not* what Ruby had expected to hear.

"Kiss—on—" Ruby opened and closed her mouth. "Coral!"

"What? You're acting like I just suggested we make a porno. It's just a kiss. A peck, even. A budding romance would boost our stats, and you know it."

"That's lying to our audience!"

The ground began to incline as they left the beach behind.

"Uh-huh," Coral said. "And how is everything else we do *not* lying? We're only telling partial truths with these videos. Neither of us shows the half of it."

"Yeah—well—that's different than faking a romance."

"Is it? What's so bad about telling a love story? It'll get the views we want. This is the secret ingredient."

"This wasn't in our Road Trip Agreement!"

"Then we can make an amendment."

They fell silent as they crossed the day-use parking lot and entered the wooded trail. The woods were so impossibly quiet that it was like being in the void of outer space.

"No," Ruby said firmly. "I'm not faking a romance to get views. Sorry."

Coral sighed. "At least give it some thought. Both of us want more engagement, and you *know* this would work."

"Would it, though?"

"Ruby, do you follow anyone on YouTube?"

"A few people."

"Okay, now imagine if one of them had a guest on their channel for a few videos, and they started flirting. Imagine that flirting led to a first kiss on camera. Wouldn't you freak out and want to know what happens next? Wouldn't you expect that video to get a shit-ton of views?"

"I—not necess—" Ruby huffed. *Dammit.* "Fine. Yeah. I see your point. But I don't like the idea of lying to our audience by faking that we're falling in love."

Coral paused. "I get that. But just think about it, okay?"

"Okay. Now, can we hurry up and get back to the van so we can get changed? I'm cold." Ruby walked faster, Calvin bounding along beside her.

Coral trailed a few steps behind, quiet.

This was over the line. Being partially truthful about her life was different from lying about dating someone. The former was about protecting her privacy and building a platform. The latter was just... fake. If her audience found out the truth, her career would be over.

Plus, something about the idea of kissing Coral for the cameras bothered her. Like, if they were going to kiss, she wanted it to be—

No. Don't go there.

They wouldn't be kissing at all.

She scowled at the path, concentrating on where she was stepping.

Pretending to be in love?

The idea was absurd.

Chapter 17
Coral

Omg, they are sooo in love!

As Coral had suspected, they'd gotten a lot of engagement on the video where they'd been splashed by the giant wave. People were losing their minds over the way they'd grabbed each other and giggled.

Sitting at the dinette, cradling her overnight oats, she stuffed another spoonful into her mouth to hide her smile.

Ruby wouldn't be able to deny her brilliant idea for much longer. Tonight, they would reach the furthest point south, which meant they were halfway through the road trip—and they still hadn't broken the barrier to more followers and more income. Fulfilling their viewers' wishes for a budding romance was their best hope.

"My phone tells me we're nine minutes from the Avenue of the Giants entrance," Ruby said, braiding her hair.

Coral hopped up to get ready. "Can't wait!"

They'd spent the night stealth camping on a side street just north of Humboldt Redwoods State Park, setting them up for a full day of exploring the forest. It was the first night of the "winging it" half of the trip, which would be an exciting change.

Admittedly, having the first half planned out had been great. It'd been nice to pull into pre-booked campsites without any stress. They probably wouldn't have been able to get last-minute sites at most of those beautiful state parks, so they would have missed out on those spots. There was something to be said for planning everything in advance—but Coral was excited to have a little less structure in the trip's second half.

Ruby hopped into the driver's seat for the first shift at the wheel.

When she turned the key, the van spluttered. *Chug, chug.* Reluctantly, it groaned to life.

"Um." Ruby's eyes widened.

Calvin tilted his head from his spot between the seats, as if he knew it wasn't supposed to sound like that.

Coral leaned over him to look at the dash. There was no indication that anything was amiss. "That was weird."

"Did I do something wrong?"

"I don't think so. Maybe something was draining the battery overnight." Coral got up to check for anything that was left plugged in but saw nothing suspicious. "I think we're fine for now."

"Do we need to take it into a shop?" Ruby asked, her voice rising in pitch.

"No, no," Coral said calmly, trying to counteract Ruby's unnecessary panic. "It'll be fine. Let's see how it does."

She'd checked everything before leaving home, and the battery wasn't old. Maybe it was something in the charging system? Whatever it was, it would be minor, and she could fix it later. Stopping at an auto parts store today would throw a wrench into their plans—a small wrench, but still a wrench. They had better things to do.

Ruby visibly tensed, her shoulders up by her ears. "What if it doesn't start at all next time, and we're in the middle of nowhere?"

"Nothing on this road trip qualifies as the middle of nowhere. Let's just keep going."

"This seems like a bit of a casual approach to a van barely starting."

"Ruby, I promise this isn't a disaster. Trust me."

Ruby drove off in silence, vague about whether or not she was choosing to trust Coral. But unless the van was literally going to catch fire, simple maintenance wasn't worth getting worked up over. Ruby should know this, having lived in a van for so long. Things broke all the time, and that was just part of it.

Coral smiled, trying to lighten the mood. "At least we have room for all the flexibility in the world now. So if we need to stop, we won't have to worry about being delayed getting to our next destination."

Ruby scowled and said nothing.

"The perks of winging it!" Coral said brightly, opening her hands.

Ruby's mouth twisted as if she were failing to hide the grin tugging at her lips.

As they turned onto the scenic highway, the Avenue of the Giants, Coral's heart fluttered in anticipation. They stopped at the entrance to grab a pamphlet and continued on.

The trees lining the road were so enormous that they cast everything into shadow. Their massive trunks dictated the curves of the road, and Ruby drove slowly, giving them time to ogle.

Coral motioned to a pullout. "Stop here."

"We've been driving for, like, two minutes!"

"I know but *look*! Oh my God, I can't handle how pretty this is." The forest was like nothing Coral had seen, which was saying something, coming from BC. But the ones back home were different, and every forest had its own unique beauty.

Ruby pulled over, and they hopped out to walk through a footpath. Sadly, most of the park didn't allow dogs on the trails, so they reluctantly left Calvin in the van. He didn't seem to mind, happy to have a bonus nap after all of that playing on the beach yesterday.

Coral ran to the nearest tree and put her palms on it. "It's so ancient," she whispered. "I feel at one with the earth."

Ruby laughed.

Coral ran her fingers up the firm ridges. "Think of what civilization was like when this tree was a sapling. What do you think, a thousand years?"

Ruby checked the pamphlet. "Give or take a few hundred years."

Her phone beeped, and she paused to reply to a text.

They walked through the network of paths, the muffled silence of the forest closing around them. Redwood sorrel bordered the trails— low-growing, bright green ground cover that looked like a dense carpet of clovers. It made the whole place look like a fairy forest.

Coral looked over to find Ruby watching her with a pinched brow. When their eyes met, Ruby looked away quickly.

Something serious was going through her head.

Are you considering my idea?

Or maybe she wasn't considering it at all. Maybe her "no" was the end of it, case closed, no further consideration necessary. In which case, Coral had to respect her answer and move on to a different idea for attracting more followers.

Which was...?

Coral bent to look through a hollow log big enough to live inside of. Neither of them spoke, as if they were in a museum. The forest's silence was a far cry from the noisy waves and wind they'd experienced all along the coast.

Ruby's phone beeped again. She stopped walking to reply.

Who was important enough to pull Ruby's attention away from the scenery like this?

As Ruby put her phone away, she caught Coral's eye.

Dammit, now I'm the one staring.

"Just my mom," Ruby said.

A trickle of relief went through Coral's chest, which she hated herself for. Why should she care who Ruby texted?

"Checking in?" Coral asked.

"Making sure I'm eating my vegetables and carrying bear spray and stuff." Ruby shrugged and kept walking, stepping over a log. "She's happy we're traveling together. She worries about my social life and thinks I'm lonely living in a van."

"I see." Coral bent to capture footage of the biggest tree yet, trying to do justice to how massive it was. She had to get Ruby in the shot for scale. "*Do* you get lonely?"

"No," Ruby said a little quickly.

Coral took a few more pictures, capturing some beautiful candid ones of Ruby looking up. "Does your mom pressure you to make friends and go on dates and stuff?"

"I wouldn't say pressure, but...yeah. She asks questions. She was asking about you, actually."

Coral's heart skipped. "Me? What was she asking?"

"If you're nice. If you're easy to talk to. If Calvin likes you. It's like she thinks…" Ruby cleared her throat, examining a tree with a Calvin-sized burl on the trunk.

"What?" Coral asked.

"Nothing. She's just being nosy."

Coral's insides danced. What was Ruby about to say? Was her mom asking about Coral because she got the impression that something was going on between them?

Or I could be totally misinterpreting her words.

"Well, it's sweet she checks in with you," Coral said. "My parents don't give a shit."

"I'm sure they do."

"They have no idea who my friends are. They've never even met anyone I've dated."

Ruby fell quiet. Maybe she wasn't sure how to respond. "What about Farrah?"

"She cares. She's normal. She knows my friends, and she's hung out with me and past girlfriends."

"That's cool. Sometimes I wish I had a sibling."

"It's nice. Like a built-in bestie. But you can also find that in close friends, right?"

Again, Ruby fell quiet. They kept walking through the fairy-forest trail, and after a long silence, she said, "I'm not great at maintaining friendships. I don't reach out enough."

"Some people are just more independent."

"I guess."

"Are you happy with your social life?" Coral asked, hoping this wasn't too bold a question.

"I think so? Maybe? I know a lot of other vanlifers. I've hung out with them here and there. But sometimes, I wish I had just one close friend."

"I can be that friend." Coral's words came out before she'd thought about them. Her cheeks warmed. "I mean, as long as you're fine with me pressuring you into doing more things like riding in dune buggies."

Ruby looked back at her, a beautiful smile stretching across her face. "Deal."

Coral's heart seemed to expand. Was Ruby serious? She wanted to be friends?

"Are you saying you want me to stay in your life after our Road Trip Agreement expires?" Coral tried for a teasing tone, but it was a real question.

Ruby nodded. "If you're not sick of me and Calvin."

"Calvin? Impossible. You? Meh, we'll see."

Ruby shoved her, laughing.

Coral's heart skipped. The promise of hanging out after the road trip was over made her step a little lighter. Where would they go next?

They returned to the van and kept driving, stopping every few minutes to walk through a new network of footpaths and take photos and videos. They found logs and stumps to stand on, hollow ones to crawl through, and all manner of other photo ops.

Ruby pointed to a tree stump big enough to fit a bed inside. "We should take a picture of you hiding inside this to send to your parents."

Coral looked from Ruby to the stump, grinning. It was sweet that Ruby remembered her story about her first memory. "Brilliant. Farrah will get a kick out of it."

Maybe she'd send it to her parents too, but they would probably just reply to tell her they had an open position waiting for her at the shop.

By the time they'd explored the whole scenic highway and let Calvin out for a play at the visitor's center, they were exhausted and ready to pull into a campsite. They snagged the last vacancy inside the park, which backed onto a river.

Coral reversed into their spot, and Ruby hopped out to hook up the van. A waft of cool air blew in, raising goosebumps on Coral's skin. Their spot was under the shade of trees, making it a little on the chilly side, but the campground was sweet and cozy. The sound of kids playing and a barking dog drifted in from a few sites down.

When Ruby came back inside, she was scowling at her phone.

Coral pulled on a hoodie. "Your mom again?"

"No, just more comments." She kept her gaze on her phone. "I swear the majority of my comments are about you and me. Not the road trip, not the scenery, but how much people ship us."

Coral's heart leaped. "Same, honestly," she said casually, trying not to convey how much she'd been thinking about this.

Ruby put her phone on the counter and met Coral's eye. She visibly swallowed. "So, um…"

Coral froze. Her lips tingled. *Oh, my God. It's happening. Is it happening?*

"I've decided…" Ruby drew a deep breath. "Yes. Let's kiss on camera."

Chapter 18
Ruby

"SERIOUSLY?" CORAL ASKED, THE WORD a squeak. She tugged the neck of her hoodie. "Oh, my God. This is huge. Okay. How should we do this? Do you want me to surprise you with it, or should we make a— Wait, who am I kidding? This is you I'm talking to. Of course you'll want a plan, right?"

Ruby couldn't help smirking at Coral's rambling. "Yes, let's plan it."

She leaned against the counter, trying to put a little more space between them to give her burning face a chance to cool. This damn tiny van.

Coral took the hint and sat at the dinette. Her eyes glimmered in the same exhilarated way they had when they fought the wind on Cannon Beach and when they'd ridden in the dune buggy.

As for Ruby, her insides were doing something wild. She was full of a jittery uncertainty, but also…excited? This idea could work. She'd agonized over the decision, and after a flood of Coral-related comments, her failure to get more followers, and even *Mom* asking about Coral as though she were a potential girlfriend…well, she'd cracked. Thousands of people obviously shipped her and Coral, and this was a painfully obvious way to get more views.

And the thing was, the prospect of kissing Coral…wasn't bad. Like, if kissing a beautiful woman was the key to getting more subscribers, this wasn't the worst idea in the world.

"Where should we do it?" Coral's gaze drifted from the bed to the door, as if she were searching for the best location.

"I was thinking the forest might be a nice place for it," Ruby said casually. In fact, when she'd imagined kissing Coral in the redwoods earlier, she was suddenly no longer sure why she'd said no. "We could stop on our way back through tomorrow."

"Sure," Coral said, sounding breathless. "Good idea."

"And *if* people respond well to the kiss, then we can consider adding a love story into our videos."

"If?" Coral's lips twisted into a cocky smile. "Ruby, they're going to die of happiness. Guaranteed."

After a dinner of Thai green curry, they took an evening stroll to the river behind the campground. The crystal-clear water rippled serenely over the river rock.

While they watched and listened in silence, Calvin waded in and laid down for a soak.

So I'm going to kiss Coral tomorrow.

It was weird to consider.

What would it be like? Would they do a quick peck or go full-on *The Notebook* and grab each other?

She'd been worried about sharing her personal life on camera, and now she was jumping both feet into broadcasting a relationship from its very first kiss. It was a fake relationship, but still. This was going to be a big change for herself and her subscribers.

And it had better work.

Coral bent to capture a close-up of the water burbling over a boulder. Calvin was basking just beyond it, his eyes closed and his snout pointing skyward. It would make for a cute shot.

Coral didn't seem to be dying inside like Ruby was. But for Ruby, this nervous anticipation wasn't unlike the first time she'd had sex. She'd talked about it with her girlfriend in the week leading up to it. She'd been nervous, looking up tips online, trying to guess what it would be like. And still, it had played out naturally. All of the worrying, planning, and guessing she'd done had gone out the window as instinct took over.

Kissing Coral would be like that. She could anticipate it all she wanted, but when it came time, all of that agonizing would go out the window.

Just do what comes naturally. Stop trying to plan everything.

A smile formed as she imagined Coral telling her that. It would have to do because trying to plan the kiss in her head was making her more anxious.

Time to wing it.

"How about here?" Ruby asked, standing between two trees flanking the path. "The light is coming through nicely, and the trees and ground cover sort of frame it."

"Hm..." Coral eyed the place Ruby was standing. "No, it'll look posed. It's also too open. We need a small space to create a more intimate feel, know what I mean?"

"I guess so. But I don't know if we're going to find an intimate feel among the world's tallest trees."

Coral sat in a hollow log that protruded over a dip in the forest floor, her feet dangling out of the end. She motioned around her head, wearing a smug expression. "Intimate."

"What, so our lips will happen to collide right in the middle of the circle? *That's* posed."

"No." Coral crawled further inside. "I'll be coming out of the log, and you'll be standing at the end waiting to help me get out, and..."

"Oh." Ruby's cheeks burned. Okay, that would work. Coral would have to hop down three feet to get out of the log, so it made sense for Ruby to offer a hand to help her get down. And if they were already holding hands...

"Let's do it." Coral jumped down and dusted off her palms.

"Now?" Ruby exclaimed, and when Coral raised an eyebrow, she pursed her lips. "Yeah, okay."

They set up Ruby's camera on a tripod. Coral would hold hers as she walked through the log so they could splice the clips together.

Ruby's heart beat faster as she adjusted the shot, making it off-center so it wouldn't be too perfect. Her mouth was dry. While Coral turned her back to climb into the log, Ruby took a sip of water and discreetly applied lip balm. This was all happening very fast. Did she remember how to kiss? It'd been a year since her last one.

Coral turned around. The log was so big that she was standing fully upright with room to spare. "Ready?"

God, she was moving this along quickly. Couldn't they have a minute to compose themselves?

"Sure," Ruby said, an embarrassing waver in her tone.

With her heart ready to pound out of her chest, she pressed record. The camera's red LED started blinking.

Was this actually happening? She was going to kiss Coral—and under these circumstances?

She caught herself pressing her lips together and forced herself to stop.

I can do this. Just let it happen. A normal, gentle kiss. Not too soft, not too hot.

"Oh, wow, it's amazing in here!" Coral exclaimed, putting on her enthusiastic camera voice. "Ruby, come check this out."

Ruby drew a breath, squared her shoulders, and put on a smile. For this to work, she had to stop acting nervous and uptight.

She walked toward the log.

"Yeah?" She leaned into the log and traced her fingers on the inside of it, as if admiring the texture. "Wow, this is so cool."

Did that sound natural? That totally didn't sound natural.

Oh-God-oh-God-oh-God.

Coral smiled down at her. It seemed like a normal smile, but there was a gleam in her eyes that was probably nerves.

She walked closer to the edge and crouched to hop down.

Ruby extended a hand to help her. "Grab on," she said as casually as she could.

Coral's soft hand closed over hers. A jolt went up Ruby's arm, settling somewhere in her chest, making it hard to breathe.

She helped Coral jump down—and there was no going back. Ruby's breath caught, and a flame seemed to ignite in her midsection.

They hadn't discussed who would initiate the kiss. What transpired would probably be a hot topic of debate in the comments. Ruby pulled Coral in, and at the same moment, Coral stepped closer.

Ruby's heart did a backflip as Coral's face came within kissing distance.

Coral's sweet breath tickled her face. Her gaze flicked between Ruby's eyes and her lips.

And even though this was planned…even though this was entirely for the cameras and it would be published for the world to see…they couldn't change the fact that this moment was between the two of them.

The silence of the forest closed in. The warmth from Coral's body tingled against Ruby's. She smelled blissful, like mango and coconut.

All Ruby wanted was to close the distance. It didn't matter why they were doing this. She just wanted Coral's lips against hers like she'd never wanted anything.

They both leaned in. Their lips met, and Ruby's head swam like she'd had too many drinks. Any logical sense of what she should do and how she should do it faded, replaced by the instinctive urge to kiss Coral harder. She tasted so good, so sweet, that Ruby opened her lips to taste more of her.

Coral responded, deepening the kiss.

Ruby reached up and ran her hands through Coral's hair, feeling the soft strands between her fingers—for the camera, of course. Obviously, it was for the camera.

For all of Coral's exuberance and boldness, her kiss was tender. Everything about her was soft to the touch. She moved gracefully in Ruby's arms, arching so their bodies fit together like puzzle pieces.

This was definitely not just a peck. They played with each other's lips, teasing, Ruby's fingers tightening in Coral's hair.

Okay, stop now. The cameras are on. Coral probably didn't intend for this to get so heated.

With a great effort, Ruby stepped back. Her lips and hands were the last things to obey, holding onto Coral like they had minds of their own.

Coral's eyelids fluttered open. Her breaths were fast and shallow. Her lips had a full, freshly kissed look that sent a blaze through Ruby's middle.

"Th-that was perfect." Coral backed up a step. She swallowed hard, averting her gaze to everything but Ruby. "That was really convincing. Nice work."

Ruby nodded, a little unbalanced.

Coral looked down at her camera, which she'd lowered to her side as they kissed. It would make for dramatic footage when they swapped from Coral's shot to Ruby's perched on the tripod.

Ruby walked to her camera, her feet moving automatically.

They both played the clips back, and the competing audio seemed extra loud as it rang through the forest.

Ruby's face grew hot. Sweat prickled under her shirt. The kiss was *not* PG. What had she been thinking? Their bodies swayed, her hands gripped Coral like she was a lifeline, and their lips moved in a way that made her question whether she'd used tongue without realizing.

"How's yours?" Coral asked.

Ruby nodded, deciding to pretend like she'd planned for the kiss to get so heated. "Looks good, I think."

Coral came over to look. As she stood over Ruby's shoulder and watched the clip. Ruby's insides danced all over again.

Get it together, she told herself, taking a slow breath.

"Hm," Coral said.

"What?"

Coral shifted. "I feel like… Well, I think you can tell we're acting. Like, we're both being a little weird and nervous."

Ruby swallowed. She played the clip again.

Coral might have had a point. Leading up to the kiss, they both moved robotically, their voices a little high-pitched.

"You think we should do it again?" Ruby asked.

"I…think so. Yeah."

Ruby nodded. *Again.* They were going to go through that *again.*

Her heart pounded as hard as ever—but for some reason, her cheeks pulled into a little smile. She bit her lip to hide it.

Coral climbed back into the log.

Ruby set up her tripod and hit record.

"Ruby, come check this out!" Coral shouted.

Ruby walked over, determined to be more nonchalant than last time. "Yeah?"

They admired the inside of the log together, and when it came time to help Coral out, Ruby extended a hand with more confidence.

Coral jumped down, smiling. Her eyes danced like before, but there was less nervousness and more playfulness in her expression.

Ruby's insides danced. She smiled back.

Their lips met more quickly than they had the first time. The kiss lasted just as long, and their bodies arched into each other as if they were picking up where they'd left off. Coral lifted her free hand to Ruby's neck, and *oh*, the tingle that went down Ruby's back.

With the first kiss out of the way, this one felt bolder, like they were both sure about what they were doing—hopefully, convincing their viewers that this was the culmination of days of sexual tension.

When they broke apart, they were both breathless.

Ruby counted to three before whispering, "Better?"

Coral opened her mouth. No sound came out. She nodded, stepping back with a flush in her cheeks and her hair in disarray.

Ruby grinned, liking this mussed-up, freshly kissed look on her.

They played the clips back.

"It looks less hesitant," Coral said.

Ruby tilted her head. "Yeah..."

"What, you don't think so?"

"I just wonder if we went too far the other way. It looks like this isn't our first kiss. Maybe we should do it one more time."

Coral's mouth opened in surprise. Ruby's cheeks warmed, and she shrugged.

Coral laughed, stepping back. "Okay. Take three, action."

She got back in the log, and Ruby set up the camera.

"Ruby, come check this out!" Coral shouted for the third time.

Ruby walked over. "Yeah?"

They admired the inside of the log.

Coral crouched to hop down.

Ruby extended her hand, and Coral took it.

Before Coral could move, Ruby stood on her toes and inclined her face.

Their lips met in a surprise peck, which made Coral let out one of her genuine, contagious laughs. The way her whole expression lit up, Ruby knew that this was the take they would use in the final video.

Coral leaned down for another, proper kiss. Ruby lifted both hands to cup her face, and their lips moved tenderly against each other.

There was something hot about this angle—standing on her toes, her face inclined, while Coral leaned down. The kiss was delicate and more tantalizing.

Okay, kissing Coral was something she could get used to. She could get on board with this fake relationship idea.

When they broke apart, they were both flushed and giggly. The moment felt sweet, PG, and it perfectly conveyed the first-kiss feeling they'd been going for.

Yep, this was the shot they would use.

Chapter 19
Coral

*Hi Coral, are you available on Saturday for dinner? We can
touch base about our agreement. We have an open position
in the shop, if you're interested.*

CORAL SIGHED AND SAT AT the picnic table of their campsite.
What a perfectly impersonal and businesslike text to get from Mom.
Also, did she seriously imply that Coral was going to fail her end of
the agreement and need to get a job at the shop?

She scowled, hovering her thumbs over the screen. Truthfully, it
didn't seem likely that she would earn enough to get her near that
thirty-grand goal. But anything could happen after their next few
videos were published, and she had to believe in that.

I won't be home Saturday. I'm on a road trip.

They'd left behind the sprawling California farmland and crossed
back into Oregon, where they'd pulled into the first RV park with
laundry facilities. Tonight would be their first chance to do laundry
on the whole trip, and it was desperately needed. While Coral set up
their site, Ruby moved around the kitchenette, making dinner under
the glow of her ring lights.

Mom's reply came in.

Right. Farrah mentioned that. Is it working?

Straight to business. No questions about whether the road trip was fun, who she was with, or what she did today. Anger twisted Coral's stomach, and her thumbs were clumsy as she punched out a reply.

> *Yes. I'll make a report for you and Dad when I get home. We can have dinner the weekend of my birthday—our agreed-upon deadline.*

> *Okay. We'll text you when we figure out our schedule that weekend.*

Coral hovered over the keyboard, debating how to reply before deciding to leave it alone. She texted Farrah instead. Maybe it was the conversation with Mom spurring her, but the need to text someone like a normal human being was strong.

> *Hey from Brookings, Oregon! How are things back home? How's Beach Guy?*

Farrah replied within a minute.

> *Still good. I might meet his brother this weekend. How's the trip?*

They texted about Farrah's love life and the sights and stops of the last couple of days. Talking to Farrah lightened her heart after that text exchange with Mom. At least Farrah was enthusiastic and supportive.

> *Is the Ruby Hayashi idea working?*

Coral frowned at Farrah's text. Calling it "the Ruby Hayashi idea" made it sound weird, like she was using Ruby for a scheme. But wasn't it accurate?

> *Teaming up with Ruby has been great. She's easy to travel with. You should totally do this road trip one day. You don't*

even need a camper – the state parks have yurts you can stay in.

There. A casual shift in topic. Telling Farrah about their fake relationship felt like a jinx. She couldn't let the secret out, not even to her sister.

Anyway, Farrah would see the kiss after Coral posted today's video. She would learn about the relationship that way and assume it was real like everyone else would.

Coral's insides squirmed in anticipation. In a few hours, the fake relationship would go public.

Awesome! I'll put it on my travel wish list. Maybe after I graduate, I can go on a celebratory road trip.

Interesting how Farrah called it a travel *wish list*. Coral had a list, but she thought of it as a to-do list. She didn't *wish* she could go—she *intended* to go.

Ruby emerged from the van with two bowls. "Dinner's ready!"

Coral sat up. "Have I told you you're the best?"

"Every day." Ruby returned her smile.

Coral had been handling their lunches in exchange for all of the dinners Ruby made, but overall, Ruby had been doing more than half of the cooking. She insisted on it. So Coral got to enjoy the benefits of road-tripping with a chef.

They ate incredible burrito bowls, and the moment they were done, they gathered their dirty laundry. Time for clean, sand-free, dog-hair-free, sunscreen-free clothes.

Coral scrounged for change in her bag. "I think I have more quarters up front..."

Ruby did the same. "I have...two."

Coral searched the cup holders, sifting through pens, receipts, lip balm, and candy wrappers. "Okay, so we have enough quarters for...one load of laundry. Well, they have a token machine that takes credit—"

Ruby lunged for her and snatched the coins out of her hand. "I'll take those, thanks!"

"Hey! Most of those are mine!" Coral grabbed for them, but Ruby was too quick to back up, fending off Coral with one hand while stuffing the quarters into her pocket.

"I need to do laundry more than you do! I have a dog."

"We both live with the dog, quarter thief!" Coral reached for Ruby's pocket.

Ruby backed up, laughing, until her legs were against the bed. "He doesn't put his muddy paws all over you on a daily basis."

From his bed, Calvin looked up at them as if affronted that they were dragging him into this.

Coral ducked under Ruby's outstretched hand and tried to dig into her pocket for the coins. She nearly had them before Ruby jerked back.

With nowhere to go, Ruby fell onto the bed. They were both giggling.

"What if we—hey!" Ruby exclaimed as Coral climbed on top of her.

Ruby tried to wiggle free, but Coral wouldn't let her. She held Ruby down by sitting on her legs and dug into her pocket. The coins tumbled out onto the bed.

"Mine—"

"No—"

They wrestled for them, their limbs tangling, uncontrollable laughter bubbling up. Something was happening to Coral's insides—a dancing, fiery sensation. She might have been enjoying this a little too much.

Ruby managed to grab all but two, and she closed her fist tightly. Still straddling her hips, Coral leaned forward, trying to pry open Ruby's fingers. She had an iron grip.

"Dammit, you're strong." Coral tried for another few seconds, then gave up. Panting, she sat back. "Fine. You go first. I'll get tokens and live in my own filth for another hour."

"Yes!" Beneath her, Ruby lay with her arms up by her head, her hair fanned out, her chest heaving as she caught her breath. Her cheeks were flushed, and her dark eyes danced. Her full lips curved into a little smile. She looked...well...

As Coral sat straddling her hips, a blazing hot sensation pooled low inside her. It was the same feeling she'd had when they kissed in the redwoods—the surprising way her body had responded to the feel of Ruby's lips and hands. She'd never had a kiss that made her so weak-kneed.

Ruby broke eye contact, and Coral blinked, pulling herself out of her thoughts.

She slid off Ruby's hips and scoffed. "Such a thief."

Ruby laughed and sat up. "Do you want to just combine loads?"

"It's okay. I'll get tokens." Coral smiled bashfully.

They took turns doing laundry. Coral was pleased when Calvin didn't fuss as Ruby left the van without him.

She scratched under his collar. "Getting used to me, huh?"

He wagged his tail.

So was Ruby, she hoped. Ruby seemed like a different person from the one who seemed agitated and uptight when they'd left Seattle.

Coral's insides were still doing flips from that wrestling match. When she'd lunged for Ruby, she hadn't expected it to go that far. Fine, she could admit that it had been a flirty move, and she'd expected a scuffle as they fought for the coins. But she hadn't expected Ruby to end up on the bed, and she didn't know what overcame her when she'd decided to climb on top.

And Ruby had laughed as hard as Coral about it. Coral couldn't let go of the image of her eyes glinting playfully beneath the soft lights above the bed.

Calvin nudged Coral's hand, which was resting on his neck. She hadn't realized she'd frozen in place.

"Want to come outside?"

He stood and wagged his tail.

She clipped on his leash in case he bolted in search of Ruby, then brought her laptop to the picnic table to start editing today's video.

She'd just sat down when Calvin's hackles went up. A low noise met her ears, and it took her a second to realize he was growling.

She looked over to see a middle-aged white man with a scruffy brown beard and a baseball cap stop in front of their campsite. "Sorry to interrupt. Do you happen to have a lighter?"

Calvin stood up. Coral held the leash a little tighter. To hell if anything bad was going to happen with Ruby's beloved pet on her watch.

Also, not knowing this guy, she understood what Ruby meant when she said Calvin was nice to have for safety. The way Calvin was puffed up, it would take a real dumbass to mess with her right now.

"Yeah, sure. One sec. Um, come on, Calvin." Coral pulled him into the van and shut the screen door. As she came back out with the lighter, keeping one hand on the door, the guy pointed to the laptop she'd left on the picnic table. "Working remotely?"

"Posting a video blog."

"Oh, yeah." He nodded. "My teenage daughter does that. Don't know how to feel about it. Do you ever get creeps on there?"

"Sometimes. You can block and report them. And it's best to avoid letting your followers know exactly where you are."

"Yeah. Good advice. I guess I should relax a little, eh?"

Coral shrugged. "It's concerning. I get it. It's worth having a conversation about it. Creeps, bullies, trolls… It's part of being on the internet, and she'll have to decide whether she's up for that. It can be hard to deal with."

Her own words bounced around her brain. So many things could backfire when posting a video online—especially one as vulnerable as this. They were about to make their first kiss *public*.

Ruby had every reason to hesitate over Coral's suggestions to be so open on camera. Was this a mistake? Her viewers had always been kind and supportive of everything she did, but she was failing to consider how the rest of the internet might respond.

"Hey, everything good?" Ruby asked, stopping behind the guy with her brow pinched.

"Yeah, just lending this man a lighter," Coral said, passing it to him.

He tipped his hat. "Thanks. And thanks for the advice."

"No problem."

As he returned to his family two campsites over, Ruby leaned around Coral to check on Calvin through the screen door. He wagged his tail.

"His hackles went up," Coral said.

"I bet. Thanks for taking him inside. You can go do laundry now, if you want. There are two machines."

Coral couldn't help smirking. Their wrestling match really had been pointless.

Maybe Ruby thought so too, because she turned away as if to hide a smile.

Coral took her laundry over inside her pillowcase, and while it ran, she and Ruby sat at the picnic table to edit their videos and update their social media. The man returned with the lighter twenty minutes later, thanking them again.

They added voiceovers and recorded additional clips to ramp up the tension before the kiss. "Neither of us can really believe this happened," Coral said. "We debated even sharing it, but...you've all been such an important part of our journey..." Awkward giggles. Shy glances. Both of them were *really* hamming this up.

After two hours of editing, it was time to publish the video. Coral's heart was in her throat.

This was it. The kiss was going public.

The conversation with that man swirled around in her brain. *Bullies. Trolls. Creeps.*

Coral glanced up, and Ruby was staring at her screen with her hands clasped tightly.

"Are you agonizing over posting the video too?" Coral asked.

Ruby cast her a guilty smile. "Yup."

Coral drew a deep breath, summoning all of her earlier confidence. "I'm sure it'll be well received. Think of all of the comments we've had so far, right?"

"I know. But I've never shared my personal life on camera. And this is just...diving right into the deep end."

Guilt churned inside Coral. Was she pressuring Ruby into doing something she didn't want to do? She reached across the table. "Hey, if you're not comfortable posting this, we don't—"

"No, I want to. This footage is amazing, and you're right. This is what our viewers want." She unclasped her hands and linked her fingers with Coral's.

A pleasant tingling went up Coral's arm and settled in her chest.

"You're right that if my favorite YouTubers started flirting on camera, I'd be glued to their channel. We've unknowingly become a *will-they-won't-they*. This is a brilliant idea, Coral."

Coral nodded, Ruby's words bringing her confidence back up.

"So let's do it." Ruby squeezed her hand. "Count of three?"

Coral squeezed back, and used her other hand to move the mouse over the button that would set the video free. "Okay."

"One?" Ruby said like a question she didn't really want the answer to.

"Two," Coral said firmly.

Ruby let out a slow breath. "Three."

They both hit publish.

There was a pause.

Ruby shut her laptop.

Coral watched her video go out into the world, and then did the same. Time to see if their *will-they-won't-they* was good enough for their audience.

Coral woke up to her phone beeping incessantly. She rolled over, groaning, and didn't even have time to look at the flood of messages when the phone started ringing.

It was Farrah.

Why was Farrah trying to contact her so urgently at seven in the morning?

Oh crap. Is it an emergency?

Coral sat up and answered the call, her heart jumping. "Hey."

"Why didn't you tell me you and Ruby were a *thing*? Holy crap, Coral, this is awesome!"

Coral winced and turned down her phone's volume. So Farrah saw the video. "Yeah. We're…a thing."

"You sound tired. Oops. What time is it? Oh, shit, sorry. I thought it was later. But yay! I just wanted to say how happy I am for you, and I can't wait to meet her, and we should totally all hang out once you're home!"

Ruby sat up, bleary-eyed, and looked at Coral with her brow furrowed. Farrah's voice must have carried.

"Sure." Coral turned the volume as low as it would go. "We'll hang out. I'll introduce you."

She would figure out how to navigate that part of the fake relationship later.

Beside her, Ruby grabbed her phone and unlocked it in a hurry. She opened Patreon, apparently getting right to checking comments.

"Well, I'll let you keep sleeping," Farrah said. "Or not. I'm just excited for you."

"Thanks." It was sweet how enthusiastic Farrah could be—and it made it worse that Coral was lying to her. She and her sister were always truthful to each other.

But she couldn't reveal this secret to anyone. This was between her and Ruby. Also, Farrah would probably have a lot to say about what a bad idea a fake romance was.

When they hung up, Ruby was still frantically scrolling through comments.

"Verdict?" Coral asked, rubbing her eyes.

Ruby sucked in a breath. "It's…good. At least on Patreon."

"Really?"

"A lot of screaming and sobbing… This person called us their new favorite internet couple. Yeah. It's good."

Coral squealed in excitement, kicking her feet under the blankets. She leaned over and flung her arms around Ruby, who hugged her back.

"You know what this means?" Coral asked, a giddy sensation filling her.

"Your idea worked and you're a genius?"

Coral's elation threatened to burst out of her in the form of a song and dance. She opened the YouTube app to find that the number of views on yesterday's video was double what it normally was at this hour—*and* she'd gotten a lot of new subscribers.

"Obviously, I am a genius," Coral said. "But I was going to say that this means we need to add romance to all of our videos. It's time to give people what they want, and that means acting like a couple."

Ruby chewed her lip, looking like she was weighing everything that could possibly go wrong. "Let me check the sentiment on YouTube first."

"Okay." Coral leaned over to look with her.

I'm so so happy for you, Ruby! You're perfect for each other!

Ruby & Coral, I can't tell you how much this video means to me. As a closeted lesbian, seeing how happy you are together fills me with hope & light. Thank you for sharing your relationship with us xoxo

They both smiled at the top comments.

Ruby scrolled farther down. "Oh, a puking emoji. That's mature."

"I've gotten that before. Those people can suck it."

"Accusing us of being attention-seeking..." Ruby mumbled. "Prayers for our souls..."

"And all of those comments have people defending us underneath them. Look." Coral reached over and expanded one of the comment threads so they could see.

Ruby nodded. Coral waited with a pounding heart for her to say something. It was hard to read how she felt about all of this.

Finally, Ruby nodded and clicked off her phone. "Okay. Do I have to call you babe on camera?"

Coral smiled. "We're going for *likable*, not annoying."

Ruby laughed.

Nerves twisted in Coral's gut. They could fake a relationship convincingly, right? And they could do this without anybody getting hurt? All of the on-camera kissing and flirting didn't have to *mean* anything—it was an amendment to their original business agreement.

Crap, maybe she should have run this past Farrah before diving in with two feet.

Too late now.

While they got ready for the day, Coral could have skipped. Her income was bound to go up. And that meant keeping the van was a possibility. She could keep living the life of her dreams.

All because of Ruby. Beautiful, wonderful Ruby.

Yes!

She slid into the driver's seat, grinning uncontrollably. They had a scenic drive ahead of them, which would make a romantic backdrop in their videos.

Ruby saw her expression and shook her head, her eyes rolling skyward. "You're way too happy about this."

"Aren't you? This is *huge*! Think of all of the extra income, Ruby. You could buy Calvin so many toys."

Ruby laughed.

Coral turned the key. "Onto the dunes!"

Click.

She froze.

"Shit," she whispered and tried again.

Click.

Ruby turned fully in the passenger's seat to face her. The disappointment—no, the *judgment*—on her face was plain.

"Um…" Coral's mouth went dry.

There was no way around it.

Something in the van was definitely broken.

Chapter 20
Ruby

RUBY SLUMPED IN HER SEAT, deflating as all of the excitement left her body in a breath.

Coral started recording a video from her phone, apparently deciding that this disaster would make for good footage. She tried to start the van twice more. Nothing but clicks.

Ruby reached forward and stopped the recording. "For fuck's sake, Coral," she said, unable to suppress her frustration. "I trusted you when you said it was fine! We should've taken the van in to get fixed the day we noticed an issue."

She thought she'd learned her lesson with her own van, yet somehow she'd ended up in the same position.

Coral shot her a glare. "It's not a big deal. We'll fix it today."

"How? You're going to use the tool kit you used for the cupboard?"

"We'll go to an auto parts store!" Coral exclaimed.

"How will we get there when the van won't start?" Ruby shouted back.

"We'll get a jump from someone!"

Calvin got out of his bed and trotted to the back of the van, where he watched them with concern.

Ruby drew a calming breath and pinched the bridge of her nose. "This delay is going to make us miss out on seeing Cannon Beach again. Do we have to extend the trip? Can we both afford that?"

"We won't be delayed. Ruby, it's probably the alternator or something." She opened the door and slid out.

"Whatever it is, we shouldn't have ignored it."

Coral sighed and popped the hood. "Fine, I should've gone to an auto parts store right when it had trouble starting. I just didn't want to derail all the plans we had. Happy?"

"No, I'm not happy. What if something's seriously wrong with it and we need a mechanic?"

Coral stared. "Ruby...I'm a piece of paper away from being a mechanic. My parents are, remember? I did the build on this van, and I do all of my own maintenance."

Ruby stared. Coral had done the *build* herself? Her parents were actual mechanics? "Coral, the only thing you told me about your parents was that they have a business."

Coral opened her mouth as if to argue, blinked, and flushed. "Right."

Ruby rubbed her face and said into her hands, "I thought when you said you do your own maintenance, you meant regular stuff like oil changes."

Coral let out a breathy laugh. "I meant all of it. Anyway, I'm going to find Lighter Dad and ask him to give us a jump. Can you map out the nearest auto parts store?"

Before Ruby could respond, Coral slid out of the driver's seat and walked away.

Heat rushed into Ruby's cheeks. Maybe she'd overreacted, but how was she supposed to know that Coral would be able to fix any problem so easily?

Calvin crept up to sniff Ruby and make sure she was okay. She patted him, and his tail wagged.

"Sorry for raising my voice, bud. This is just a hiccup, apparently."

They got a jump start from the man who borrowed their lighter, who was tent camping with his wife and two daughters and had a pickup truck.

"What goes around comes around." He tipped his hat. "Good luck, ladies."

They left the campground, and Coral drove them to the parts store that Ruby picked out on the map.

They parked at the back of the lot, and Ruby filmed Coral while she popped the hood and used a multimeter from her toolbox to diagnose the problem. "Yep. It's the alternator. It's not letting the battery charge. Back in a sec."

She went inside and, minutes later, returned with a box the size of a toaster.

"I'm—um—impressed that you know how to do all of this. And jealous," Ruby said as Coral got to work. Her chest was less tight now that she understood why Coral had been so nonchalant about all of this.

"I could teach you some things." Coral was already disconnecting parts of the engine. "You could save a lot of money doing your own oil changes, for one."

Ruby moved the tripod for a better angle. "That would be awesome. You'll need to have patience because I don't know a thing about cars."

Vanlife would be so much easier if Ruby could have fixed her van's many problems herself. How many times had little things gone wrong? Water leaks, the fridge, propane, batteries, brakes, and now the entire damned transmission.

The muscles in Coral's arms flexed as she worked, and loose strands from her ponytail fell across her eyes. She wasn't afraid to get dirty, she knew how to problem-solve, she was brilliant, she was fully prepared for the realities of living in a van... She was, in short, a badass.

Ruby's most pressing matter bubbled up inside her. "Have you ever dealt with transmission problems?"

"Yeah, totally. First thing I did to this van was give it a new transmission."

Holy shit. What if Coral could share some tips or help her get parts for cheaper?

The silence must have gone on for too long because Coral looked up with her brow pinched. "Why?"

Ruby's heart skipped. The time had come to tell Coral what was wrong with her van.

She reached for the tripod and stopped recording. "Okay, the reason I wanted to take your van on this road trip is because mine is actually broken. It won't even drive." Her lips were numb as the words spilled out.

There was a long pause while Coral stared as if processing what she'd just heard.

"Ruby, why didn't you say anything?" Her shoulders sagged, her eyebrows pulled down, and her expression became so sad that Ruby almost regretted the confession. One thing Ruby hated—*despised*—was looks of pity. She'd had enough of those in recent years to last a lifetime.

"I can't tell my followers that my van is broken," Ruby said firmly, "because that isn't the purpose of my channel. I don't get my views from creating drama and hardship. My fans want to watch a close-up shot of me pouring a cup of tea and gazing out the window—not moaning about a broken-down van while I huddle on the side of the road."

"I get it," Coral said. "Your channel doesn't have space for broken things. I won't tell anyone. But I think you're underestimating how loyal your viewers—"

"I'm not telling them my van is broken."

"Okay. That's fine."

There was a pause. Ruby's face heated up. She didn't mean to be snappy. She pressed the heels of her hands against her forehead, letting out a breath. As her broken home weighed down on her, she leaned against the van for support, directing her gaze to the engine instead of Coral's eyes.

"It's not just that." She'd never allowed the thought to materialize, even in her own head, so saying it aloud was difficult. But she forced the words out, letting them come however they may. "I keep thinking about my dad. He wouldn't have wanted me to be open and vulnerable on camera. He was a very private man. He barely even told my mom and I when something was bugging him. We only knew by his body language. It took weeks for us to even know he was sick. All of this relationship stuff…all of the details about what's wrong with my van and my life…I can't help wondering how he would feel about me broadcasting it."

Coral waited, silent, her hands immobile under the hood.

Ruby's eyes prickled, and she blinked it away. "He's the only reason I could afford to buy my van. He left me some money when he died. I wanted to put it toward his medical bills or maybe have my mom use it for her shop, but she insisted that I use it for myself. So I bought the van. And then—I let it break." Her voice cracked, her throat too tight to keep talking.

"And you think your dad would be disappointed in you for that," Coral said gently.

Ruby drew a big breath and let it out in a huff, trying to loosen the tightness in her throat. "He would be. And so would my mom."

"Maybe not. Maybe they would understand that things break, and it's outside of your control."

She met Coral's gaze. It was soft, understanding.

"I should have taken it into the shop sooner. I made a mistake. First, I was in denial that something was wrong—like maybe if I ignored the problem, it would disappear. And then I didn't want to prioritize fixing it over helping my mom. It was so..." Ruby shook her head, furious with herself. "How can I keep helping her if my source of income goes away? I don't know why I thought—"

"Everybody makes mistakes. Don't be so hard on yourself. I think your parents would forgive you. I think your happiness is more important to them."

Ruby swallowed hard. Hadn't Mom always said something along those lines? She shifted her weight from foot to foot, her body lighter than it had been a moment ago. Her eyes stung, and her throat was tight, but a tingling sensation started in her chest and spread outward.

"It's just a van, Ruby," Coral said with a little smile.

Ruby nodded. She'd been taking a page out of Dad's book, holding in her emotions, not telling anybody what caused her stress. But that wasn't helpful. She should've confessed everything to Mom, and Coral, and even told some of it to her audience because nobody would be as hard on her as she was on herself. She'd tied so much guilt to her broken van, but it didn't have to carry all of the meaning she'd assigned to it. It didn't have to represent a broken home, a promise to Dad, a light for herself and Mom.

It's just a van.

"Thanks," she said to Coral.

Coral smiled. She removed a piece of the engine that must have been the old alternator. "I'll help you fix your transmission. When we get home, I can rebuild it."

"Oh—no, I didn't mean—" Discomfort tightened in Ruby's gut. This was way too much for Coral to promise. Now she thought Ruby was asking her to fix a several-thousand dollar problem. "I'll get it repaired at a shop. I just wondered if you knew of a cheaper way to—"

"I want to do it. Let me fix it for you. I just need you to pay for the parts, which I can get for a lot cheaper than you'll find anywhere else. You'll save thousands on labor."

"Then I should pay you for the labor."

Coral kept working, her hands moving nimbly to clean the area around the alternator. "Ruby, come on. After everything we've been through on this trip, I want to do this. As your friend."

Ruby's eyes prickled. *Dammit.*

"Plus, it'll be nice to hang out while I do it," Coral said, keeping her head bowed.

Was she blushing?

Ruby's jaw was tight as she fought the tears threatening to well up. Coral's offer was seriously nice. What did Ruby do to deserve her?

Without consciously deciding to, Ruby stepped in and wrapped Coral in a hug. "Thank you." Her voice was muffled against Coral's shoulder.

Coral hugged her back. "Of course."

Ruby let out a breath. God, Coral's arms felt good around her waist.

Too good.

Ruby stepped back, breaking the hug. She returned her attention to the camera, which had shut itself off.

Coral cleared her throat. "Hey, what you said earlier about missing Cannon Beach again—"

"I didn't realize how quick it would be to fix this," Ruby said. "I'm sorry. I feel like a drama queen."

"No, it's fine," Coral said, opening the box she'd just bought. "I was just going to say that Cannon Beach will be our last stop, so we can totally stay there for an extra day if we want to. We have nowhere to be, right?"

She had a point. They didn't have to worry about being late to their final stop because they could stay longer if they needed to. They'd said ten days, but they could make it eleven. Or twelve.

Ruby grinned, liking the sound of this. She resumed recording. "I say we wing it and see what happens."

Chapter 21
Coral

WITH THE NEW ALTERNATOR RUNNING strong, they continued down the highway. They pulled off to get footage at Sisters Rock State Park, a rocky headland with three peaks rising from the waves. A gravel path wound down to the shore.

"Hold my hand for the cameras," Coral said in sing-song, and Ruby laughed.

They walked down the path hand-in-hand, their shoes crunching over the gravel, Calvin trotting off-leash beside them.

Coral never considered herself to be good at acting, but with Ruby to feed off of, it was easy to pretend to be infatuated. They tugged each other along, leaned into each other while looking at the views, and smiled like they were totally smitten.

With nobody else around, this scenery would make for excellent footage.

Ruby scanned their surroundings. "We should probably get a kissing picture for Instagram and the featured image."

Coral's lips tingled. "Right. Sure."

They set up Ruby's camera on a tripod facing the shore. Coral fixed her ponytail, her heart pounding as hard as it had the first time they'd kissed. Maybe this was a sign that she'd been single for too long—she was excited and nervous about a planned, nonromantic kiss.

They started a ten-second timer and stood in the midst of the rock formations. While Calvin sniffed around behind them, Coral took both of Ruby's hands in hers.

"Ready?" Coral asked.

Ruby nodded firmly. "Hit me."

Coral laughed. "So romantic."

Both smiling, they leaned in.

Coral's insides did a little jig as their lips met. This happened in the woods too—a totally disproportionate reaction to how nonspontaneous and contrived the kiss was. But Ruby's lips were so soft, and she smelled like springtime, and something about her kisses just...worked. She was good at it. The way her lips gently claimed Coral's, it was all Coral could do to stay standing.

They stayed with their lips touching for a second until the camera clicked, and then broke apart.

Coral pressed her lips together as they walked back to the camera, tasting Ruby's mango lip balm.

Ruby looked at the photo and laughed. "You popped your foot up!"

"It looks cute!" Coral said defensively, leaning in to see it. It was a nice photo. The shadows from the surrounding rocks cast them into darkness so they were almost silhouettes.

"Or cheesy."

"Come on, we're adorable." Yes, Coral had popped her foot up, but only a little. She'd lifted it, like, a couple of inches off the ground, just to make the picture look like there was some movement to it.

Ruby caught her lower lip on her teeth, thinking. "I guess it adds something to the picture."

"Does it get your approval?" Coral had the urge to ask for another picture but couldn't summon the bravery.

Ruby nodded. "Looks good."

So they only got one take today. Coral couldn't decide whether to regret not asking for a second. Maybe it was for the best. Her heart was still beating fast.

As they headed back to the van, Coral walked a couple of paces ahead, needing to stop holding Ruby's hand for a minute.

Why did she keep getting so fluttery when they kissed? These kisses were supposed to be strategic. This was about numbers. Statistics. Fluttery stomachs had no place here.

They got back on the road and stopped for lunch in North Bend, both of them craving diner food. It would be a nice break from their healthy meals. They got a table at a tiny, unassuming restaurant on the side of the highway with a cute, retro interior. Calvin hung out in the van while they went inside.

Everything on the menu had some form of eggs, dairy, or meat, so Ruby made up her own menu item and ordered a hash brown veggie scramble. Coral ordered a Denver omelet with a side of pancakes.

"Mmm," she moaned loudly as she took her first bite of omelet.

An elderly couple seated nearby glanced over.

"This is a family restaurant," Ruby whispered, on the verge of giggling.

"I've been mostly vegan on this trip, and, yes, I feel energized, healthy, and ethical…but sometimes, a girl just needs greasy ham and cheese."

Ruby wrinkled her nose. "You lost me at *greasy ham.*"

Coral grinned and stuffed a bite of the massive, fluffy pancake in her mouth. She moaned again.

"This is hitting the spot, I admit," Ruby said.

They shoveled food down for a couple of minutes, and then Coral reached over to the cameras perched between them, which had been recording since they sat down. "That's enough, yeah?"

"Yup," Ruby said through a mouthful.

Coral pushed the button on each of them, regretting her sticky syrup fingers. She would have to wipe off the cameras later.

"So, *Ruby,*" Coral said, settling deeper into the booth. "If we're going to have a fake relationship, we should fake get to know each other a little better."

Ruby raised an eyebrow, reaching for her coffee. "What else do you want to know about me?"

"I don't know. Tell me about your exes. Why did your past relationships end?"

"Wow, is this what you talk about on first dates?"

Coral waved her fork through the air. "Would you rather small-talk? Tell me about your family, where you've traveled, what your hobbies are, blah blah blah…"

"Fair point." Ruby sat back, cradling her mug. She'd made a sizable dent in the enormous mound of food on her plate, and Coral wasn't doing so bad herself—although she was slowing down on this Frisbee-sized pancake.

"I've dated here and there, but nothing serious," Ruby said. "My most serious relationship lasted almost a year, and I broke up with her when my dad got sick. I came to this realization that when you really love someone, you want them there with you when you're going through a rough time. They become your anchor, your light. But...I didn't want her there. I wanted to be with my parents, and when she was there, it just felt intrusive." Ruby tapped her fingers on her mug, not meeting Coral's eye.

Coral's heart ached for Ruby. She wanted to hug her and make her pain go away, but she didn't know what to say. Maybe there was nothing to say. It was more about listening. Being there.

"I've never missed her," Ruby said. "Not once. I think when I was with her, I was just going through the motions of a relationship. I thought I was in love, but I wasn't. And I decided I didn't want to do that again. I'd rather be single than be in a relationship with someone who I'm not crazy about."

"I get that," Coral said. "Agreeing to another date because you think, '*Why not? They're nice.*' Not realizing that there's a spark missing. I've done that."

"Yeah?" Ruby met her eye again.

Coral prodded at the mangled remains of her pancake, too full for another bite. "My last girlfriend was super cool and artistic but not outdoorsy at all...like, she would rather get dirty in a pottery class than in the forest. It was cute at first, like opposites attract, but a few months in, it kind of wrecked the relationship. We had nothing holding us together. Like, we could never agree on a movie or a song or a meal or what to do on the weekend. Her idea of a fun Friday was a paint night, which was fun to try once, but I'm really not into it—and I felt bad taking her snowshoeing or whatever because she clearly hated it."

Ruby smirked. "I can see why a relationship with someone who hates camping might be hard for you. Why'd you even think that was a good idea?"

"This was before I started vanlife! In a way, she helped me realize who I was and what I liked. So I thank her for that." Coral raised her mug in a toast. She'd become a whole other person since dating Kass. She'd traveled, moved into a van, launched an online platform. And now she was faking a relationship with the most beautiful woman she'd ever met.

What a life.

"And what about your other girlfriend?" Ruby asked. "You said you had two?"

Coral grinned. "Interesting that you remembered."

Ruby opened her mouth, and no sound came out. She sipped her coffee.

"We were sixteen," Coral said. "We kind of broke up with each other. We were never soulmates or anything—just each other's first crush. There are no hard feelings. I appreciate the experience I had with her. She helped me find myself."

"That's sweet."

"Who helped you find yourself?" Coral asked.

Ruby bit her lip as if to hide a smile. She made the most adorable, mischievous expression that promised a good story.

"Go on," Coral urged.

"Okay, I was fourteen. There was…"

"Yes?" Coral leaned her elbows on the table and rested her chin in her hands.

Ruby smirked. "There was a butch girl in school who got all the babes. She had more girlfriends than any of the jocks, I swear. Those guys were so jealous of her. But she was *smooth*." Ruby gazed out the window with a wistful expression, and Coral laughed.

"Like your experience, she was definitely not my soulmate," Ruby said. "We had nothing in common other than being gay. But I was curious, so I sidled up to her one day after school under the pretense of asking about homework. She knew right away. She picked up on my shy flirting. We made out in the bathroom." Ruby shrugged. "That was it. One blissful day. I knew I was a lesbian ever since."

"Damn, Ruby!" Coral said, drinking in the juicy story. "I can't believe it took you so long to tell me this. God, that's good. I can just picture you..." She trailed off as heat bloomed in her midsection. Picturing Ruby making out with a girl was doing something to her.

She crossed her legs.

The server came by to offer them coffee top-ups, and they both accepted. Coral was grateful for the break in the conversation, needing a minute to cool down.

"Could we get the check, please?" Ruby asked, then faced Coral again. "Sorry, I hope that's okay. Don't want to leave Calvin in there for too long."

"Yeah, totally. I should stop drinking coffee, anyway. I'm jittery."

Jittery, hot, and bothered.

When they got back in the van, Coral drove them another hour to Jessie M. Honeyman Memorial State Park. It was a massive campground just north of Dunes City, and they got a site without a problem.

Thank God. Between the alternator situation and all of the stops they'd made along the way, it'd been a long day.

Their neighbors were all here for the dunes, with toy trailers, ATVs, and dirt bikes filling every campsite. The roar of dirt bikes could be heard in the distance.

"Should we rent a dune buggy again?" Coral asked teasingly.

Ruby grimaced. "Yeah, you go ahead. I'll be here reading a book."

"How about a walk instead?"

"That's more my style."

Energized from their bottomless coffees at the diner, they followed a trail to a little lake that backed onto the dunes. A huge, sandy beach sloped steeply upward, and they played with Calvin in the sand until all three of them were out of breath and their freshly laundered clothes were filthy.

The way Ruby smiled when she played with her dog was so pure and unguarded that Coral was sure these were the moments when Ruby was at her happiest. Coral couldn't help watching her as they all ran in circles, just to see her beautiful smile light up the world.

Chapter 22
Ruby

AFTER SUNSET, RUBY STARTED EDITING the day's video while Coral went for a shower. Calvin leaned heavily against her knees, his head on her lap, where he knew he would get absent-minded pets for hours if he stayed there while she worked.

Playing all of the clips back, Ruby's cheeks warmed. It was strange to watch herself and Coral flirt on camera. It looked normal, like they were a real couple, which made it weirder, knowing it was all fake.

But something about the two of them worked. They played their parts well. No wonder people were losing their minds over it.

It was hard to believe they would be in Cannon Beach tomorrow. She wasn't ready to end the road trip yet—but at least Coral wasn't either. They would hopefully extend their stay for another day or two like they'd talked about.

She hadn't heard from Mom today, so she picked up her phone and called. It rang a few times, then went to voicemail.

Ruby furrowed her brow. Was Mom in bed? It was almost ten, so it was a possibility. But it was weird that Mom hadn't texted her at all today, when normally she checked in.

Ruby's heart double-skipped. Her brain immediately went to a place of disaster.

Don't overreact. She's probably just busy.

Calvin looked up, maybe sensing a shift in her mood. She petted him again, and his big, seal-like eyes got heavy and tired.

She opened her text messages and composed one to Mom. If Mom didn't answer within the next half-hour, she'd call again. And then maybe try Yui.

Hey Mom! Hope you had a good day. We're driving back to Cannon Beach tomorrow. Love you lots.

She went back to video editing but found it hard to concentrate. Finally, a reply came in.
Ruby let out a breath, feeling silly for overreacting.

Hi Ruby. Sorry I missed your call. Just getting a few things done around here. Love you too, and I can't wait to see you!

Ruby smiled at the message, relieved to hear everything was fine.

At least, it seemed fine? It was unusual Mom hadn't messaged her today. But maybe she really was busy doing errands.

The van door opened, and Ruby put her phone down, eager to be pulled out of her spiraling, anxious thoughts. She tended to overreact when it came to issues of Mom's well-being. She tried to go easy on herself for it—with everything their family had been through, she had good reason to be concerned.

As Coral stepped inside the van and shut the door, Ruby let out a breath and relaxed her shoulders. It was interesting how Coral's presence calmed her. She hadn't noticed that until now. Calvin helped keep her mind busy, but there was something to be said for human company.

"Ahh, it felt amazing to get all of that crusty sand off," Coral said. "Ten out of ten, would recommend." She combed her fingers through her wet hair and took off her sweater, dumping it and her shower tote on the passenger's seat.

Ruby's heart tripped over itself. She'd seen Coral with wet hair after the shower multiple times, but today, something swooped in her belly. Coral wore a beige tank top, her nipples showing through the thin material. Her bare shoulders were smooth and damp, and Ruby had the urge to run her hands over them and down her arms.

"Great." She averted her gaze to Calvin on the floor. "Can't wait for my turn."

These feelings had to stop. This was still supposed to be a business-oriented road trip. Clearly, these fake relationship feelings were messing with her mind and making her think she had real feelings.

She glanced back at Coral, who was brushing her hair, her toned arms flexing. The tank top moved up and down, revealing a tease of her sun-kissed midsection.

Ugh, Ruby couldn't deny it anymore. She *did* have real feelings. Coral had made her feel so alive on this trip. She was smart, fun, and sexy. Kissing her was mind-blowing. Ruby couldn't remember ever having a kiss like that.

It was easy to imagine what it would be like to be in a real relationship with her.

But she wasn't supposed to have real feelings for Coral. Their relationship was fake—an amendment to a business agreement. No part of Ruby should be considering what it would be like to peel off her clothes, crawl on top of her, and...

Stop it.

This was bad. She was tingling between her legs, and some unnamed feeling swelled in her chest.

I am in so much trouble.

If Coral realized how Ruby felt, she would get so awkward. This plan was clearly working, and they'd both gained followers, but if Coral knew that Ruby was starting to catch real feelings, she might try to do the noble thing and call off the fake relationship.

And with Ruby's entire online career at stake...she absolutely could not let that happen.

She had to put a lid on this. The fake relationship was working, and she couldn't let her gay panic sabotage that.

She went for a shower—a *cold* shower—and when she got back, Coral was bundled under the blankets like a burrito.

"I'm freezing," Coral moaned. "Help. Let me steal your body heat."

Ruby smirked. "Okay, okay, I'm coming."

Ruby climbed into bed next to Coral, who shimmied closer. Her feet were like ice cubes against Ruby's thigh.

"Don't press your ice feet against me!" Ruby cried.

"Do you want them to fall off from frostbite?"

"Oh my God, drama queen."

Coral made a show of shivering. "S-so...c-cold..."

Ruby laughed. "How do you survive in your van alone?"

"I don't know. A hundred blankets."

Ruby flung her arms and legs over Coral and hugged her tightly. "Is that warmer?"

Coral laughed, the tightness of Ruby's hug making her come unraveled from the ball she'd been huddled into. "A little."

Ruby squeezed her harder.

"Perfect," Coral said, muffled because her face was squished against Ruby's arm. "Just stay like that all night."

"Okay. G'night!" Fighting laughter, Ruby kept holding Coral tightly, refusing to be the first to crack.

This was not doing anything for her feelings. A sensation filled her belly that should not have been there. She had to tame this—starting tomorrow.

"Ruby?" Coral said, still muffled.

"Yeah?"

"My grandma would be disappointed."

This seemed like such a strange thing to say that Ruby loosened her arms and legs. "Huh?"

"We aren't leaving room for Jesus."

The words took a moment to sink in, and then Ruby dissolved into laughter. She let go of Coral, overcome with it.

Coral started laughing too, uncontrollable until they had to roll onto their backs and catch their breath.

A week ago, she never would have guessed that she would be like this with Coral. But Coral brought something out in her that she didn't know she had—something silly, open, and free.

Coral shimmied close again, and they huddled in each other's arms for warmth.

Sure, they could have turned on the heater. They were plugged into shore power, and it would have warmed up the van in twenty seconds.

Except the thing was…it wasn't actually that cold in the van.

And Coral was looking right at Ruby, her perfect, heart-shaped lips parted.

Chapter 23
Coral

CORAL'S HEART WAS BEATING OUT of her chest.

She said she's not interested in a relationship.

Ruby wasn't the type to play games, so there was no doubt she meant what she said.

But dating and hooking up were two different things. And right now, Coral's libido was telling her that she would be fine with either.

She ached for Ruby, needing more than fake kisses.

They lay face-to-face, a breath apart, their arms draped over each other.

Ruby shifted, and under the covers, her leg brushed against Coral's. She was so soft and gentle that Coral's breath caught and a tingle went through her. Ruby was barely doing anything and managing to drive her wild.

Tentatively, she moved her hand to Ruby's waist. She ran her fingers up and down, the thin material of her camisole between them.

Ruby's eyes fluttered closed. She let out a breath through her nose.

Coral stopped moving her hand, unsure how to read Ruby. Somehow, in the course of this evening, she'd gone from believing Ruby would never be interested in her to wondering if there was actually the possibility of something happening.

Maybe she's not out of my league?

Ruby's eyes opened, and she gave Coral a blazing look that couldn't be misinterpreted.

Coral moved in, and so did Ruby, and Coral's mind spiraled into a haze as she caught Ruby's lips in hers. They moved closer, their bodies arching together under the covers.

Ruby's breath hitched, a sound that sent a flame through Coral's middle.

She kissed Ruby with more heat than she'd given her on camera, holding her face, teasing her with her tongue. Ruby teased her back, sucking her lower lip, deepening the kiss—and Coral melted. She sank into Ruby's arms, breathing in her sweet scent, feeling the way their bodies undulated beneath the covers.

Ruby reached down, her fingers brushing the bare skin at Coral's waist where her tank top had bunched up.

The feel of Ruby's fingers on her skin sent her head spinning, and she brought her knee up, pulling Ruby's hips closer with her leg.

Ruby let out a hiss, wrapping a fist in Coral's hair. She kissed Coral hungrily, soft noises escaping that made desire pool in Coral's middle.

Coral propped herself up on an elbow, ready to climb on top—and Ruby pulled back.

"What are we doing?" Ruby let out a shaky breath that might have been an attempt at a laugh. "The cameras aren't even on."

Coral swallowed hard, heat rising in her cheeks. *Crap.* "I—I don't know. Carried away?"

She tried for a casual laugh, but her tone was anything but casual. She was panting and aching, and this abrupt stop left her voice strained. She shifted, uncomfortably aware of what was going on between her legs.

Ruby let out another awkward laugh. "I've never been in a fake relationship before. I think my brain is confused."

She shimmied up her pillow, a clear indication that Coral should roll back to her side of the bed.

Coral did, heat burning in her face. She felt empty, her body missing where Ruby was pressed against her a moment ago.

"I'm sorry," Ruby said. "We've got a good thing going with this fake relationship for the cameras. I don't want to mess that up."

"Yeah, of course," Coral said a little too loudly.

Ruby turned her head to meet Coral's eyes. "You agree, right?"

Coral nodded, forcing a smile. "Faking it can really mess up a person's emotions, I guess."

What had she been thinking, going in for a kiss? Ruby said she didn't have time for a relationship. Anything real was off the table, and it always had been.

"Anyway, I'm excited to be back in Cannon Beach tomorrow night," Ruby said, a pitiful attempt at changing the subject.

Coral swallowed hard, her heart wilting. Her lips tingled, wanting more of what she couldn't have.

Apparently, she was way more into Ruby than she'd thought.

"Me too," she finally said.

As she rolled over and stared at the ceiling, willing her racing pulse to calm down, it became painfully clear that this fake relationship had been a terrible idea.

Chapter 24
Ruby

"DON'T FREAK OUT, BUT THERE'S a trending article about us." Coral frowned at her phone, leaning against the counter with her half-made bowl of oatmeal at her elbow.

On the bench, Ruby paused while mixing hers. "Um, what?"

"*How Two Lesbian YouTubers Are Stealing Our Hearts.*"

Ruby let out something like a gasp and an attempted laugh at the same time, and it came out as a splutter.

"I can't decide whether to be excited or freaked out," Coral said. "Like, this is big and will probably get us more followers, but also…"

"It's weird?"

"Super weird. Hang on." Coral scrolled through the article while absently eating her oatmeal with raisins and maple syrup.

Ruby continued making hers, adding hemp seeds, almond butter, blueberries, cinnamon, and sunflower seeds. She tended to put so much in her oatmeal that she was usually still making it by the time Coral was done eating hers.

"Okay, they're basically just recapping our videos," Coral said finally. "There are some screenshots of us allegedly flirting, and then the forest kiss…the cave yesterday… I guess this is good, right?"

As if on cue, Ruby's phone lit up with an email informing her that she had another new Patreon member. She grinned. "Very good."

Both of them had gotten way more followers and views, and in time, this would translate to income. This morning, Coral had surpassed a hundred thousand followers, and Ruby had surpassed 1.1 million.

If they kept going with this fake relationship—which would probably be in everyone's best interest—their stats would likely keep going up.

They just had to avoid crossing the line like they had last night.

Whatever that was.

They hadn't talked about it, as if it didn't happen. Their casualness this morning had started off a little forced, but now they were back to normal, and it was as if last night were a fading dream.

We got caught up in the charade. That's all.

Ruby refused to mess up this great thing they had going by mixing in real feelings. The plan was working, and crossing the line into real feelings would complicate it—especially once they got home. They lived in different countries, and seeing each other wouldn't fit into her busy life. She had Mom's well-being to worry about, and the more she thought about it, the more she realized what she had to do: she had to help Mom with the tea shop. She could work in the store part-time, even if it impacted her ability to travel, and she could help with social media, ads, and other marketing. With that, in addition to maintaining her vanlife platform, she would have no time left.

After breakfast, they packed everything up and got back on the highway. They would arrive in Cannon Beach tonight, giving them all day tomorrow to explore it.

And after that… Well, it would be fun to stay a day or two longer to see Cannon Beach properly this time. She wanted to soak up as much as she could before returning to reality.

They stopped to top up on groceries, then stretched their legs at Neskowin Beach, where they walked along the shoreline to see the Ghost Forest. It was aptly named, casting a chill over Ruby as she looked out at the ancient tree stumps jutting out of the sandy beach.

Calvin trotted around and sniffed everything, his nose working loudly as he investigated the strange landscape.

Coral faced the camera to explain the sight to their viewers. "This was a forest a long time ago until an earthquake destroyed it and left us with just these stumps."

Ruby walked closer and took Coral's hand for the cameras. "It's…a little creepy-looking, to be honest."

"Creepy but beautiful. A reminder of the power of nature."

"A reminder that a natural disaster could kill us all," Ruby said.

Coral threw her a horrified look. "What is the matter with you?"

Ruby nudged her, flashing a teasing smile.

When they got back in the van, Ruby said, "Let's stop in Tillamook."

"Sure!" Coral side-eyed her. "Why?"

"Ice cream. I seem to recall you saying something about getting violent over chocolate chip cookie dough." She wanted Coral to try the famous ice cream, and to see the delight on her face as she tasted it. After a whole trip of making her eat vegan food, she owed it to her.

"This is true." Coral laughed. "But what about you? You don't eat dairy."

"I'll get sorbet."

Coral grinned. "You know the way to my heart, Ruby Hayashi."

Chapter 25
Coral

CORAL OGLED THE TILLAMOOK CREAMERY storefront. "I wouldn't have thought a dairy farm could be a tourist attraction. This feels more like the entrance to a theme park."

A gigantic picture of a cow greeted them over the doors while streams of people flooded in and out. The people leaving carried cheese, ice cream, T-shirts, cheese-shaped stress balls, and all manner of other merchandise from the gift shop. Signs pointed toward guided tours.

"Welcome to America," Ruby said. "Come on, we're going that way."

She tugged Coral to the left, where more doors led into a cafeteria.

With the cameras rolling, their hands stayed clasped, their smiles were big, and their flirting was in full force. Coral's belly swooped as Ruby cast her a look of adoration.

And then Ruby turned her camera off...and it was like a flipped switch. She let go of Coral's hand, her smile dropped, and she even avoided eye contact.

Coral furrowed her brow, searching the side of Ruby's face. Ruby had done this on the drive too, but Coral had brushed it off.

What was going on? Was Ruby trying to respect boundaries or was she having regrets?

While Ruby and Calvin waited outside at a shaded bench, Coral ordered a waffle cone of chocolate chip cookie dough ice cream and a cup of mango sorbet. She joined Ruby outside, where Calvin begged and drooled until Ruby took pity on him and fished a dog treat out of her bag.

The ice cream was so good that Coral closed her eyes and sighed. "Heaven. I owe you for bringing me here."

Ruby smiled into her mango sorbet. "Glad you like it."

She made no eye contact.

Of course, the cameras were off.

Coral held up her camera. "Quick clip of us eating?"

Ruby nodded. Predictably, she smiled, laughed, and leaned in affectionately while Coral recorded. Then, as Coral put the camera away, they returned to silence.

Coral frowned. The difference between on-camera and off-camera Ruby was exaggerated today. It was like she physically leaned away when they weren't recording.

But what about everything else that'd happened off camera? Why did Ruby kiss her in bed the other night? Even though she'd stopped the kiss, it didn't change the fact that she'd done it in the first place.

There must have been some feelings there.

Then there was all of the cuddling, the flirting, and that hug after Coral offered to help with her transmission when they got home. Early in the road trip, Ruby told Coral that hugs meant a lot to her—and yesterday, she'd given Coral a seriously good, long hug.

That had to mean something too.

Coral's knee bounced as she licked her ice cream cone.

What do I expect from her? She's doing what we agreed on. She's acting in love in front of the cameras.

But it left Coral wanting.

Ruby was doing what they agreed on—and Coral wanted more.

She couldn't deny it. It was painfully obvious in the way her heart thrummed that her crush was real. Given the way her stomach did flips since the day she'd set eyes on Ruby, it'd probably never been fake at all.

If there was a chance that Ruby felt the same, then they could stop faking it and start an actual relationship. They could spend time together once this road trip was done and open their hearts to each other, and their kisses could be for *them* instead of for an audience. And they could do a lot more than kiss.

But Ruby's body language said plainly how she felt. She wouldn't be so distant if she were interested. She was probably trying to hint that Coral was coming on too strong while the cameras were off.

Coral broke off a piece of the waffle cone, getting to the end of her dessert. Today was a reality check. All of the flirting was confusing her and making her feel like Ruby was interested, when logically, she *knew* this was all fake. Days ago, Ruby had flat-out said she didn't have time for dating. Coral's body needed to cooperate and stop getting all fluttery when Ruby touched her.

"Well, that was heaven on a cone," Coral announced as she took the last bite, satisfied and a little nauseous from too much of a good thing.

"Glad you liked it." Ruby put a hand on her stomach and groaned. "You might have to roll me back to the van."

They got back on the highway and continued north. They passed through Wheeler, a cute seaside town, and pulled into Nehalem Bay State Park. They would spend the night just south of Cannon Beach and drive into town first thing in the morning to spend the day there.

They'd stayed in this park on the way up, but it'd been too dark to see, so coming here again was like visiting a new world. The campground was on a sand spit, which made for different views than the rest of their stops along the coast. Grassy dunes separated them from the beach, and the surrounding trees were short with twisty trunks. The wind blew strong, so they spent the evening in the comfort of the van.

They were an hour into doing their social media updates when Coral came across something that made her heart plummet.

Oh. Shit.

Did she have to tell Ruby about this? Could she just ignore it and hope it went away?

There was a chance it would go away.

But also not.

A few minutes passed before guilt forced her to speak.

"Hey, Ruby? There's another viral post about us."

"Really?" Ruby kept her gaze on her laptop. "What's it this time?"

"Um…"

Ruby looked up, her brow pinched. "What's wrong?"

Coral took her laptop across the van and sat beside Ruby on the bed. With a sick feeling churning in her gut, she unplugged her headphones and played the video. Ruby watched over her shoulder, silent.

He was a round-faced, twentysomething white guy sitting in front of a podcast microphone. His smug smile made Coral want to punch him before he even opened his mouth.

"Hey, and welcome back to The Joe Show, where we talk about what's going on around the internet today."

The urge to punch became stronger as his over-the-top radio host voice filled the van.

"If you follow the *hashtag-vanlife* trend on social media, you've probably come across these two by now."

A picture of Coral and Ruby appeared at the upper right corner of the video. It was the featured image from one of their first videos together, both of them smiling inside the van with the back doors open to a view of the beach.

Coral's pulse picked up. Watching this guy talk about her life made her stomach roil.

"Now, I admit, I hadn't heard about them until this morning," he continued. "And then I got a tip from a listener who sent me this video. Check this out."

He cut to a clip of them in Tillamook today. It was a shaky, grainy phone video taken from the side. Someone had videoed them eating ice cream on the benches outside of the creamery. There was Ruby rummaging in her bag for a treat for Calvin. The video continued for about thirty seconds as they ate, talked, and took videos of each other.

The video cut back to the podcast host. "Now, you may not think this is a very exciting video, but when you understand a bit of background, their body language becomes interesting. See, just a couple of days ago, these two started publicly dating."

A picture of their first kiss in the forest appeared in the top right.

"But if you look at this video, you can clearly see that they're only being affectionate when the cameras are on. They're holding hands and flirting while the cameras are rolling, but the second those cameras are off, they aren't acting very coupley. This begs the question: are Coral Lavoie and Ruby Hayashi already *fighting*? Are they even *really dating*? Are they *lying* to their viewers to get attention? Let's dive in on today's episode."

The video was twenty-six minutes of him painstakingly going through everything they'd posted since the start of the trip, sometimes frame by frame, to analyze their emotions. The ass probably would have gone back to analyze their older videos too if he'd had more time.

When it was over, Ruby's hands were over her mouth, and her eyes were wide. "I can't believe someone was watching us in Tillamook."

"This was uploaded an hour ago. One of my patrons sent it to me. Whoever recorded that phone video must have sent it to him right away."

"Fuck. What do we do? We can't tell him to take it down."

"I think we have to ignore it and hope that not many people see it."

"They'll see it. The entire internet is going to think we're frauds," Ruby said, her pitch rising.

Coral shook her head firmly. "It's just speculation. Some people in the comments are already defending us."

"*Some* comments? What about the rest of them?"

Coral said nothing. She scrolled through the comment section, searching for supportive ones, but there were just as many trolls—if not more.

"Well, what do you expect from a podcast called The Joe Show?" Coral said in an attempt to lighten the mood. "Feminists? Allies? People who want the two of us to succeed?"

"Coral, this is exactly what I was afraid of!" Ruby exclaimed. "If people know we're lying, we're ruined!"

Coral shut her laptop and leaned back on her hands, drawing a deep breath. She didn't want to admit that this made her nervous. They could lose their entire audiences and be in a worse position than when they'd started this road trip. "I don't know how many people will take him seri—"

"We should've tried a different tactic to get more subscribers. This is a disaster."

Coral's heart sank, and not just because Ruby was doubting her plan. She liked the flirting and kissing, even if it was fake. "Don't say that. We're doing great, and this guy is an idiot."

"How big is his audience, though?"

"The important question is, how much of our audiences overlap? And I think it's next to none. I doubt that any of our followers watch him, Ruby."

"Our followers *will* see this because he put our freaking names in the video title!"

Oof. That was true.

"They'll come to our defense," Coral argued, determined not to let this guy win. "Anyone who likes us will think this guy's a dumbass."

Ruby inhaled slowly, shaking out her hands. "Yeah," she said as if trying to convince herself. "Total douche."

"What kind of man spends time recording a *gossip* video about two vanlifers, anyway?"

At this, Ruby cracked a smile.

Guilt simmered in Coral's gut. Ruby had so much more to lose than she did. Coral could survive if she lost her followers and had to sell the van—but this was Ruby's entire livelihood. Her mom and dog also depended on her.

"Let's give them no reason to think we're lying," Coral said, putting as much confidence as she could into her tone. "We'll just have to make sure we act coupley in Cannon Beach tomorrow in case anyone spots us."

"I guess so..." Ruby grimaced. "This is so weird. I feel like a celebrity being stalked by paparazzi or something."

"I know. I don't like this either."

Well, she didn't like the fact that random people were gossiping about them. She didn't mind the idea of acting more hands-on with Ruby, though.

Throwing caution to the wind, Coral leaned over and pecked Ruby on the lips.

Ruby's mouth opened in surprise. She glanced at the cameras on the dinette, which were very much off.

Coral shrugged. "What do you think? If we act more convincing, both on camera and off, then we'll give nobody any reason to suspect that we're faking it."

Ruby's dark gaze searched Coral's face. Coral's heart beat faster as the fear of rejection crept in, making it hard to breathe.

A smile tugged at Ruby's cheeks. "Okay, honeybunch. Nothing to lose by trying, right?"

Coral nodded firmly. "Nothing to lose."

She hoped those words were true, but God, she couldn't help feeling otherwise.

Chapter 26
Ruby

IN THE MORNING, THEY PARKED in a day-use lot near the visitor center and set off on foot to see all the shops. Most were dog-friendly, and for those that weren't, they took turns holding Calvin's leash outside while the other went in to look around.

Being back in Cannon Beach was bittersweet. It was nice to have the day to explore the town this time. But would tonight be their last night, or would they stay another after that?

Ruby had gotten used to Coral's company, and the van would be lonely and quiet without her. Plus, how were they supposed to continue this relationship charade when they lived in different countries?

Unless they faked a breakup.

The thought of breaking up, however fake, made Ruby's insides hollow out. Hopefully, it wouldn't come to that.

They entered a shop full of stylish outdoorsy clothes, rustic home decor, and a lot of high price tags. It was quiet, smelling like the homemade pine candles on a large table in the center. A few other people milled through the tables and racks.

"My Aunt Nina used to take me window shopping when I was younger," Coral said. "Kitchen stores were our favorites. All of the random stuff you can get, like egg peelers and hot dog slicers."

It was the second time Coral had brought up her aunt, and for the second time, she seemed to have better memories with her aunt than her parents. Curious but not wanting to pry, Ruby said, "Sounds like your aunt is pretty cool."

"Yeah, she is. I haven't seen her much in the last year because she's been traveling a lot."

"Do you miss her?"

Coral pulled a mint green sweater off the rack, examined it, looked at the price tag, and put it back. "I usually see her every weekend, so yeah."

"Is she on your mom or dad's side?"

"My mom's sister. She doesn't have kids, so Farrah and I get all the attention from her...which is funny when I look at my mom, like..." Coral shrugged. "I don't know. I don't know where I'm going with this."

Ruby flipped through a stack of vintage postcards of the state parks while Calvin sat patiently at her feet. She could tell this topic made Coral uncomfortable, but there was something else underneath—maybe relief for talking about it with someone. The glimpse into Coral's life was nice, as if a rope were tugging them closer together with every confession.

"You think she felt like more of a mom to you than your actual mom did?" Ruby asked.

Coral said nothing, a pink tinge in her cheeks.

"Maybe your relationship with Aunt Nina is so good *because* she's your aunt," Ruby said. "Things would be different between you if she were your mom."

Coral traced her fingers along a rack of shirts. "Yeah, that makes sense. You're probably right."

"Does she support your vanlife career more than your parents do?"

"Well, she never made me sign an agreement that I would make a certain income or else give up the van," Coral said bitterly.

Ruby hesitated over the question on her lips. She wanted to ask whether Coral thought she would be able to fulfill her end of the agreement and keep the van, but she didn't want to ruin Coral's day if the answer was no. Plus, finances were a tricky and often private topic—she'd learned this from years of trying to broach the subject with her mom. "Are you...feeling okay about that agreement?" she asked vaguely.

To her surprise, Coral smiled. "Whether my parents are satisfied or not, I can tell you one thing. I'm glad we went on this road trip."

Ruby smiled back. "Me too. Thanks for inviting me."

"Thanks for saying yes."

There was a pause. Coral looked like she wanted to say more. Her gaze darted over Ruby's face. Whatever was going on behind her eyes made a flutter rise in Ruby's belly.

"There's a top behind you calling my name," Coral said abruptly, pointing. "Do you mind if I try it on?"

"Go for it."

Coral grabbed it off the rack and bounced over to the change room. While she was there, Ruby bought a couple of the state park postcards so she could put them on the corkboard in her van. She missed her van, but not as much as she thought she would. Coral's company turned out to be a fair exchange.

"Ruby?" Coral poked her head around the corner. "Come tell me if this looks good or not."

Ruby put away her wallet and slid the postcards into her bag, then led Calvin to the changerooms.

"Is it okay?" Coral asked.

It was a pearl-white, tight-fitting top that could have passed for a bikini. It curved in a heart shape above her breasts and came to a twist in her cleavage, emphasizing the line down the middle of her stomach.

Paired with her high-waisted jean shorts, she looked irresistible.

"Y-yep." Ruby's mouth went dry. "That definitely works. It's a really—um—very attractive top."

At her obvious stuttering, Coral laughed and tilted her head. "Cool. I think I have my answer."

"Cool."

Coral wiggled her shoulders, shamelessly teasing Ruby.

Ruby stepped in and hooked a finger over the twist of material between Coral's breasts. She stopped before she pulled Coral in, not wanting to go too far. "Tease," she said, then let go and backed away. "You'd better buy that, or else I'll buy it for you."

Coral's cheeks flushed. She opened her mouth, and after a pause, nodded and shut the curtain.

Ruby waited outside with Calvin, drawing a breath. *Did I cross a line?*

She didn't know what came over her, touching Coral like that.

Why did Coral have to be so sexy? Her flirting and boldness were making it hard to figure out boundaries.

Coral bought the shirt, and they continued on.

The next store was a pet store, and Coral offered every single toy to Calvin to see which one he liked best.

Ruby laughed. "His favorite is anything he can play tug with."

"Okay, that's fair. How about this rope?"

She offered Calvin a rope with a tennis ball on the end, and he grabbed it and started pulling.

"Yes!" Coral played tug-o-war with him. "We have a winner."

She let him win, and he galloped a victory lap around Ruby.

By the time Ruby untangled herself from the leash, Coral was at the cash register. "I'll take the tug rope and a bag of those bacon cookies, please."

Ruby rushed over. "Coral, you don't have to!"

"I want to. Calvin has been a very good boy this whole trip, and I owe him a present for letting me into your lives like this."

Ruby flushed. "You really don't have to. But thank you. He's going to be thrilled."

Calvin didn't let go of the toy as they left the store, strutting proudly with it like he'd caught it in the wild himself.

God, Coral was too sweet. Ruby could have melted into a puddle over how cute she was. She twisted her fingers together, fighting the urge to pull Coral into a kiss—and not just one of those gentle smooches they were doing for show. She wanted to *really* kiss her, like they'd done in bed the other night.

This plan to keep up the charade when the cameras were off was turning into a disaster. Before, there had been a division between the flirty, on-camera version of Coral and the regular version, but now, there was no difference. She was a hundred percent affectionate, all over Ruby, turning up her charm to level ten even when the cameras were off.

And it drove Ruby wild. She couldn't get enough of the way Coral smiled at her, the way she felt, her sweet smell when they stood so close…

Coral slipped into the next store, and Ruby checked the sign. A florist.

"Hey, look at this." Coral returned to take Ruby's hand.

Ruby's heart flipped over as their hands clasped. Their fingers entwined, and Coral's soft palm pressed against hers. It took Ruby a moment to notice what Coral was doing.

She pulled Ruby up to a bouquet of sunflowers and cast her a cheeky smile. "Look! Your favorite!"

Ruby stepped back from the yellow-and-black arrangement. "Ew, why?"

Coral tugged her forward again. "They're so pretty. It's like sunshine in a vase."

"They have faces!" Half-laughing, Ruby tried to pull Coral out of the shop.

Coral clasped her hand in both of her own, holding her in place. "Okay, okay, no sunflowers." She dug her heels in to keep Ruby inside the shop.

Ruby stopped pulling, and the sudden shift in balance made Coral stumble.

Ruby caught her around the waist, pulling her close. Coral's breath hitched. Before Ruby could think about it, she leaned in and kissed Coral on the lips.

After all the times they'd kissed, the cameras were off this time. This one was for them. Whether Coral felt it, Ruby didn't know, but time seemed to stop as their lips met.

Ruby parted her lips, inviting Coral in, and Coral responded eagerly. Everything else faded as the kiss deepened. Ruby teased Coral with her tongue, a gentle brush across her lower lip. Coral reacted by pressing closer, sliding a hand around the back of Ruby's neck. The whole world became the feel of Coral's body against hers, and their noses brushing, and her soft, sweet breath.

They moved against each other, the temperature of the kiss rising from a simmer to a boil, and then…

The noise of a group of people getting closer. The feel of Calvin leaning against her leg. The scent of the flower shop.

Ruby's brain stumbled back into action, and the first emotion to hit her was embarrassment for this over-the-top public display of affection. She'd meant to go in for a regular kiss, hadn't she? When did it evolve into full-on making out?

Her brain clouded. She couldn't remember even deciding to kiss Coral. Her body just took over.

Ruby pulled back a little, and Coral's breath hit her lips, coming faster than a moment ago.

Coral swallowed hard. "That was…"

"Should we continue?" Ruby murmured.

Coral blinked, then nodded, looking dazed.

Ruby let her go, and Calvin led the way out of the shop.

"Ruby, wait," Coral said.

Ruby tensed, bracing herself for something she didn't want to hear—but when she turned around, Coral was holding a bouquet of red tulips.

"How about this?"

Ruby smiled.

Before she could protest, Coral was at the cash register paying for the tulips. Ruby thanked her profusely as they walked back to the van with the gorgeous arrangement and their other shopping bags.

"You really didn't have to do that." Inside, she was dancing. No one had ever bought her flowers before.

"You've been cooking for me all trip," Coral said. "I appreciate it. Besides, consider this something to remember me by after we get home."

"As if I'm going to forget you."

Coral chewed her lip, searching Ruby's face.

They entered the van, breathing sighs of relief as they got out of the hot sun. It was cool and comfortable, especially with the sunshade over the front window.

Silence engulfed them. As Ruby shut the door behind them, the sound of the lock clicking shut seemed to echo.

Was the van always this quiet and isolated? Why did it feel extra small right now?

Calvin flopped in his bed, eager for a nap, his new toy cuddled between his front paws. He closed his eyes and let out a big breath, apparently exhausted after that big day of shopping.

Ruby put the gorgeous red flowers on the counter, her pulse quickening for some reason. "That was really fun today."

"It was."

They both put down their bags. Coral's sweet scent seemed to fill the van, making it hard to function.

"I'm glad we got to see Cannon Beach properly this time," Ruby said.

"Mm," Coral said. "And I'm glad you kissed me in the flower shop."

Ruby's heart seemed to stop beating. Her lips tingled, and then the sensation moved lower. Should she explain that kiss? What *was* her explanation, anyway?

She turned. Coral sat on the bed. The van closed in on them, feeling smaller than ever.

"Should—should we get dinner at a patio restaurant?" Ruby asked, not even sure what she was saying. Her mouth was dry.

Coral shimmied further back on the bed. She toyed with the hem of her flannel shirt—that cute oversize one that had been teasing Ruby since the day they met.

God, Ruby wanted to run her hands up and down those smooth, tan thighs.

Coral reached over to pull the curtains shut on the rear window. The light inside the van dimmed, casting her into shadow.

Then, slowly, she lifted her shirt over her head.

She wore a pale pink bralet. Her chest and stomach were so smooth, begging to be kissed.

Ruby's heart pounded faster, slamming into her ribs.

They'd had to get changed in front of each other countless times on this trip, but this was different. Coral was looking at her, her lips parted, a blazing look in her blue eyes.

Ruby was frozen in place, a decision hovering thickly in the air between them.

Coral unclasped her bralet. She let it fall, exposing her perfect breasts and hard, pink nipples.

Ruby couldn't handle another second of that sultry look in her eyes.

"Coral, you drive me crazy," she whispered.

She walked forward, and Coral inclined her face as Ruby made it to the bed. Taking Coral's face in both hands, she kissed her hard, ready to follow through on everything she'd wanted to do since the day they met.

Chapter 27
Coral

CORAL KISSED RUBY BACK, MOVING her lips eagerly. She lifted her hands to Ruby's face, cupping her cheeks, pulling her closer. Her body reacted instinctively, sizzling from her lips to her toes, heat building low inside her as they finally gave into each other.

She'd wanted this for too many days. She wanted to unravel Ruby, to make her let go of all of the inhibitions that'd been holding her back from getting what she wanted.

Ruby rasped out a breath, knotting a fist in Coral's hair and sliding the other around her waist. The sensation of Ruby's soft hands on her bare skin sent a shiver through her that made her breath hitch.

Ruby pushed her onto her back and climbed on top, her movements firm. The boldness caught Coral by surprise as she fell back, sending a jolt of desire through her core. She moaned and pulled Ruby in with her thighs.

"The things I've wanted to do to you," Ruby murmured.

Coral gasped. "Then—stop making me wait."

Beneath a canopy of Ruby's hair, a burning desire like nothing she'd ever felt trickled through her middle, turning her mind into a fog. She pinned Ruby between her knees, and they rocked against each other.

Ruby parted Coral's lips with her tongue. Coral welcomed her, exploring Ruby's mouth like she'd wanted to do since their first kiss in the woods—not just their lips meeting gently, but fully claiming her, teasing her tongue, sucking her bottom lip. Ruby moaned, reacting to the kiss by grinding harder against Coral's hips.

Everything that had been building up since they met came flooding out, making them both frantic. Coral let her body take over, responding to Ruby's movements, arching into her soft hands. She tugged Ruby's shirt, and they paused to take it off. Ruby tossed the shirt aside and then her bra. At the sight of Ruby's perfect, round breasts, desire pooled between Coral's legs. She ran her hands over them, rolling her hard nipples under her palms.

Ruby leaned down, and Coral's breath hitched as their bare skin touched.

Oh, fuck. Ruby's hot skin on hers made her ache, and she arched her body to feel more of her.

"You're so gorgeous," Ruby murmured, kissing Coral's neck.

Coral responded with an incoherent whimper.

Ruby kissed lower, running her lips over Coral's chest. Coral's eyes fluttered shut as she savored the sensation. Ruby swirled her tongue around a nipple, and Coral gasped, arching into it.

"Ruby—that—f-feels—*oh*…"

Ruby flicked her tongue and sucked, sending a ripple of pleasure through Coral's body. Then she moved to the other one.

Coral couldn't take this. She was going to melt into the bed. The way Ruby took control had caught her by surprise—but really, didn't it fit? Ruby was always in control. Every detail of her life was planned, organized, perfect.

Right now, she had to be given permission to surrender.

Coral caught Ruby's chin and pulled her back up to her lips, and before Ruby could react, she rolled them over. Ruby let out a gasp of indignation.

Suspended over Ruby, Coral cast a wicked grin. Ruby was flushed, her full lips parted. Her chest heaved as her breaths came fast.

A wild sensation filled her chest as she looked down at Ruby spread beneath her, her hair fanned out on the pillows.

"My turn on top." Coral reached between Ruby's legs, massaging her over her shorts.

Ruby moaned, parting her legs.

"Can I?" Coral whispered into her lips, tugging the waistband.

Ruby was already helping her remove them. "Yes."

She turned to Coral's shorts next, and Coral helped her take them off.

They were both naked, and oh, *God.* Coral's skin prickled as the temperature in the van rose. She ran her palm up and down Ruby's thighs, teasing her.

Ruby whimpered. "Coral..."

With a knee on either side of Ruby's hips, Coral leaned down, kissing her so gently that Ruby hissed in frustration. Ruby reached between Coral's legs—and before Coral had time to ready herself for what was coming, Ruby's fingers traced down, up, down...

And Coral lost all sense of who and where she was. She moaned, unable to stop the sound from escaping. The feel of Ruby's fingers as she straddled her hips was agonizingly good, making it hard to stay suspended.

Dizzy, she reached between Ruby's legs, finding her wet and swollen. The gasp Ruby made was so sexy that a lick of heat blazed through Coral's middle.

They massaged each other, their kisses getting slower, deeper. Ruby was so wet on her fingers that it was obvious she'd wanted this just as badly. God, how long had they both wanted this and held back because of their agreement?

"What are you smiling at?" Ruby murmured, a smile forming on her own lips.

"Nothing." Coral silenced her with another kiss.

Coral rocked her hips against Ruby's hand, her body taking over. Ruby pushed a finger inside her, and Coral gasped, tightening her fist in Ruby's hair. She lost herself as their hands moved between each other's legs, their fingers sliding in and out, exploring what made each other cry out.

Sweat dampened Coral's skin. She moved a knee down to push Ruby's legs further apart, and Ruby gasped, tipping her head back.

"Coral—oh—that's amazing..."

Ruby's wetness coated her fingers, driving her wild. Coral lifted her fingers to her mouth, needing a taste. She held Ruby's gaze as she licked her fingers, then slid one back inside her.

Ruby moaned, her fingers tightening over the back of Coral's neck. A fiery expression Coral had never seen came over her.

Heat gathered in Coral's middle, intensifying. Her thighs trembled. She gasped into Ruby's lips, her coordination failing as she could only focus on the sensation of Ruby's hand and the heat building inside her. She braced herself on her elbows, her mouth by Ruby's ear, breathing in the scent of her hair. "Yes—yes—"

"Come for me," Ruby whispered.

The words sent Coral over the edge. She cried out as waves of pleasure overtook her, her mind spinning. Her arms lost strength, and she leaned into Ruby, lips pressed against her neck.

Ruby ran her fingers through Coral's hair and kissed behind her ear. The movement was so tender, so personal, it was like they'd been dating for months.

As she recovered, gasping for breath, her body still sizzled as if static played across her skin—like no matter how long they spent in this bed, it wouldn't be enough.

She lifted herself up, and a rush of cool air hit her front where their sweaty bodies had been pressed together. She kissed Ruby deeply, hoping to show how much this meant to her—that this wasn't just sex. She wanted to give Ruby every pleasure in the world, to make her forget about the stresses that sent her on this road trip in the first place. This moment was entirely theirs, and for once, nobody but them had to know.

"Your turn." Coral dipped her head lower, kissing Ruby's stomach. "I've waited a long time to taste you."

Ruby moaned. "I—if—okay—"

Coral moved lower, kissing her inner thighs. "You're in for a long night."

She kissed Ruby at the apex between her legs, then ran her tongue in a long, slow lick.

Ruby gasped. "Y-you're going to kill me."

"Not a bad way to go." She closed her eyes, the taste of Ruby intoxicating.

Ruby gripped the duvet, her legs trembling.

Coral licked her again, needing her. She moved her tongue gently, savoring how swollen she was, reveling in the knowledge that it was for her.

Coral circled her tongue, moving faster. When she brought her hands up to push Ruby's legs further apart, Ruby whimpered incoherently, reaching down to run her fingers through Coral's hair.

"Oh, God, Coral—"

Coral ran her hands over Ruby's thighs, up her stomach, to her breasts, where she flicked her nipples.

Ruby trembled all over, gripping the duvet, at Coral's mercy.

Coral had grown so used to seeing Ruby in full control of herself, calm, composed. But *this* Ruby? The sounds she made, the involuntary movements of her hands and legs, the way she writhed with each flick of the tongue... Seeing her losing herself like this made Coral hungry for more. She held back nothing, needing Ruby to let go and relinquish full control.

"Mmm..." Coral slid her arms around Ruby's thighs, relishing the feel of her soft skin. She tingled between her legs, every sound out of Ruby's lips making her ready for more.

"Yes..." Ruby moaned, tipping her head back in ecstasy. She writhed on the bed, tensing, curling her toes. "Yes—"

Coral grinned as Ruby gasped and gripped the bed—and then she tipped over the edge, letting go of her last shred of control. She wrapped her fingers in Coral's hair as her orgasm rose up and completely unraveled her, making her cry out. The way she moved and the whimpers rising from her lips were instinctive, unrestrained—a moment of trust Coral had ached for from day one.

She held onto Ruby's thighs, making the moment last, until Ruby fell back onto the pillows, gasping for breath.

"Holy—crap," she said between breaths. "That was..."

As Coral climbed up to lay beside her, their gazes locked.

The most beautiful, pure smile broke across Ruby's face, which Coral returned.

"I...needed that," Ruby said.

"We both did. And we should have done it a lot sooner."

A mischievous expression played at Ruby's eyebrows. "Then we'd better make up for lost time."

After pausing to drive to a parking lot to stealth camp, they immediately jumped back into bed, clawing at each other's clothes. True to Ruby's words, they had to make up for all of the sex they could've been having over these last few nights.

By the time they lay beside each other, gasping for breath, it was well into the middle of the night, and Coral's whole body was exhausted and hypersensitive—and she couldn't stop smiling.

"So that was the VIP experience you were talking about," Ruby said weakly. "I have to admit, I would choose that over a free Michelin meal any day."

Coral burst into laughter.

Seeing Ruby smiling on the pillows beside her, naked, flush-faced, her hair a mess, sent a ripple of pleasure through her.

"What's the plan for tomorrow?" Coral asked, a flutter of nerves in her belly.

Ruby hummed. "Maybe we should go see Haystack Rock again and try some of the other hikes and beaches around here."

"And stay another night?"

Ruby nodded. "What do you think?"

Coral leaned over and pecked her on the lips one more time. "Yes. I think we should extend the trip so we can fit in a few more things."

Chapter 28
Ruby

RUBY AWOKE TO A BEEPING sound. She rolled over, grabbing blindly for her phone. The mid-morning sun beamed through the cracks in the curtains—they'd slept in.

It was a text from Mom.

You're home tonight, right?

Ruby frowned at the message, a ball of dread tightening in her stomach. She hadn't intended to be home tonight, but did Mom need her? She typed a reply.

Yeah. Why?

Good. Just checking. I might need your help with something when you get home. Hope that's okay.

The ball of dread turned into a boulder. Something happened.

She sat up. The covers slid off her, and cool air rushed in, reminding her she was topless.

Mom, what's going on?

It's fine. There was a leak under the sink, and I have to empty the cupboards. Don't worry, it's under control.

Ruby swore under her breath. She slid out of bed and pulled on her pajamas. Quietly, she opened the door to step outside. Calvin got up from his bed to follow.

The sun attacked her as she left the van, so bright that she couldn't see for a few seconds. It was already hot. A glance at her phone told her it was ten. She hadn't slept in this late since she was seventeen. Then again, she'd never stayed up all night until she was sore between her legs and her jaw muscles were cramped.

She stepped away from the van and into the shade of a wispy tree, where she called Mom. The view wasn't as nice as any of the campgrounds they'd stayed at—they'd found a gravel parking lot beside the highway for the night—but it was just meant to be a stopover on the way home.

"Hi, Ruby." Mom sounded tired.

"Hey. So the apartment is flooded?"

"Not flooded. It's just the kitchen. I called the building manager."

"Is it still coming in?"

"No, no. We turned off the water, and a plumber is coming tomorrow."

Ruby closed her eyes, rubbing her face. "Okay. When did this happen?"

"Yesterday morning."

Yesterday? This has been a problem for a full twenty-four hours?

"You called your insurance?"

"Yes."

Ruby paced, absently following Calvin as he sniffed around some decorative shrubs and peed on everything in sight. Cars whooshed by in a steady rhythm on the highway. "Mom, why didn't you tell me about this right away?"

"I didn't want to ruin your trip."

"I appreciate that, but you know you're my priority. I would have come home to help you."

"That's just it. I didn't want you to do that for me."

Ruby sighed. "I'll be home tonight, and we can get everything sorted. Is it just the cupboards?"

"Yes. I've emptied most of the damaged ones…but I still have to soak up some of the water…"

Ruby pinched her brow. Something was off. "Are you okay?"

Silence.

"Mom."

"I slipped on the water and fractured my wrist. It's in a cast, so don't wor—"

"What? Oh my God. Okay, I'm coming home." Ruby's heart jumped into action, and she bit her tongue to stop from swearing. Mom had been in the hospital while Ruby was having a romp with Coral and not sparing half a thought for anyone else.

"I'm fine! See, this is why I didn't tell you. Yui took me to the hospital and helped me soak up the water. It's all under c—"

"You won't change my mind, Mom."

Mom's breath hit the phone—resigned, defeated. Ruby's heart ached, her eyes burning as she pictured Mom alone with her arm in a cast right now.

What kind of daughter am I?

"Okay," Mom said. "Don't rush. I don't want you speeding home and getting a ticket."

Ruby's brain churned faster, like a train gaining speed.

What would Dad have done? Call the right people. Fix the problem. Go to the hardware store.

"There are extra towels and blankets in my van we can use to soak up the remaining water, and we'll get everything out of the cupboards in time for the plumber. I'll get some fans we can use to dry the cupboards before they mold."

"Thanks. See you soon—and I promise I'll be fine until you get here."

When Ruby stepped back inside the van, Coral was awake but still in bed. She sat up, topless, her hair a disaster from the frenzy of the night before. A tendril of heat wound through Ruby's middle, making all of this worse.

A crease appeared between Coral's eyebrows. "What's wrong?"

"That was my mom. I have to go home."

A silence passed as Coral seemed to process this.

Calvin walked over to the bed to say good morning to Coral, his tail wagging. She reached out to scratch his ears.

"What happened?" Coral asked.

"Her kitchen is flooded, and she fractured her wrist slipping in the water. She needs help cleaning it up."

"Oh. Crap, I'm sorry to hear that. Did she call the building manager and stuff?"

"Yeah. I have to help her clear out the cupboards for the plumber and dry everything."

"Can't her friends or neighbors help out with that?"

Ruby shot Coral a glare.

"I just don't know what you're supposed to do," Coral said quickly. "You're hours away, so can't someone closer go help?"

"She's my mother!" Ruby exclaimed. "How would you feel if you had a leak *and a broken wrist,* and your own family didn't come help you?"

"I have had a leak," Coral said flatly. "And I've had a sprained wrist. And I've managed to get on with things by myself."

Ruby's chest tightened. She huffed. "Well, some of us are less independent than that."

Coral's brow pinched. "But now we have to end our trip—"

"Our trip was over anyway."

Their conversation about staying longer hovered between them, filling the air, making it hard to breathe.

"It's just—I told you, I have priorities—" Ruby's throat seemed to close. Maybe that wasn't the right thing to say, because it implied that Coral was a lower priority in her life. She tried again. "I know it's hard for you to understand because of your relationship with your parents. Like, your van is your own problem, and their problems are theirs, and you've probably never been expected to rush over and help them with anything...and even though you're close with Farrah, she's always busy with school..." Ruby swallowed hard. She was rambling, and it was definitely not helping.

Coral's expression hardened. She got up and rummaged for an outfit. "I'll drive. Do what you need to do."

"Thanks," Ruby said, barely a whisper.

She turned away to get the oatmeal out of the cupboard, a lump in her throat.

She hadn't meant to insult Coral's relationships with her family. In truth, the thought of not having someone to depend on made her chest tighten. It would be hard to have independence forced upon you, making you solve problems alone when it would be less stressful having loved ones to help. Coral deserved to have people there for her.

Should Ruby try to explain what she meant?

She looked over. Coral was getting dressed, pulling on her clothes with jerky motions. A deep scowl pinched her face.

Ruby looked away. She didn't have the emotional capacity to dwell on this right now. They were going home, and she would help Mom fix this mess, and that was what mattered.

"I'm going to pee in the cafe." Coral glanced out the window at the lonely cafe at the back of the gravel lot. "Want anything?"

Ruby shook her head.

Coral left the van, slamming the door a little hard.

In the heavy, pressing silence, Ruby's eyes welled, wishing this morning-after could have gone a lot differently.

Chapter 29
Coral

CORAL PULLED OFF IN TUMWATER for a stretch and a snack, following the signs for the historical park. Ruby tensed, maybe about to tell Coral they didn't have time to stop, but then Calvin began to whine. They all needed a break.

The day was cool and overcast, threatening rain. As they exited the van, a wave of sadness washed over Coral. This was their last stop. Their next one would be at Ruby's mom's place, and then Coral would drive back to Canada. Where would she sleep tonight? The prospect of parking the van somewhere alone and continuing life as it was left her hollow.

Ruby leashed a bouncing Calvin. "Should we walk a bit?"

"Sure."

Brewery Park was an interesting little oasis in the middle of Tumwater with a pretty river running through it. They followed the footpath toward the river, Calvin trotting in the lead. The purr of a waterfall filled the air.

The word *priorities* swirled around in Coral's brain from their earlier conversation. Maybe Ruby had a point, and whatever last night had been, it wasn't as important as everything else in their lives. Ruby had her mom to worry about, and Coral had to think about her future in the van. The point of this road trip was to address the bigger, more pressing issue of needing to boost their platforms. *Those* were the priorities. Coral shouldn't be wasting time thinking about a relationship with Ruby. She should be thinking about whether she was on track to earn a thirty-thousand-dollar annual income, and more realistically, whether she could buy the van off her parents or ask for more time. Maybe they would look at the upward trend in her follower count and consider that enough.

A series of waterfalls tumbled down alongside the path, and large grates let them see into the stream below their feet as they walked. Calvin avoided these, walking on the narrow strip of concrete beside the grates.

"I think this is a fish ladder," Coral said, looking down. "Pools to help the fish swim around the waterfalls so they can get upstream to spawn."

She was forcing lightness, trying to show Ruby that she wasn't mad about earlier. Even though she was a little bit. Even though Ruby had said hurtful things about how alone Coral was. But fighting during these last moments of the road trip could mean the end of their friendship, so Coral needed to put that hurt aside.

"Hm. Cool that they built the park around the waterfalls." Ruby kept her gaze on her feet. Her eyes were glassy, and she had a distant, defeated look about her. Was she sad? Was she also wondering where they stood?

Priorities aside, Coral was dying to know what would happen next for them. She didn't want to say goodbye.

"How long do you think it'll take to get your mom's place sorted?" Coral asked, her heart beating faster.

"I don't know. A few days."

"Do you want help?"

I could be there for you. Let me be the person you want to pull closer in times like this.

Ruby looked over, her mouth open, and then back at her feet. "No. That's okay. Thanks."

A sinking feeling pulled Coral's insides downward. The answer was no, then. Ruby didn't want Coral there during hard times, and she obviously didn't have the same feelings.

What did last night mean, though?

They kept walking, the grates and pools beneath their feet hypnotizing.

"And…what about afterward?" Coral asked, her mouth dry.

"What about it?"

Coral glanced at her, not sure how to elaborate without asking bluntly.

Ruby blinked, seeming to clue in. "Oh. After I'm done helping her…" Her gaze darted from Coral to the river and then around the park, like she didn't know where to look. She sighed. "I don't know if we should keep this up."

Coral had the sensation that she'd jumped into the river beside them. "Why not?"

"That guy's video has tens of thousands of views. People are guessing that we're faking it, and we're going viral for the wrong reasons."

"But we're also going viral for the *right* reasons!" Coral exclaimed. She hadn't known that gossip video had so many views—although she had seen an uptick in trollish comments under her videos.

Uhh how convenient that you happened to catch your "first kiss" on camera. But hey, sex sells, right?

woowww this channel is about as real and unscripted as reality tv.

Came here from The Joe Show. Was not disappointed. Someone get these girls acting lessons. It hurts.

The truth settled over Coral like a raincloud: her brilliant plan was teetering on the edge.

But they could get over one guy's gossip video. Their stats were still way up, and the majority of their audiences didn't think they were faking it.

In fact, the majority saw what both of them had spent so long denying. They saw the real feelings that couldn't be faked.

She shook her head. "You're putting too much weight on that guy's video. People will forget about it soon. Who cares what—"

"We *have* to care about stuff like that, Coral. It matters what people think! Without a loyal audience, we have no platform. We risk losing everything. I'll lose my entire livelihood." Ruby's voice cracked.

"I won't let that happen! Come on, we can prove him wrong."

Ruby threw her hands in the air. "We can't just *fake it harder!*"

"Don't let that guy ruin what we have—"

"What we *have*? Enlighten me on what that is, please. Everything about this feels wrong. We're using each other for clicks. Everything about *us*—" She made air quotes. "—is contrived. We're fake, and I hate it!"

"Well, what if this wasn't fake? What if we made it real?" Coral shouted—and the words were out, and she couldn't take them back. Icy dread rushed through her veins as the words swelled in the air between them.

Calvin stepped away from them and sat down, whining.

Ruby let out a breath. More quietly, she said, "We can't. We don't even live in the same country. I have too much going on without a relationship to worry about."

Ruby's answer came so easily, it was as though she'd spent time thinking about it.

Had she thought about it? And was this truly her reason for saying no, or was that a gentle way of rejecting Coral because the feelings weren't there?

"Right." Heat rose in Coral's cheeks. She stepped back. "No, you're right. It would never work, and I know you don't have time for it. I guess we took it too far last night."

Ruby blinked. Her eyes were a little red. "Too far. Yeah."

They kept walking, the air ringing with their words. Coral's throat was tight, and she tried to breathe deeply. The rejection was biting, the pain swelling like a wasp sting.

At the top of the waterfalls, windows offered a peek into the murky river, where little silver fish darted in and out of view. Beyond it was an area where the fish were farmed—a sign labeled them as Chinook. Glimpses of movement revealed the chaotic swarm of fish below the calm surface.

Coral considered filming this but couldn't bring herself to do it. She didn't want to press the record button, didn't want to smile for the cameras, didn't want to try and sound happy.

"Should we go?" Ruby asked.

Coral nodded and turned back to the parking lot.

Ruby's movements were heavy, her tone sad, which made anger spark in Coral's gut. Why was Ruby the one acting morose? They were doing exactly what she wanted. They were going home so she could help her mom, and then they would part ways and their whole fake relationship would be over.

It doesn't have to end this way, Coral wanted to shout.

But she'd taken her shot. She'd asked Ruby if they could make it real. And Ruby had said no.

They shut the van doors, muffling the waterfall and plunging them into a stifling silence.

As they left Tumwater behind, fat rain drops hit the windshield, and Coral clenched her jaw to stop her tears from falling.

By the time they made it to Ruby's mom's place, the silence in the van was so thick that Calvin kept looking between them in confusion.

They parked the van next to Ruby's, and while Ruby ran up to get the keys, Coral started taking all of Ruby's stuff out of drawers and cupboards. The parkade was cold and dim, casting a chill over her that dampened her already bad mood.

Ruby returned, opened her van, and haphazardly shoved things inside. Clothes. Kitchen supplies. The vase of tulips.

How could they be ending the road trip this way? They had such a good time. Coral had really enjoyed herself, and last night left her floating. But Ruby's cold rejection put an unexpected bookend on the trip. How was she supposed to recover from that?

"It was worth it, right?" Coral asked, hoping for a less ugly bookend. "This whole road trip?"

Ruby pulled a box of Coral's winter equipment out of her van. "Yeah, I think so. We'll have to see how many paying subscribers we've lost or gained. We'll find out when we get our payouts over the next couple months."

The chill settled more deeply over Coral. That was it? That was all the whole road trip amounted to—statistics?

Obviously. We have a signed and dated agreement to prove it.

"Are you going to make a video to tell people we broke up?" Coral asked through numb lips.

"I guess so. We can email to talk about what we want to say and make sure we don't contradict each other's story."

Coral nodded. She wouldn't be posting any such video. She would go back to her usual content without mention of Ruby. Recording a video to tell her audience that they broke up felt too personal, and she might not be able to get the words out.

When they were done, dread tightened Coral's chest, making her breaths shallow. She bent to say goodbye to Calvin. "Bye, buddy. Thanks for letting me into your life."

He whined in delight, wiggling his whole body, smacking his tail against her and the van as he tried to squirm around to lick her face.

She was going to miss his smiles.

Coral stood, finding it hard to meet Ruby's eye. "See you, then."

Ruby waved. "Bye."

A wave. Not a kiss, not even a quick hug. Just a wave from six feet away.

Coral got into her van, shut the door, and turned the key.

She put the van into reverse, and as she rolled up the window, Calvin's whine of despair echoed through the parking garage.

Chapter 30
Ruby

RUBY RODE THE ELEVATOR UP to Mom's place with a bag of essentials, her plants, and the tulips Coral had bought her in Cannon Beach. Everything else stayed unceremoniously dumped onto the floor of her van. The van was the messiest it'd ever been, but there would be time to address that later. First, she had a more important task.

She'd gotten a glimpse of the apartment when she came up to get the keys, and although Mom had mopped up the water, the damage was obvious. Mom would need new floors, cupboards, and God knew what else.

Calvin hip-hopped in the elevator, and when the doors opened, he barked and ran down the hallway toward Mom's place so fast that he jerked the leash right out of Coral's hand.

"No barking," she hissed.

Mom opened the door, and there was an explosion of whining and "Hello, hello, my sweet friend!"

Ruby shouldered her way in. "I called the hardware store while we were on the road. They have those big industrial fans for rent. I'll run out and get one, and we'll leave it pointed at the cupboards all night."

She'd thought about it, and that was what Dad would have done. He would have gone to the hardware store to buy or rent whatever they needed to fix the problem.

Except with a broken van, she would have to borrow Mom's sedan to get it home. Hopefully, Mom wouldn't ask questions.

"We can do all of that in a minute." Mom rushed over to help her juggle all of her stuff. She was one-armed, her right one in a cast and a sling, but insisted on carrying something anyway. They put it all down in the bedroom, and Calvin continued to jump and wiggle.

When Ruby's arms were free, Mom pulled her into a big, swaying hug.

The hug went on for so long that Calvin got bored and went to the kitchen to sniff around. He was probably wondering why everything was soggy.

"How was the road trip?" Mom asked.

"Fine. Good. It was great, actually." *Right up until the last day. Why did we have to complicate things last night?* "What'd the insurance company say?"

"Ruby, stop. Let's say hello for a minute before we get to business."

Ruby sighed, following her to the kitchen. The floor was rippled and discolored.

"Can I make you something?" Mom opened the cupboards and pulled out udon noodles, moving awkwardly with her non-dominant hand.

When Ruby paused to think about it, she was starving. "Sure. Thanks. I'll help."

Mom pulled carrots, cabbage, red pepper, and green onions out of the fridge. "What was your favorite place?"

"Cannon Beach," Ruby said automatically, and then flushed. Well, yes, her favorite stop had been the last one, but that was because of the way things were with Coral. They'd been happy yesterday—giddy, even. The whole day was fun and exciting. "I mean, the entire Oregon coast was amazing, and it's hard to compare the views when they're all a ten out of ten. The redwood forest was a ten too. I don't think I have a favorite spot."

"I'm so happy you got to go." Mom brewed her favorite blend of peppermint tea for them to sip while they cooked. "How was Coral?"

Ruby's stomach flipped over. "Good. She was nice."

Silence. There was a heavy thump as Calvin flopped on the floor in the living room.

"That's it?" Mom asked. "Where are all of the details?"

Ruby's mouth twisted into a guilty smile. She scanned the soggy kitchen floor. "We really should get a fan in here tonight. Maybe two. We could also use hair dryers."

"Mm. I tried to rent a big carpet cleaner to suck up the water—I remember your dad doing that when the washing machine leaked—but..." She glanced at Ruby, something like concern lingering behind her dark eyes. "Well, I didn't know if it would fit in my car, so I thought I would take your van, and..."

Ruby's heart jumped. "You tried to drive the van?"

Mom grimaced at the stove. "How long has it been broken?"

Crap.

"Why did you think you could bring a carpet cleaner home with a broken arm?"

Mom didn't fall for the topic change. "Ruby. How long?"

Her insides burned with the uncomfortable sensation of being caught in a lie. "It happened the morning I showed up here before the road trip. I got it towed to your parking garage."

Mom faced her, slumping. "Is it expensive to fix?"

Ruby hesitated. Having no energy for another lie, she nodded. "That's why I haven't brought it to the shop yet. But I got a lot of new paying subscribers on the road trip, so I'll be able to fix it soon. Don't worry."

"I feel awful."

"Don't. Please don't feel awful because of me." Ruby blinked, trying to make her eyes stop stinging. "I didn't tell you because I didn't want to add that pressure to you."

"You add no pressure to my life. Don't say that. Why are you crying?"

"I'm not." Dammit, she was. "I just—I didn't want to disappoint you. I let the van break. *Our* van."

Mom slumped as she caught on. "Vehicles break, and it's not your fault. Don't let a lump of metal represent something it shouldn't." She shimmied closer, putting her face close to Ruby's. "Dad left you that money so you could follow your dreams and be happy. He would be proud of you for everything you've accomplished. Okay?"

Ruby nodded, fighting the swelling sensation in her eyes and nose and throat. Hearing it from Mom was everything she needed—like she needed permission to believe this.

Mom returned to cooking, struggling to chop vegetables with one hand. "Anyway, the shop is recovering, and I'll be able to cover all of my bills next month, so—"

"It's okay," Ruby said before Mom could try to do something valiant, like refuse Ruby's financial help. "I'll be able to fix the van soon. The point of the road trip was to get more subscribers and boost our channels, and it worked."

Mom raised her eyebrows. "*That* was the point of the road trip? Not to have fun? Not to see the coast?"

"Well—that, too—" Ruby's stomach twisted. Of course enjoyment was the *main* point of the road trip, right?

Except, what had been at the front of their minds the whole way down the coast? What was the motivation behind everything they'd done, including their entire fake relationship?

"The pictures and videos you posted were top-notch, Ruby. You really are one of the best channels out there. I'm so amazed by you. I haven't seen anyone who comes close to your quality and finesse."

Ruby's cheeks warmed. Typical Mom, thinking everything Ruby did was perfect and wonderful. "Thanks, Mom. That's—wait—" A hot feeling bubbled in her stomach as the words sank in. "You still watch my channel?"

Mom smiled.

Ruby covered her mouth. She'd been under the impression that Mom didn't keep up with every one of her videos—not since her first year of vanlife.

Oh, God! What sorts of embarrassing things had Ruby said and done? Ugh, this meant Mom had seen her and Coral kiss!

"I've never stopped. I haven't told you because I didn't want you to be self-conscious about what you decided to post."

"I—well—I appreciate that, I guess." Ruby's face was on fire. How mortifying.

"I leave comments too. You've replied to a lot of them."

"I have?"

Mom took a sip of tea.

"What's your username?" Ruby's face was numb.

On the floor behind Ruby, Calvin sighed dramatically.

Mom looked down at her tea, a little smile on her lips. She swished it around so the peppermint leaves twirled.

"You're Mrs. Peppermint!" Ruby cried. "But… Mom, do you subscribe to my Patreon page?"

"I do."

"You give me money every month?" Ruby exclaimed. "You don't have to do that! You're my mom!"

"And that's exactly why I want to. I want to support your career. I'm so proud of everything you've done with your channel. Your dad would be too."

A lump formed in Ruby's throat. She nodded, unable to get any words out.

They scooped the yaki udon into two large bowls and settled onto stools at the kitchen island. The vase of tulips sat in front of them, the brightest thing in the kitchen.

"Did Coral go home?" Mom asked.

Ruby's insides went cold. If Mom watched her videos, then she saw the entire fake relationship. "Yes."

"Are you going to keep seeing her?"

Ruby's cheeks burned until steam from their bowls might as well have been coming from her face. "No."

Mom's face sank. She looked genuinely sad. "Why not? I was looking forward to meeting her."

"Mom, that whole relationship…" Ruby swallowed hard. "It was fake. We were pretending to be in love for the cameras. It worked. We got more followers. But it's over now."

A crease appeared between Mom's eyebrows. She looked at Ruby for so long that Ruby dropped her gaze to her food.

"Fake," Mom said.

"Yeah."

Ruby's mouth was too dry to eat. She poked at the noodles, blinking a lot.

Mom leaned closer, forcing Ruby to meet her eye. "I don't want you to take this the wrong way, but when you were in high school, you weren't that great at drama class. I mean, you're good at everything you do, but acting...wasn't your forte. Not like the way you were with cooking and other skills."

"Um. Okay?" This might have been the first time ever that Mom told Ruby she wasn't good at something.

"So you'll have to forgive me if I'm having a hard time believing that all of that with Coral was acting."

Impossibly, Ruby's face became even hotter. "Mom, don't."

"I know you don't want to talk about this with me. But why does that relationship with Coral have to end? Was it on her terms or yours?"

"Both—we agreed—well, on my terms, I guess." Ruby shifted on the hard barstool.

Mom's eyes were watery. Was she going to cry? Dammit. Ruby couldn't handle watching Mom cry.

"You spend so much time trying to make sure I'm happy."

"Because I love you! I want to be there—"

"And you are, Ruby! Trust me. I'm happy. I have you, and I get to watch you flourish and live a full life. Now please think about yourself. What do you want? Let yourself be selfish."

"I don't want to be selfish!"

"Everybody has to be a little bit. It's not a bad thing. If you spend your whole life living for other people, you'll never be happy."

"But you need me." Ruby's voice broke. She blinked at the ceiling, drawing a breath. "I want to help out with the shop. I'll do your social media and marketing, and I could even work part-time—"

Mom put her hand on Ruby's arm. "Stop. You're not working in the shop. It's doing fine, and we can talk about marketing, but I'm going to have to reject your application for employment."

"Why? Let me help you. Or at least hire a student to help out. You're going to exhaust yourself with these long hours."

Mom considered, drumming her fingers on the counter. She nodded. "I'll look into hiring help for the busier months."

Ruby let out a breath. "Good."

"Ruby, I appreciate you more than you know. You're my whole world. But I'm strong. I've been through a lot in life, and I can handle myself."

Ruby cracked a smile.

"You have to live your own life. Take care of yourself before you take care of others. When you prioritize your own happiness, then you can bring your best self into the world, right? Isn't that part of living intentionally?"

Ruby nodded. Maybe Mom was right. Ruby spent so much time thinking about Mom, her followers, and what everybody else in the world wanted from her. Maybe part of it was that she just loved Mom and wanted her to be okay. And maybe the other part was that focusing on others was easier than facing her own feelings and needs since losing Dad.

Mom rubbed Ruby's arm affectionately. "Remember how hard you fought me when you thought you should stop living in the van and move back in with me? Remember our conversation?"

Ruby nodded, a little smile tugging her lips. "If you call that a conversation." She vividly recalled getting cold feet and trying to move back in with Mom a few months into vanlife, but Mom had been adamant that Ruby should keep following her dream and building her online platform. She'd literally locked Ruby out of the house during that argument.

To this day, Ruby was grateful for it. She wouldn't be this successful if Mom hadn't forced her to keep going. Mom saw through her. She knew what Ruby truly wanted, and she'd helped her see through all of her doubts and fears.

"So, right now, I need you to think about what would truly make you happy." Smiling, Mom reached out to touch one of the tulips on the counter—bright, vibrant, beautiful. "What does that picture include?"

Now it was Ruby's turn for the watery eyes. Because she knew exactly what that picture would include.

And the subject was currently driving back to Canada.

Chapter 31
Coral

AUNT NINA ANSWERED THE VIDEO call on the third ring. A blur of tanned skin, dark blond hair, and white teeth flashed across the screen before she steadied her phone. "Hey, Coral!"

Coral tried to smile, but even the joy of seeing her aunt couldn't lighten her mood. "Hey. Whatcha doing?"

Aunt Nina turned the phone to show where she was—poolside. Greenery leaned over the pool deck from all angles, and a waterfall descended into the hot tub. "Spoiling myself at this hotel for a couple of days. I haven't moved from this seat for three hours. My ass is numb. What's up?"

"I just wanted to...to talk..." Shit, her eyes were welling. She blinked and looked up, trying to swallow down the tightness in her throat. It was dark in the van—she'd drawn the curtains while hiding out in a department store parking lot in Vancouver—but even in the darkness, it was obvious she was on the brink of tears.

Aunt Nina sat taller on her deck chair, frowning. "Spill."

Coral drew a deep breath, wiping her eyes. "I don't know how you do it. I won't be able to keep living the life I want. I'm going to have to give up everything and get a nine-to-five job, and I'm going to be miserable."

She was dodging the topic that squeezed her heart the most—but the wound Ruby left was so fresh that she hadn't had time to process it. Plus, nothing Aunt Nina said could lessen that pain.

Aunt Nina nodded, like she'd expected this. "I talked to your mom last week and she mentioned your deadline is coming up. She's right that your career is important, but I had to argue with her because so is your happiness. You can have both. You *should* have both. You shouldn't have to give up your dream and go two feet into the career they expect you to have."

"What did she say?"

The corner of Aunt Nina's mouth twitched upward. "She said, 'You and Coral are so alike it's ridiculous.' I'll take it as a compliment."

Coral smiled, warmed by the comparison. She curled her knees to her chest and drew a steadying breath. "How am I supposed to convince them they're wrong?"

"The thing is…" Aunt Nina twisted her mouth. "They're not entirely wrong. A little but not fully. Life is full of bills and expenses, and you need to be able to pay them. I might travel a lot, but I fund my adventures with a great career as a nurse."

"I thought I could pay my bills by being a creator. And I am earning an income. It's just taking a long time to build that audience—time I don't have."

Aunt Nina tilted her head. "Maybe you should think of yourself as an artist. So many have day jobs to pay the bills. You can live in the van while you do an apprenticeship or whatever it is that strikes your fancy."

Coral nodded slowly. That wasn't a bad way to think of it. She could argue that her videos and photos were a form of art. But could she find a job that would allow her to be a nomad? "Maybe… But my parents still want me to sell the van. That was our deal."

"Yeah, that part sucks." Aunt Nina squinted into the distance, a frown on her lips. "I think you should go talk to them. Be honest about your dreams. I promise they are human beings, even if it doesn't seem like it sometimes."

Coral rolled her eyes. "I find that hard to believe."

Aunt Nina looked past the phone and nodded to someone before bringing the phone closer to her face. "Listen. One time, when your mom was seventeen, she called in sick to her job at the hardware store to bring a baby squirrel into a wildlife rescue. Yes, she prioritized humanity over work once. She has that capability."

Coral twisted her lips. Aunt Nina let the silence drag on, refusing to break it, until Coral sighed. "Fine. I'll talk to them."

Her pleading would go nowhere, but she might as well try. It was her last hope.

"Good. And how's Ruby?"

Coral's heart jumped into her throat. Her mouth went dry. "Fine."

"Anything you want to talk about there?"

She knew something was wrong. Of course she did. But talking about it would unleash the tears Coral was trying so hard to hold back—so she shook her head, dropping her gaze to her knees. "Thanks for the talk."

"Sure. Call me anytime you need me. I'm just hanging out by the pool—oh, crap, spider monkeys." She turned the camera to show Coral at least a dozen spider monkeys swinging into the pool area. Aunt Nina's hand stretched out to protect her belongings.

Coral might have laughed if only her heart weren't on the brink of shattering into a million pieces.

Coral knocked on the front door of her parents' house. It was after seven, so they should hopefully be home. She wasn't sure what she would say. She didn't usually show up unannounced.

The door opened, and Dad stood there with a look of surprise. He wore a flannel shirt, grease-stained jeans, and a baseball cap over his receding hairline. Dark strands stuck out of the bottom of the cap, wispy and in need of a cut. His mustache was as neatly trimmed as ever, and the rest of his tanned, freckled face was clean-shaven. He looked the same as always, all the way back to Coral's earliest memories.

"Coral!"

She opened her mouth to explain why she was here, but nothing came out.

After a pause, she burst into tears.

"Ah, crap," Dad said, typically casual when one of the women in his life started crying. He stepped back and waved her inside. "What happened?"

Mom rushed over, wrapped in a bathrobe, her blond hair in a messy bun. "Doug? Oh, Coral! What's wrong?"

"Did you say, 'Coral'?" Farrah asked, appearing behind them with a cookie in her hand. "Hey—oh, shit. Did something happen on the road trip?"

Coral stepped inside, embarrassed for breaking down in front of her whole family. She wiped an arm across her streaming eyes.

"The road trip was good. It was great. I got a lot more followers, and—" She choked on her words. Blinking away tears, she drew a breath. Between the reality of how things ended with Ruby and the conversation with Aunt Nina, she had the sensation of disintegrating. "I failed. I'll be twenty-four in less than two weeks, and I won't be earning enough to fulfill our agreement."

Farrah took a bite of cookie and said through a mouthful, "*That's* your first thought about the road trip? Not all the cool stuff you did with Ruby, not all the sights and scenery?"

"That was the whole point of the road trip! Now I have to sell the van!"

"Okay, okay, let's have a meeting." Dad calmly shut the door, and they all shuffled to the living room.

"What'd I tell you before you left?" Farrah asked. "Remember? Don't focus so much on work that you forget to experience the *actual road trip*?"

Coral opened her mouth to argue, let the words sink in, and closed it. Sure, she'd enjoyed the road trip and the scenery, but Farrah might have had a point. Coral had been so desperate to get followers that she'd suggested a fake relationship without considering that she might have wanted a real one with Ruby. She'd let the "business" part of the trip overshadow her feelings.

Still, she glared at her sister. "I enjoyed the *actual road trip*, thank you."

Farrah raised an eyebrow in an *uh-huh* look.

They all sat on the leather couches facing the TV, where golf was on. It'd been weeks since Coral last visited, and the place looked the same—the huge TV on the wall flanked by dusty DVD racks full of movies that nobody had time to watch, high school graduation photos of Coral and Farrah on the left wall, a painting of a '57 Chevy on the right wall.

"Let's talk about our agreement," Dad said.

Coral's eyes welled up again. The idea of having to sell the van hurt worse than ever. She had so many memories inside that thing. "Can I have an extension? Just a few more months. I can show you my growing audience and engagement stats."

Dad shook his head. "The point of that contract was to get you to think more seriously about your career. We wanted you to see that being an influencer is not a—"

"I'm a creator! I spend hours creating content that people pay for. I showed you the stats. You know how much money—"

Dad extended a hand. "A creator, then. It has unpredictable income. This was a good trial, and I'm sure you learned a lot, but you can't keep doing this forever."

"You don't know that. I'm gaining followers, and I want to keep doing it."

"For how long? It's a frivolous career path."

"Just because you don't understand something doesn't make it frivolous," Farrah said.

Dad shot her a glare before returning his attention to Coral. "Your early twenties should be about setting yourself up with a good career. Something that will pay the bills. You need a plan."

"I have a plan!" Coral's arguments with Ruby over planning vs. winging it came rushing back, making her drop her gaze. Fine, some things needed Ruby-like planning, and her career was one of them. But she could make a plan without giving up the thing she loved most.

"You need a backup plan, then."

"You and Mom don't have a backup plan. What would happen if your business went under?"

"I think you underestimate how much time we spend learning new skills and adapting to the market," Mom said. "Mechanical skills translate, and we could find work elsewhere."

"I'm always learning new—" Coral closed her eyes and drew a breath.

Breathe. I'm getting defensive.

Maybe there was some truth here. Ruby had brought it up when they went for that windy stroll to Haystack Rock on their first night. If Coral stepped away from vanlife, what would she do next? It was a real possibility—she might get sick of being in the public eye, or her followers might abandon her, or one of the platforms she depended on might disappear.

"Our terms were that you'll come work for us if you don't meet your target," Mom said, "but you can also go to school. You have the foundation for a career in business or marketing. We can amend the terms. You can work for us *or* you can apply to a university or college."

"I don't..." A dull ache started behind Coral's eyes. She couldn't picture herself in an office job, and she really didn't want to follow Farrah's path of being stressed out in university for four years.

"Why does it have to be so black-and-white with you two?" Farrah asked. "Instead of telling her to sell the van and go to school, can't she keep doing this and build other skills on the side? Can't she have both?"

They all looked at her. Coral's heart jumped as Farrah's words lined up with Aunt Nina's suggestion to get a job to support her goals.

"And—" Farrah dusted cookie crumbs from her hoodie. "Maybe if you made suggestions like parents instead of coming at her with *terms* and *contracts* as if you're her lawyers, this conversation would go a lot better. Jesus. I'm going to make coffee."

She got up and shuffled to the kitchen, mumbling to herself.

Coral rubbed her forehead. Having a conversation that didn't feel like a contract negotiation would be a lot easier.

"We can amend our—suggestions," Dad said stiffly. "We'd like to suggest that you take classes and..." He glanced to Mom, who wrinkled her nose.

There was a pause. The sound of the coffee maker drifted in from the kitchen.

Mom let out a breath. "Okay, let's try this again. Coral, I talked to Aunt Nina, and I think she has it right. Sure, she's always off traveling somewhere, but when she isn't traveling, she's working so she can afford to do it. We want that for you. We want you to afford to live the life you want."

Coral nodded. "I get that you need money in order to live. I just don't want to work all the time like you and Dad, and I'm not sure how much I'd like university. It's not my calling, and it wouldn't make me happy."

Farrah leaned against the doorway to the kitchen, listening in while the coffee brewed.

Mom searched Coral's face with her brow pinched. "That's fine. You don't have to work as much as we do."

"We want you to be happy," Dad said.

Coral wiped her cheeks, which had gotten puffy and wet. She'd never had a conversation like this with her parents. They'd never told her these things. They just told her what they expected from her.

"If you care about my happiness, then why do you never ask about my personal life? You're never around. I'm shocked to find all three of you here, actually."

"I was just yelling at them about the same thing." Farrah narrowed her eyes at them. "They're aware of their crimes."

"Coral, we're so sorry." Mom gripped her knee. "We should have been more involved."

Dad nodded. "We understand that we've been too focused on work."

"You're missing out on life," Coral said.

Mom and Dad exchanged a defeated look, looking so ashamed that Coral's anger dissipated. She felt sorry for them—and sorry for snapping at them.

"We were negotiat—discussing—chatting with Farrah about how we can fix this," Mom said, shifting as if uncomfortable using such casual language. "What would you think if we made time for each other once a week? We could all hang out, go for a walk, do whatever we want."

Coral nodded. "That'd be nice."

It would have been nicer when she was a kid or a teenager, but better late than never.

Farrah walked into the room and leaned her elbows on the back of the couch. "About the university thing... Coral, I know you look at me suffering through it and use that to justify not wanting to go.

And I get it. It's not easy. But it's also a lot of fun. Like, when I'm not studying, I'm having the best years of my life living in a dorm, meeting new people, trying new things. I paddled a longboat last weekend with a bunch of new friends, and we won second place in a race and got obliterated at a beer garden afterwards."

Mom and Dad cast her disapproving looks.

"Responsibly obliterated," Farrah amended. "Anyway, I'm trying to say it's not all bad. It's actually a cool experience, and at the end of it, I'll have a degree and be able to get a great job—so the stressful parts will be worth it."

Coral returned her sister's smile. She hadn't thought about the social part of university, but when she pieced together all of the little details Farrah talked about, it did sound like fun. Farrah went to more parties and festivals in one year than Coral ever had in her whole life.

Maybe I've been a bit self-righteous for thinking Farrah doesn't know what she got herself into.

"I guess I've been worried that by doing something like going to university, I'll lose the freedom I have in the van," Coral said. "I don't want to give up this lifestyle."

Farrah nodded. "When we were at Kits beach, you told me you like that you get to go on a different adventure every day. I was thinking a lot about that, and… I feel like I have a lot of adventures too—just a different kind. And I feel like at the end of my degree, I'm going to have the freedom to do what I want. Adventures come in different forms. It doesn't matter what path you're on in life because if you want fun and excitement, you'll be able to find it. So I wouldn't worry so much about what you do. You're the type of person who lives for adventures, and you'll be able to get that no matter what."

Coral blinked. She'd never thought about it that way. A light sensation filled her. She'd been clinging to the van because she was afraid of who she would be without it—but it wasn't the van making her free and adventurous. She'd gravitated to vanlife because she already had that sense of adventure inside of her.

"Thanks for the perspective. It helps, actually."

Farrah smiled.

Coral let out a breath and rubbed her face. "I like doing maintenance on my van. I'm good at it. I'll...I'll get certified as a mechanic."

It was the most logical backup plan she could think of—one that made her excited instead of full of dread.

Both of her parents lit up.

"That sounds perfect," Mom said.

Dad nodded. "I'd say it fulfills the terms of our agreement."

Farrah sighed dramatically.

"Sorry," Dad mumbled. "Can't take the business out of a businessman."

"But I'd like to keep the van while I work on my certification." Coral's heart pounded as the words came out. This was her last shot. "Living on the road makes me so happy. Please."

Her parents looked at each other.

Coral's heart seemed to stop beating.

Mom's chin dipped in the tiniest of nods, and when they faced her again, both smiled.

Coral smiled back, filled with the sensation of floating into the ceiling. Finally, a plan they could all agree on. "Thank you." She slumped, letting her shoulders drop. "I—I'm sorry for fighting you so hard on this."

Her parents exchanged another look, still grinning.

"What?" Coral asked suspiciously.

"That's the thing about you," Mom said. "You fight so hard for what means a lot to you, and you never let us tell you that you can't follow your dream. That's such a good quality."

Coral's heart swelled. Wow, now a compliment. She should have burst into tears in front of her parents years ago.

But there was something Coral hadn't fought hard enough for—some*one*. The girl who meant more to her than the van and her channel and her platform.

Farrah brought over the coffee pot and four mugs. "Your slumpy shoulders and sad eyebrows are telling me that something happened with Ruby."

Mom looked between them. "Ruby? Who's that?"

"Her girlfriend," Farrah said. "Which you should know about, if you'd thought to ask, by the way."

Mom and Dad looked at each other, guilty again.

"She's not my girlfriend," Coral said.

Farrah gasped. "You broke up?"

"No. She never was. We faked it. We faked the relationship to get more views."

There was a long silence.

Farrah pinched the bridge of her nose. "Okay. Um. There is so much I want to say here. But I'll just say this: are you *sure* it was fake for both of you?"

Coral's eyes burned. She looked at the ceiling and drew a shaky breath. "No."

"Could you make a real one work?"

"I…" Sure, they lived on opposite sides of a border, but Coral was willing to put in the effort. They could take turns driving across to see each other. And really, they could live wherever and however they wanted, because wasn't that the whole point of living in a van? The freedom to do what they wanted?

In the silence, Farrah said firmly, "I think you need to find out before you say it's over."

Coral nodded, nerves churning in her gut.

"And, um, if it works out…" Dad glanced to each of them. "We'd love to meet her."

Coral smiled. Maybe there was hope for Mom and Dad.

She leaned over to hug them, something she hadn't done in a long time. The hug was so warm, and so needed, that she could have cried all over again.

She decided to stay the night, sleeping in her old bedroom for the first time since high school. Farrah stayed too, wanting a break from her university dorm.

The queen bed felt massive. As Coral sprawled across it, relishing the space, she grabbed her phone and opened YouTube.

Ruby hadn't posted a video today either. There was also no email in Coral's inbox hashing out the details of their fake breakup, which Ruby had promised to send.

Coral flipped to the photo app, scrolling back through the hundreds of pictures she'd taken on the trip—all the way back to the first selfie of all three of them at Haystack Rock. They'd thought at the time that the picture wasn't good enough to post, but looking at it now, it was perfect. Their smiles were big and exhilarated, and even Calvin seemed to be grinning.

Coral's heart beat faster. If Ruby wanted to part ways forever, fine—but Coral wouldn't give up on them this easily. She had to give it one more shot.

Tomorrow morning, she would drive back to Seattle to tell Ruby how she felt. She had to ask more than just a vague question about whether to make the fake relationship real, like she'd done at Tumwater. She had to make a real confession and tell Ruby everything she felt and everything she hoped for.

She rolled over, her pulse racing. By noon tomorrow, she was determined to have an answer from Ruby, one way or another.

Chapter 32
Ruby

RUBY ENDED THE CALL WITH the mechanic and rubbed her face. "Okay. They'll come get my van later today."

"That's great!" Mom's voice was muffled as she examined the damage inside the soggy, warped cupboards. The fans had done their jobs overnight, but the wood might be beyond saving.

"Yeah. I'll probably be busy with the tow truck and stuff all afternoon, so go ahead and have dinner without me today."

Ugh, this was going to be a busy day.

She slid off the barstool and stretched. It was almost noon. "Anything else we need for groceries?"

"You can add bananas to the list. My car keys are by the door. Thanks."

Ruby grabbed Mom's keys and headed down to the parking garage.

She'd buckled up and turned the car on when she realized she'd forgotten her phone.

"Dammit," she whispered.

Well, she could survive without it for a grocery run.

Except as it turned out, she had to detour around construction, and by the time she figured out where she was going without a maps app to guide her, her quick trip took two hours.

She fumbled back into the apartment in a bad mood, weighed down by groceries.

When she pushed through the door, Calvin jumped against her legs and Mom greeted her from the living room, where she was reading a book. "Your phone's been ringing like crazy."

Shit. It was probably the mechanic trying to call her back with something important. What if she'd missed the window to get the van into the shop?

"Okay. Thanks."

She picked up her phone—and her heart skipped. The missed calls were from Coral. There were no texts, just calls.

What does she want?

Curiosity ate her stomach. She wanted to hear Coral's voice but wasn't ready to talk to her. With Mom's disaster to worry about, she didn't have the emotional strength to navigate a conversation about feelings.

Except Mom's advice from yesterday echoed in her brain, telling her to think about what would make her happy. It was time to think about what she wanted and what to say to Coral. She owed it to herself.

Ruby stared at her phone. Her battery was at five percent. Did she forget to charge it last night?

The phone lit up with another incoming call from Coral, making her heart leap—and then the screen went black as the battery died.

Her chest tightened. With a huff, she plugged in her phone and unloaded the groceries. She would call Coral back after they were put away.

But minutes later, with the groceries done, she crossed her arms and stared at her phone.

What does she want? What do I say in response to whatever it is?

The words Ruby needed to say swam through her brain, jumbled, murky, not ready to take shape.

Okay, she would call Coral back after lunch. She was too hungry to think.

She made sandwiches, and all the while, the tulips on the counter stared at her. They weren't as vibrant as yesterday. In a few more days, they would wilt, and she would have to get rid of them.

When they'd finished eating, she grabbed Calvin's leash and her phone. The battery had charged to fourteen percent, and it would have to do.

"I'm taking Calvin out."

"Okay."

She brought him down the elevator, fidgety. She would call Coral outside where Mom couldn't listen in.

She knew what she needed to say: she had to apologize. She'd been an idiot to push Coral away. Coral's absence left an ache inside her—and when she let her imagination go to a place where they could be together, she felt warmer and happier than she had in years.

"Ruby!"

Ruby's heart did a somersault. Coral's van was parked on the side of the street. Coral stepped out, looking achingly gorgeous in white shorts, a peach crop top, and a high ponytail. They were in the same place as when she'd first set eyes on Coral—right outside the apartment building, the sun shining, pedestrians minding their own business while strolling past on the sidewalk.

So much had changed since then.

Calvin pulled the leash out of Ruby's hands, which seemed to have lost all strength. He galloped up to Coral, all barks and wiggles.

Coral bent to welcome him with open arms. "Hi, buddy!"

"What are you doing here?" Ruby asked, breathless.

Coral stood. "I promised I would rebuild your transmission. Well, here I am."

Ruby's chest tightened, as if her heart had gotten too big for it. "What? Oh. You don't have to do that."

"I want to."

"That's such a ridiculous amount of work!"

"Consider this a career-building thing."

Ruby furrowed her brow. "What do you mean?"

Coral shifted, drawing a breath. "I don't spend enough time planning anything—or any time at all—but you've helped me realize that sometimes it's nice to have a plan. So in the interest of planning my life a little better, I'm going to get certified as a mechanic."

"Wow! Coral, that's awesome."

Coral nodded. "Fixing your van will look pretty good on my resume, so you'd really be helping me out by letting me do this, actually."

Ruby laughed.

Coral shrugged, looking a little shy.

"Okay," Ruby said. "I guess I could do you this one favor."

Coral stepped closer. "You helped me realize a lot of things. Who I am, what I want, where I'm going. The real reason I came here is so that I could apologize in person."

The grin slid off Ruby's face. "For what?"

"I'm sorry I used you to get more subscribers."

"Coral, we both used each other to—"

"I'm sorry I suggested a fake relationship, especially since what I really should have done was asked you out for real."

Heat rose in Ruby's cheeks. "Coral—"

"I'm sorry I made you drive a dune buggy."

Ruby laughed.

"And," Coral said, sounding out of breath, "I'm sorry I made you feel bad for wanting to end the road trip to go help your mom. That was shitty, and I was being selfish."

Ruby's chest squeezed. The jumble of words in her brain took a moment to form. "Thanks. I'm sorry I pushed you away." She swallowed hard. "Since my dad died, it's just been me and my mom. We're there for each other no matter what. She was having a crisis, and I had to come home even if it meant cutting my plans short."

"Of course. I get it."

"But I shouldn't have made you feel like you were less of a priority. It doesn't mean I don't care about you."

"You care about me?"

Ruby's cheeks burned hotter. "Well, yeah."

Coral twisted her fingers together. "So when I asked if you wanted help, and you said no… Is this like how you felt with your ex? During hard times, you don't want me there?"

Ruby shook her head firmly, alarmed that she came off that way. "No! That's not it. I didn't want to burden you. I thought you were just asking to be nice."

"I was asking because I want to be there for you, Ruby."

Ruby's chest felt full, like her heart was expanding with every thump. As they looked at each other, the air seemed to grow still between them. Ruby had never met anyone who made her feel this way. "I'm sorry for saying those things about your family not being there to help you."

Coral nodded, looking serious. "About that. It's true that Farrah's always busy, but she's there for me. She helped me come up with the whole idea for the road trip. And my parents are business-minded and frustrating, but they're still my parents, and—I know they'd be there for me if I really needed it. If I called them crying over a flood, they would help me."

Ruby's eyes burned. It hurt to hear Coral have to defend her relationships with her family because of something senseless she'd said. "I know. I'm sorry. I shouldn't have said those things. I didn't mean to make you feel bad."

"Okay. Thanks."

Ruby stepped even closer until they were an arm's length away. She knew what she needed to say. "I never realized it until the road trip, but before we met, my life was pretty hollow. My schedule was always full, and yet I was missing something big. Something important. You make me want to seize every day and live the life I should've been living all along." Her voice became louder, and she waved her hands, and for once, she let it happen. She didn't want to control everything that was pouring out of her. "There's something about you that makes me feel alive. I never thought I would go on a road trip and just *wing it*, but with you, it wasn't scary. And maybe riding a dune buggy isn't my thing but I—" Seeing Coral here and feeling everything that was going on inside her chest, she knew without question what she wanted. "There are lots of other kinds of adventures, and I want to go on all of them with you!"

Ruby's heart pounded as her words came out strong. Warmth tingled through her as the hot summer sun beat down on them.

Coral's lips pulled into a wide, genuine smile. It was the most beautiful sight Ruby had ever seen, making her more breathless than the sight of any beach, forest, or dune ever could.

"I never see you get fired up," Coral said.

Ruby bit her lip. "I prefer not to."

"There was a time when I thought you didn't have it in you. I guess I was wrong."

Ruby eyed her, unsure whether to consider this a compliment or an insult.

"I like it," Coral said. "We all need to get fired up sometimes."

"It's your fault for bringing out the worst in me."

They stepped closer. So did Calvin, leaning into each of them and wagging his tail, apparently thinking they were playing a game.

"I really like you," Coral said, a quaver in her voice, "and I wasn't faking it. These last few days, I was making excuses to kiss you and hold you, but, really, it wasn't about the cameras. It was about you."

Ruby had the sensation that she was floating into the sky. "Good. Because I was making excuses too, and I like you a lot."

Coral's breath hitched. "For real?"

Ruby smiled. "It's always been real, Coral."

Coral swallowed. A pink tinge rose in her cheeks. "Same."

Ruby drew a breath, summoning every drop of bravery she had. "Do you want to be my real girlfriend?"

Coral's mouth fell open. Then her whole expression brightened, and a huge smile stretched across her face. "Yes!" she said, breathless. "I do."

Ruby smiled back. "Good."

She'd barely gotten the word out when Coral flung herself forward.

Ruby met her kiss with open arms, pulling her close. Their lips moved tenderly, passion licking between them as if they were kissing for the first time. And it was their first kiss, in a way. There were no questions behind it, no terms or clauses, no uncertainty about what it meant.

"Thank you for coming back," Ruby whispered into Coral's lips.

"Of course I did." Coral ran her hands through Ruby's hair in a way that sent a tingle down her back.

The way she fit in Ruby's arms, it was as if she were meant to be there. She was everything Ruby needed. Ruby could have stood there kissing her soft lips and feeling the heat of her body for hours.

"Once we fix your van," Coral murmured, "do you want to take it on a celebratory road trip?"

"Yes." Ruby kissed her again.

"Where to?"

"It doesn't matter. Anywhere."

"Utah? Arizona? Vancouver Island? Alberta?"

Ruby nodded. "Yes."

Coral laughed.

Something pressed against Ruby's leg, and she looked down to find Calvin gazing up at her with his big, baby-seal eyes, his tail wagging.

"And you're coming too, of course!" she said, and he barked happily.

Standing on the bustling Seattle sidewalk, lost in their own private world, the promise of adventure crackled in the air between them. They were free to start their next journey, whenever and wherever they wanted.

Chapter 33
Coral

Two Months Later

"Welcome to Intentional Living with Ruby Hayashi," Ruby said in her classic, soothing camera voice. "Today, I'm making a vegan deep-dish pizza in the slow cooker, which was Coral's idea."

She turned the camera to Coral, who waved and flashed a smile from the dinette.

Coral watched Ruby carefully prepare the ingredients and coordinate the recipe like a dance. She would never get sick of watching her girlfriend work.

They'd parked at Green Lake near Whistler, which was one of Coral's favorite spots. Following their plan to alternate whose van they stayed in, they would spend the next two weeks exploring the area in Ruby's—and Coral had yet to get used to how clean and bright it was compared to her own. The succulents, hanging fruit net, white wallpaper, rose gold knobs, and all of the other little details were perfect, minimal, beautiful, and just so *Ruby*. Coral loved every inch of it.

When Ruby started the slow cooker and shut off her camera, Coral stepped in for a kiss. "Lovely as ever. Ready for a swim?"

Ruby gathered her hair into a ponytail. "As ready as I'll ever be. You promise it won't be terrifying?"

"There's, like, half a second of terror, tops."

"I think I can handle that."

They changed into bikinis, gathered their stuff, and headed out. Calvin perked up from his nap in the middle of the floor, hopping alongside them in excitement.

"My mom's shop had a line out the door this morning," Ruby said as they walked to the lake. "She texted me a picture."

Coral gasped. "That's amazing!"

Ruby grabbed her hand, giving it a squeeze. She seemed lighter since getting her van back, her smiles coming more easily. With her mom's shop standing on its own legs and her livelihood no longer compromised, she was free to focus on herself—and that meant Coral got to enjoy more time with her.

As for Coral? Running her channel and living the life of her dreams turned out to be a lot easier when she had no career-ending contracts to weigh her down. It also helped that she wasn't stressed about how she would fund her lifestyle. While doing her apprenticeship at her parents' shop, she'd posted a few videos to her channel, showing people how to do their own van maintenance, which opened a whole new door to getting more views.

"Rubes!" someone shouted down the trail.

They looked up. A couple in their twenties was walking toward them.

"Oh, hey, you two!" Ruby exclaimed. "Coral, this is Annie and Parm."

Coral waved. "Nice to meet you."

"*Coral Lavoie Adventures*," Parm said. "We know all about you. We've been following Ruby's channel for some time—"

"And we've followed yours as well since the road trip," Annie said.

"I was getting to that," Parm said.

"Well, it's nice to meet you in person," Annie said to Coral.

Coral smiled. "You too."

"What are you doing here?" Ruby asked.

"A little romantic getaway." Annie took Parm's hand and gave him a gooey-eyed look.

"We're staying with friends because we're having some trouble with our ride," Parm said. "The roof's got a big crack in it."

"Sorry to hear that," Ruby said. She didn't sound surprised for some reason.

"Made for a dramatic video, though," Parm said.

Calvin whined, pulling Ruby toward the lake. He was as eager to swim as Coral was.

"Anyway, we're going kayaking later," Annie said. "Do you two want to come?"

Ruby looked at Coral, who nodded.

"Yes, kayaking sounds great," Ruby said, and Coral smiled wider.

"Cool," Annie said. "We'll text you later."

Coral and Ruby continued to the lake, where Ruby confirmed that disasters were a regular part of Annie and Parm's life.

"They would benefit from learning some basic van maintenance, honestly," Ruby said.

"It never hurts."

"Lucky for me, I have you." She leaned over and kissed Coral's cheek.

They made it to the lake, and Coral led Ruby to her favorite jumping spot.

The low cliff had a worn path on the side from all of the people who did this jump.

"Calvin, sit. Stay," Ruby said, making him wait at the base.

He sat obediently, watching them climb up.

"He's *so* going to swim after us the second we hit the water," Coral said.

"Oh, he'll definitely try to rescue us. Good boy, Calvin."

He wagged his tail, watching them curiously as they approached the edge.

Coral grimaced. It was a little higher than it seemed when they'd looked up at it. She curled her toes over the gritty rock, her adrenaline spiking. "You still have time to go back to the bottom and be the videographer, if you want."

"No, I can do it. I want to," Ruby said.

"Okay. Hold my hand?"

They clasped hands, and Coral's heart fluttered as hard as it did every time they touched. Ruby returned her smile, looking energized.

Coral's world seemed to expand with each day they spent together. Ruby made her feel like every moment of every day was one worth savoring—like she was living out her best story.

They hadn't said "the words" yet, but over the last few days, Coral had felt ready to.

Was now the time? The thought of speaking those words aloud set her heart racing worse than the anticipation of jumping off the cliff.

Ruby searched Coral's face, her brown eyes calculating. A breeze swept up locks of her hair, framing them around her perfect face.

One of us has to say it first. Should it be me? Maybe she needs more time—

"I love you, Coral," Ruby said, her breath catching.

Coral blinked, unsure if these words had really happened or if her imagination had gotten away on her. "What?"

Ruby brushed her fingers gently along Coral's jaw. "I love you."

Coral's heart seemed to leap off the cliff without her. Her face broke into an uncontrollable grin. "I love you too!"

Ruby let out a breath, and Coral stepped into her arms. They kissed, perched on top of the world, a warm breeze tickling Coral's skin. She could have stood like this for hours.

Calvin barked in protest. They broke apart and looked down to see him standing up as if he were contemplating climbing after them.

"Come on." Ruby took Coral's hand.

With Coral's other hand, she held the GoPro at the end of her selfie stick.

Their palms were sweaty. They exchanged a nervous grin. The lake shimmered twenty feet below, and paddle boarders and kayakers coasted by, off on their own adventures.

"Ready?" Coral pressed the record button.

"Go," Ruby said.

Gripping each other's hand tightly, they ran for the edge of the cliff.

Below, Calvin ran into the water after them, barking excitedly.

Coral and Ruby pushed off, and both of them let out exhilarated screams.

As they soared through the air together, the sense of freedom lifted Coral into the sky. *This* was why she'd chosen this life. She wanted to be in no other place with no other person. Everything about this day, this summer, this moment with the woman she loved, was absolute perfection.

Other Books from Ylva Publishing

www.ylva-publishing.com

From Fan to Forever
Tiana Warner

ISBN: 978-3-96324-691-3
Length: 202 pages (67,000 words)

When student Rachel meets her crush, A-list actress Cate, it leads to a shocking offer to become a science consultant on Cate's new film.

An age-gap lesbian celebrity romance about how much you'd risk to have your dream.

Not the Marrying Kind
Jae

ISBN: 978-3-96324-194-9
Length: 314 pages (113,000 words)

Small-town florist Ashley loves creating wedding bouquets. Her own love life is far from blossoming since she's stuck in the closet.

Sasha isn't faring much better. Her bakery keeps her too busy for romance anyway.

When the town's first lesbian wedding forces them to work together, Sasha is soon tempting more than just Ash's sweet tooth.

What else is on the menu in this delicious lesbian romance?

Puppy Love
L.T. Smith

ISBN: 978-3-96324-493-3
Length: 149 pages (40,000 words)

Ellie Anderson has given up on love. Her philosophy is "Why let someone in when all they do is leave?" So instead, she fills her life with work and dodges her sister's matchmaking. Then she meets Charlie—a gorgeous, brown-eyed Border Terrier. Charlie is in need of love and a home, prompting Ellie to open the doors to feeling once again. However, she isn't the only one who is falling for the pup…

The Business of Love
Charley Clarke

ISBN: 978-3-96324-752-1
Length: 308 pages (97,000 words)

Driven Mack wants to take over her family company to secure her sister's future. Except the company's CEO must be married and a relationship's the last thing on her mind.

A year of playing Mack's wife will get barista Taylor out of debt. Good thing Mack's too pretentious and arrogant for Taylor to ever fall for her. Right?

About Tiana Warner

Tiana Warner is a writer and outdoor enthusiast from British Columbia, Canada. She is best known for her critically acclaimed "Mermaids of Eriana Kwai" trilogy and its comic adaptation. Tiana is a lifelong horseback rider, a former programmer with a Computer Science degree, and a dog mom to a hyperactive rescue mutt named Joey.

CONNECT WITH TIANA

Website: tianawarner.com
Facebook: facebook.com/TianaWarnerAuthor
Twitter: twitter.com/tianawarner
Instagram: instagram.com/tianawarner
TikTok: tiktok.com/@tiana_warner

Credits
Edited by Miranda Miller and Michelle Aguilar
Cover Design and Print Layout by Streetlight Graphics